A History of Running Away

Also by Paula McGrath

Generation

A History of Running Away

Paula McGrath

JOHN MURRAY

First published in Great Britain in 2017 by John Murray (Publishers)
An Hachette UK Company

1

© Paula McGrath 2017

The right of Paula McGrath to be identified as the Author of the Work has been
asserted by her in accordance with the Copyright, Designs and Patents Act 1988.

A CIP catalogue record for this title is available from the British Library

ISBN 978-1-47364-175-4
Trade paperback ISBN 978-1-47364-176-1
Ebook ISBN 978-1-47364-177-8

Typeset in Sabon MT by Hewer Text UK Ltd, Edinburgh
Printed and bound by Clays Ltd, St Ives plc

John Murray policy is to use papers that are natural, renewable and
recyclable products and made from wood grown in sustainable forests.
The logging and manufacturing processes are expected to conform
to the environmental regulations of the country of origin.

John Murray (Publishers)
Carmelite House
50 Victoria Embankment
London EC4Y 0DZ

www.johnmurray.co.uk

For Pauline McGrath

Dublin, 2012

She is beginning to think this meeting will never end. Round and round they go, though they must know they won't reach any conclusions. How could they? The law is the law, and unless it changes, all they can do is what they've always done: their best. God, would Sean ever shut up. He doesn't have the details; no one does. It's all speculation. Would have, could have, should have. So much for his scientific training.

She tunes him out. The strips of sky between the vertical blinds have darkened as rainclouds gather in the late afternoon. It's looking unlikely that it will hold off until tonight, as forecast. If they would only finish up here, she might manage to get her run in before it starts. But it is her professional experience that meetings are not about coming to conclusions. Rather, they act as safety valves, where frustrations can be expressed to prevent them being expressed in less appropriate circumstances. Unfortunately, a lot of hot air gets released in the process. It's always the same one or two, the ones who love to hear themselves speak. She's never understood it herself. When her opinion is sought, or when she has one to express, she states it succinctly, so much so that her contributions to the minutes have become a standing joke: a page from Sean, followed by one line from her.

—It could be our turn tomorrow. Then what? We're still none the wiser on where we stand. We don't want to get caught up in a scenario like that, dragged through the legal system. If the legal system itself doesn't know what it wants, how are we supposed to know?

On and on. This latest medical scandal is a very real concern, and it has her on edge as much as the rest of her colleagues. Morale is low, and more and more staff are requesting time off for anxiety-related illness. But more than worry, what she is feeling is guilt. NMP, one of her patients told her yesterday, when her breakfast tray slipped accidentally, dousing the bedclothes in tea and cornflakes. She had to ask what it meant: Not My Problem, the new mother told her – as, in fact, propped up in her bed feeding her infant, it was not. And increasingly it looks as if this current debate will not be her problem for much longer: Ken's email arrived this morning.

A heads-up to let you know the job is yours. Offer in the post. Hoping you will be leading the team very soon, K.

Ken, Jeffrey's protégé. She doesn't appreciate his little insider's *heads-up*. Even the term grates.

—We do need clarity, she agrees, when she realises Sean is looking at her. But her attempt to show support backfires, and he launches into lengthy agreement with his own argument. She sits back in resignation, maintaining the neutral expression she has perfected over decades of dealing with the same topic, behind which she hides her impatience with the futility of his tirade, and her urgent desire to walk out on the whole pointless debate. But she hasn't made up her mind if she can go as far as to leave the country.

A sudden spattering against the windowpane announces the rain, and by the time she escapes it's coming down hard. It's not just the meeting that has her on edge, it's also Jeffrey. A long-distance relationship was always going to be unsettling. Though if she's honest, her current restlessness preceded Jeffrey. Somewhere in the past year, the life she had been content with for a long time had begun to feel as if it was not enough. Or too much. And it makes her feel like an idiot that she doesn't know which. Like sometimes when she's running, and for a panicky moment she doesn't know whether she's inhaling or exhaling. Perhaps she even agreed to Jeffrey's attentions more readily than she might otherwise because of it. Now *there* was a new, anxiety-provoking thought.

She hails a taxi, and just as she's climbing in and trying to close both her umbrella and the door at the same time, her phone rings. She's ages fumbling in her bag before she finds it. It's Jeffrey, the man she's planning on spending her life with, but somehow the thought of a conversation with him exhausts her. That can't be right. By the time she swipes from green to red, it has stopped. Oh well, she excuses herself, she'll get back to him once she gets home.

Besides, she knows what he will have wanted, and by the time she gets home it will be too late. Have the taxi take you to the airport instead, I'll send a driver to pick you up at this end. Everything is so easy for Jeffrey. But it's unfair of him to compli-cate her guilt like this; he knows how she spends her evenings. Once, she let herself be persuaded. She phoned the home and explained that she had an unexpected work commitment – she didn't know why she didn't just tell the truth – and left it to Ana, the Filipina nurse, to soothe her conscience. *Don't worry. We will explain. She won't even know.* She had gone to London, where Jeffrey went out of his way to spoil her with oysters and champagne, and impossible-to-get tickets to the opening night of the play everyone was talking about, he said. But she couldn't relax, and in the end she flew back to Dublin on the Saturday evening, wasting the tickets. She felt bad, but there was no getting around the facts: she was all her mother had.

The rain is coming down in sheets now. The driver has the wipers going full speed.

—You can drop me at the gate, she tells him, as they draw closer to the nursing home.

She researched for weeks, following up on every promising lead and recommendation from colleagues with at least two visits, until she settled on this one. It's the best place for

Alzheimer's, and they do everything they can to make her mother comfortable. But still her visits leave her feeling disappointed, as if somehow everything can be blamed on her because of her choice of institution. Each evening, she finds her mother propped in an armchair, not quite looking at the wall-mounted TV permanently on low in the background. Her heavily sedated state is for her own safety, after the lightbulb incident: her mother had apparently unscrewed a lightbulb and crushed it in her hand, then smeared the broken glass across her face and tried to rub it into her skin, *like a moisturiser*. The carer on duty had been alerted by the screams of another patient. Luckily, the cuts were superficial, and had healed well.

—Are you sure? the driver asks.

—I'm sure.

She needs the air.

She makes a run for it, pushing her umbrella open as she goes but getting drenched anyway, so that, just for a moment, it's a relief to get indoors. Then the sudden heat jolts her back, into the home. She checks in with Sheila, as always, then seeks out the duty nurse to get a detailed update. She examines her mother's chart carefully, though there is rarely any variation. When she can postpone it no longer, she goes in.

Her mother doesn't recognise her; she doesn't even register the fact that she has a visitor, so there is little to do once she has smoothed down the throw. She says hello to May's visitors, and walks over to look out the window. May's family is always happy to make small talk, but in the pause after the initial observations on the weather, or the shortening of the evenings, or the heavy traffic, everyone remembers why they are there. This evening they all agree that it's a dirty evening, and that the rain is the proper, wet kind. Then she turns to her mother and fusses over her slippers, while May's daughter rustles up a newspaper and begins to read bits out. *She likes to keep up with the news*, they've told her many times. May is just as sedated as her mother, so it's highly unlikely. But she mustn't presume. No one really knows what May, or her mother, is aware of. After one or two articles, clearly chosen for their lightness of content, May's visitors leave, but she can hear them out in the corridor, where they stand for ages chatting.

Eventually, she gets up to leave too. But just as she reaches the door, her mother says something, which is an almost unprecedented occurrence. It's a mumble, as if she is talking to herself, but audible nonetheless. *There you are, off running again when someone needs you.* This, from her mother who has not been cogent for decades – first from drink, then dementia – her mother who knows nothing about running, and who certainly doesn't know about the job in London. No one does, except the board and Jeffrey. For goodness sake, she hasn't even received the official offer yet. And when she does, she hasn't decided what she will do.

—What did you say, Mam? she asks. Unfairly. She knows what she said, and she knows that there is no point in asking her to repeat it. Sure enough, her mother has resumed her staring off into whatever unreachable realm she usually inhabits, and there is no repeat of the words, or any words, though she waits for several minutes longer. When finally she leaves, and slips past the close group of May's family, she is suddenly envious of the simple comfort of their numbers.

In the visitors' toilet, she takes her running gear and rolled-up backpack out of her Longchamp bag. She puts on leggings, T-shirt, visibility vest and runners, then she puts her neatly folded suit and blouse, shoes and her now-folded bag into the backpack. *Quite the routine*, Jeffrey said, when she told him about it. She couldn't gauge his tone.

She has a book, *What I Talk About When I Talk About Running*, one of the few she owns that's not a textbook, which she returns to again and again like a Bible. Running is the closest she comes to religion, the one thread that is woven through her entire adult life. Sometimes she thinks it's what keeps her going. When she slips the straps of her pack over her shoulders it feels as if she is putting on wings. She walks through the front doors of the home, barely able to contain herself until she has rounded the bend in the driveway, then breaks into a run.

But there is too much getting in the way for her usual sense of peace to kick in. May's visitors had left the newspaper lying on a chair, with its cover photograph of the beautiful woman who had died, perhaps because doctors were not allowed to help her; it's what this afternoon's meeting was about, and what they're all full of at work: the mothers, the midwives, security and visitors, as well as her colleagues. They're all talking about it in the UK too, Jeffrey told her. Such a stupid death, such hypocrisy, they're saying, and they know all about it over there, since they are the ones who have to deal with it. She is professionally embarrassed, and much more. *Isn't it shocking*, May's daughter had said as she put the paper down, and they had all nodded, helplessly. She can't remember if her mother glanced at it before she spoke. Was this what she had meant? She tries to reassure herself that she did not apply for the new job because it's only a matter of time before it happens in her own hospital. She tries to suppress an instinct that tells her this is the very reason she should stay. *Off running*. Was that the same as running off? Of course, her mother has long been a stranger to reason, and it was highly likely that her strange little speech meant nothing at all. Or meant something else entirely; between them, after all, there was a history of running away.

Maryland, 2012

The deck chair is close to tipping point, but I straighten my knees another fraction until I'm leaning right over the gap between the pier and the boat. I perfected this art of hovering between land and water when I was a kid. Though I fell in plenty of times too. Maxie passes the fat joint he's been rolling and I reach for it carefully; at this angle, the least movement is all it takes, and the water below is black and greasy. I take a toke. What's the plan? Maxie wants to know, and I see him glance at the urn on the ground next to me as he asks. I inspect the joint, hoping it might offer some kind of answer, but the tip just smoulders and the ash hangs there, suspended. I bring the feet of the chair back down, right as the ash falls. I hand the joint back.

—Tell you the truth, Maxie, I don't exactly have a plan.

—You want any help with . . .?

—You did plenty already, you know, coming with me to . . . and everything . . .

I don't exactly have the vocabulary for this conversation, but Maxie's nodding like he gets it anyway.

—Do you think she'd like if I took the boat out in the bay and, you know, sprinkled . . .?

Mom liked to get out on the water as often as she could. But it was also what she did whenever there was something she needed to figure out, some problem to solve. Or when we got in a fight about something. *Let's take it out on the water*, she'd say, meaning the disagreement as much as the boat. By the time we got back we forgot what it was even about, because out there you have to work together, and you're way too busy to fight. But it's more than that. It's how helpless you are in your little boat against the hugeness of the ocean, makes all the other stuff seem, I don't know, trivial.

But Maxie shrugs at what I'm suggesting. I get why he's not into it. It's because Mom wasn't into making big deals out of stuff. She sure as hell didn't leave instructions for this eventuality. In the movies, dead people already have music and poems picked out. Always seemed control-freaky to me, but hey, what do I know? Maybe I'll do all that shit myself when I get old. But it wasn't Mom's thing.

—No relatives?

—Not that I know.

Maxie lets that one sit there. Most of the long-timers down here have stuff they either don't know, don't want to know, or don't want you to know. Which amounts to the same thing. You don't pry.

—Well, that simplifies things, he says finally.

—I guess so.

Neither of us says anything for a while. Which is cool.

—All right, Ali Baba. He hauls himself up. —You just let me know if you need anything.

—I don't need anything, I tell his retreating back as he shuffles off up the slipway.

It's true. I've been here alone plenty of times before. And apart from that first night, when Maxie and Jess refused to leave me by myself, I've been staying on the boat alone. The trick is not to think too much, because no amount of thinking can change what happened. And nothing could've prevented it, either, because Mom would never have wanted to live anywhere but the boat. That makes it easier.

But this morning was way tough. I didn't see it coming; I figured seeing her in the morgue was as bad as it could get, all yellow and swollen, not even close to what she really looked

8

like, except it was definitely her. I ran out of there and ugly-cried all the way back to the marina in Maxie's car. But this morning was even worse. Just a handful of us in some room that was not a church but was like one, all soft music and those big, stinking lilies that she hated. She'd of preferred to open all the windows and let the air in. Then I remembered the coffin, and how she was right at that moment being shoved into a furnace and burned. That's when I had kind of a meltdown. Maxie got me out into the parking lot where we hung out by his car smoking weed until I was able to calm down.

I'm okay now. I can handle it. I just have to figure out what to do with her ashes. I'm thinking I'll put the urn below deck, at least for starters, and I'm dragging myself up out of my chair when I notice the car pull up. It's not a fancy marina by a long shot, and we don't get cars like this one too often. It's long and shiny and black, and the driver has wound down his window to talk to Maxie. Max can't have told him much because he only stops for, like, two seconds, but when he's leaving he glances towards me, like a sort of warning. I figure he's got it wrong, because what would someone in a car like that want with me?

It takes them for ever to get out, and then I see why. One of them is an old woman with a walking frame, and the other one has a stick. The driver, who looks older than Maxie – and Maxie is old enough to be my granddad – is guiding them along the sidewalk and on to the pier. He's clutching a folder under his arm, and he looks like he can't decide which one of them needs the most attention, so he scurries back and forth between them. It's kind of funny, so I stay where I am to watch, the old leading the ancient, all of them wearing expensive-looking black clothes, which look way too warm for the day.

Duh, the clothes were the clue, but I missed it. I even smile as they make their way towards me; Maxie was right, they *are* coming to see me. When the young-old guy spots me, he hurries ahead with his arm stuck out in front of him the whole way down to the boat.

—Philip Goldman, of Goldman, Zimmerman and Boyce, he announces when he gets close.

I say *Hi*, ignoring his hand until I hear what he has to say.

—We're—

He checks on the ancients' progress; they're about halfway down the finger.

—We're looking for Ms Alison Dougherty. Are you she?

I shake my head. He looks disbelieving.

—This is number 24, is it not?

I shrug, instinct kicking in too late to tell me to be wary. But he's not about to be put off that easily. He leans back on his heels and squints at the slip number, which is just about visible on the board beside my chair.

—Twenty-four. It says it right here. Your *friend* agreed that you were Alison.

He says it like Maxie's something unsavoury he has to hold away from his nose. I'm starting to get a bad feeling about all this. By now, his two companions have arrived. They look from him to me expectantly.

—Are you Alison Dougherty or not? he demands, losing patience.

—I am Alison, I am not Alison Dougherty, I tell him reluctantly.

The old lady can't contain herself any longer. She edges her walker forward and peers into my face.

—Yes, yes. It's her. She must use Delahunt, the mother's name. You're Alison Delahunt, aren't you?

I nod. She seems to know everything anyway.

—I knew it, she says, sounding satisfied. —I am your grandmother, Moira Dougherty. And this is my husband, Richard, your grandfather.

I don't know what to say. I didn't know I had other grandparents. I guess Mom let me think that they had died somewhere down the line, like her parents had. Or had they, really? I'm starting to doubt all kinds of stuff when the guy with the folder clears his throat.

—I am under instruction . . .

He pulls a paper out of the folder and waves it, like I'm supposed to be able to read it like that. Then he's talking a lot of stuff I don't understand. The old pair look excited, or at least, she does. Old Richard looks like he'd prefer to be just about anywhere else. I know how he feels.

—Do you understand? he finally asks. He's their attorney. I caught that part.

—No. Now if you'll excuse me.

I need to get away from them. Something's taken a turn, and I don't like the sound of it. I pick up the urn, but I'm starting to feel like its contents are the cause of all my new problems. Your mother, he kept saying, while he waved his paper around. I caught a glimpse of a signature on it that I recognised. My mom, who liked to talk about living with nature, off nature, off the grid, but who, it seems, also had legal representation.

—You're coming to live with us, the old lady cut in again.

I'm shaking my head as I step on to the boat deck.

—I live here.

The attorney intervenes again.

—You are a minor, and your mother has made provision. Your paternal grandparents are now your legal guardians.

—You're crazy, I tell him. I'm not thinking straight, but I'm thinking straight enough to start untying the boat.

A shiny black shoe plants itself on to the rope.

—Hey!

—I'm afraid you must come with us. Now. The courts have already issued the order.

Rathlowney, 1982

She couldn't empty her bank account in case Audrey, the cashier, told her mam, as unlikely as it was that she would bump into her, so she withdrew as much as she dared, and at the last minute she went through Mam's bag and took another twenty pounds. She left a note on the hall table: *By the time you read this I'll be gone.* It sounded like something off the telly when she read it back, but how else were you supposed to say it? She added another bit at the bottom. *I'm going to stay with a cousin of a girl from school in England. I'll ring when I get there. Jasmine.*

There was no cousin, and no girl from school unless you counted Lisa Whelan, who at that very moment was down the road getting into her uniform. She thought of Lisa because her uncle had got her tickets for *Top of the Pops*. Jasmine, and everyone else in the class, tuned in that Thursday night to watch, and for a couple of seconds you could see her, swaying self-consciously to Blondie, in her yellow jumper and her gypsy skirt. But that wasn't why she decided to go to England. It was what came next. 'Night Fever'. It wasn't really her thing, but the Bee Gees weren't able to be there, David Jensen said, so Legs & Co. danced instead. That was what did it. Not that she wanted to dance like them – some of the moves were so corny you'd get laughed out of it if you tried them in the Rugby Club disco – it was the nerve of them. There they were, with their daft moves and their ridiculous see-through nighties with their silver knickers showing, and they didn't give a damn. They tossed their hair back and threw their arms up, shoulders and hips swinging, as they advanced up the stage which ran right into the audience, looking invincible. Jasmine wanted to know how that felt, and she wouldn't find out by staying in Rathlowney. Though apart from London, her plan was vague, to say the least.

Mam was out of it as usual; she wouldn't wake up for hours yet. Besides, she could hardly pretend she hadn't seen it coming. Jasmine didn't know exactly how things had gone so wrong, or when it had happened. It used to be okay, back when she still liked school, and her mam kept busy, always painting a room or making a new rockery. Or baking. She baked far more cakes and butterfly buns than they could ever eat; Dr Jessop had told her that keeping busy was the best thing to do, in the circumstances.

It was around the time Jasmine started secondary school that she'd come home to find Mam still in her dressing gown, confused about the time of day. She took over the cooking then, because it was a matter of having to. She started with beans and packet soup and sandwiches, but when she got sick of those she learned how to make stews, and various things with eggs. It was a while before she realised that fridges and toilets and baths had to be cleaned, so she did that too. Her mam stayed in bed with the curtains closed most days and had to be cajoled into eating, and when the room started to stink, Jasmine had to fight with her to have a bath. Their relationship had somehow turned upside down.

Occasionally the butcher or someone in the supermarket would ask after her. They hadn't seen her in a while, they'd say, and Jasmine would reply that she was fine, just busy. One day Sister Enda asked if everything was okay at home, and Jasmine wondered if she should finally say something, but before she could decide, the nun had launched into a lecture on the state of her uniform, which was a disgrace, and which she needed to tend to immediately or her mother would be called in. She started avoiding classes then, and by the time she was in fifth year she was taking full days off. She'd go down the river, or if it was wet she'd just sneak around downstairs, reading *Jackie* and *Blue Jeans*, and listening to her transistor on its lowest setting. Mam was oblivious upstairs, with her bottle of whatever it was.

Jasmine didn't know when that had started either.

The day the inspector came, she spotted him through the net curtains, and she was shaking when she answered the door. But she managed to brazen it out. She told him she had been very sick, but that she was better now and she'd be in tomorrow. He issued a stern warning before turning and striding down the path. She closed the door in relief, hardly able to believe she had got away with it. Only, to her dismay, her mother had chosen that day to get out of bed for the first time in weeks, and she was standing in her dressing gown, swaying, at the top of the stairs. She wanted to know who was at the door, but when Jasmine stammered something about a friend from school, her mother let loose in a way Jasmine had never seen. She had HEARD THE WHOLE THING. She didn't want to be LIED TO. Jasmine was a LITTLE RIP. The shock of her mother shouting, and the unfairness of it all, made her shout back, which was another shock. She had never answered back before. To her surprise, it made her feel better.

It happened again the next day. She actually did go to school, but when she got home her mother was waiting, glass in hand, demanding to know what sort of time it was to be getting home. Jasmine was bewildered. It was only half four. She had stopped at the butchers, she began.

—Don't give me any of your LIES, her mother screamed.

The unreasonableness scared her, so she did what she could to appease her, and finally persuaded her to go back to bed. It marked the start of the bad phase. She couldn't predict her mother's moods from one hour to the next, because it depended on whether she was drinking, and which tablets she had taken. She knew she should be more patient, but she was already under pressure from school, and doing everything in the house and for her mam, so she ended up fighting back. In the end, she couldn't work out whether the rows were all her fault, or all her mam's, and it didn't really matter; all they'd done for months was scream at each other.

She had threatened to run away lots of times, only now she was really doing it. She swung her old khaki rucksack on to her back, closed the door quietly, and made her way up the town to Murphy's Bar, where the Dublin bus stopped every morning.

Imelda Lawlor's father, who drove the bus, asked her where she was off to, but she had her story ready. She was getting fitted for uniforms in Arnotts, she told him.

—Is it that time of the year already? he asked, but he hadn't a clue. Most fathers didn't, she gathered from listening to her classmates. She wondered how different things would have been if hers hadn't died, but she nipped that line of thought in the bud, because what was the point?

By the time they were pulling up along the quays she was bursting with excitement. It suddenly felt real. She was starting her new life. She gave Imelda's father a breezy *See ya*, and headed off towards O'Connell Bridge.

She had to ask a man the way to the ferry, and the walk, past grim-looking warehouses covered in graffiti, was longer than she expected. Her rucksack was getting heavier with every step, and by the time she got to the P&O ferry ticket office she was wrecked. She paused outside the door, worried that someone might try to stop her getting on to the boat. Someone should, surely, a girl on her own? But the woman took her money and issued the ticket, and told her she could change her punts into sterling on the boat. Jasmine took the ticket and her change and thanked her. It hadn't even occurred to her that the money would be different.

—Which way . . .?

—Over there, love.

She pointed to where little clusters of people had gathered. They were a grey-faced, miserable-looking bunch. One lad who looked about her own age was surrounded by his family, and they were all crying. As Jasmine got closer, she saw them step back a bit to give him time with a red-haired girl; his girlfriend, presumably. As they clung to each other, his freckled hand on her waist to keep her close, Jasmine heard him promise that he'd write. She wondered what it would feel like to have a fella's hand on your waist, and if he would keep his promise. She couldn't imagine any of the yahoos she knew sitting down with paper and a pen, writing to a girl. No, it was more likely that he'd forget all about the girl back home, waiting for the postman every morning. Still, she hoped she was wrong.

Maryland, 2012

—Come on, Ali. We're leaving.

   —I want to drive.

   —You can't, so scoot back, and stop being a pain in the ass.

   —You're the pain in the ass.

But he's right, I can't. It's something I need to fix. How hard can it be if Callum can do it? I could take off on my own, not have to put up with these assholes. Get out on the open road, stop when and where I want. But I haven't figured out how I'll do any of that. My money's not going to last for ever. Besides, I'm scared even to use the ATM because it'll give my location away. I'll lose this bunch of dickheads as soon as. Meanwhile, they're useful, or at least Callum is. I scoot, and he climbs on. He'd like if I'd press into him, wrap my arms around him, be his back warmer, like he said when I got on the first time. I told him I was no one's back warmer. So I hold on to the seat behind me and he revs up and takes off.

I figure he likes to leave before the others so he doesn't feel all emasculated and shit when the guys with the big dicks, I mean, bikes, roar past and smother his little Honda in their dust. Either way, they'll already be sculling beers and toasting their smores by the time this lame pile of junk rocks up. Not that I'm complaining. It's getting me where I want to go. Which is far away from Federal Hill Park, Baltimore.

I tried. I mean, it wasn't like I had much choice. But two months of that dump was as much as I could take. The old pair are like clockwork, always up at the same time, eating the same things, mostly stuff to keep them regular. Gross. And I'm supposed to join them? Rita's nice, always sure to make something I might like when they weren't looking. I miss her enchiladas already. But I don't miss that shit school they sent me to. The girls there were unbearable, so I quit. Next thing you know, they're talking about boarding school. I mean, shit, why grab me out of my life where I was perfectly happy, then send me off to some bullshit private school? It's like, they liked the idea, doing the right thing by their only grandchild and all, but when it came down to it, I was just getting in the way of their stuffy boring lives, making noise and mess and trouble. That's what I figured, anyhow. I called Maxie because I wanted to hear a friendly voice. I wasn't about to admit it to my so-called grandparents, or even to Maxie, but the thought of being locked up in some fancy school scared the hell out of me. I was doing just fine with you guys, I told him, trying not to sound like I was whining. But instead of reassuring me, he told me the boat was letting in a lot of water, and that I should count myself lucky that my fairy grandparents had turned up when they did. Fuck you, Maxie, I told him, and hung up.

I wasn't surprised about the boat. The thing was ancient, and is probably at the bottom of Chesapeake Bay by now. But that was when I made my mind up to leave. Maybe I couldn't go back to the marina, but I sure as hell wasn't staying in Federal Hills to get sent off to school. I feel kind of bad about Maxie. None of this is his fault. But I can't call him back because I pitched my phone into the dust soon as we got out of the city so I couldn't be traced.

We roar out of the gas station and up the street, making heads turn. Callum gave me his other jacket. It's way too big, but it keeps the wind off. It got pretty chilly crossing Hanover Street Bridge in just a sweater. I pulled my jeans on over my shorts too. It was scary weaving through the cars like that at first, and it's not like I trust Callum – I don't even know him that well – but I don't have a choice, so when he tells me to lean, I lean.

It gets better once we get out of the burbs into the country. It's kind of cool, watching the trees whizz by. I haven't been out this way before – by which I mean west of Maryland – which, I know, sounds crazy. But me and my mom always went east, straight out from the bay to the Atlantic. Mom never liked to be far from the ocean. She said she couldn't breathe right in there, meaning inland. When we had to take a trip to the Supercentre, three, four times a year, she'd prepare like we were going into the wild. Maps, phone all charged up, burners all turned off on the boat. Then she'd pile her inhalers into the glove compartment. And right before we left the marina she'd wind down the window and smoke a little something. She did it, like, a lot, but she specially needed it if she had to drive inland. Everyone who didn't live on a boat was crazy, as far as she was concerned. But I get it. When you grow up tasting salt every time you take a breath it's hard to imagine anything else. All the stuff the old couple bought for me, the fancy laptop and phone, the big-screen TV, doesn't come close to having the ocean for your playground. The big plan was one day to sail all the way to Bermuda, just her and me, a two-woman crew. Guess that's not going to happen now.

Every mile that passes I'm wondering what I'll do *out west*. Callum thinks he's Sal fucking Paradise, with all his big plans. When I told him, he said *Who?* See what I'm dealing with? Couldn't find his ass with two hands and a compass. Worst partner ever in Shop, totally clueless. All he wanted was to get out of school, which is how I figured he was my ticket out of Federal Hill Park. Only I hadn't seen him since I moved schools, and when I tried to track him down, I heard he'd already dropped out and was hanging with his loser biker cousins. When I called by his house, his mom said he was *around*. She was backing away while she said it, real cagey, like I was the cops or something. She was still standing there inside the screen door when I left, I guess making sure to see me off the property. Wanting to get back to her vodka grapefruit, Callum said when

I told him how suspicious she was acting. I found him outside his cousin's house. They were passing around a reefer and necking bottles of Bud Lite at, like, ten in the morning. They hadn't been to bed, he told me. I guess they're not so different, Callum and ol' Sal.

I'm not like that, just taking off without any planning. I like to think ahead. It's part of growing up on a boat, and because of my mom being the way she is. Was. I don't think I'll ever get used to saying that. The so-called grandparents like to imply that she neglected me. I heard them tell the social worker it was my *alternative upbringing* when she came round to see how I was settling in. Like it was my mom's fault that I hated their house and their neighbourhood and their boring lives and the shit school they sent me to. It wasn't like they did such a great job with my dad, as far as I can tell, taking off like that when I was a baby, leaving my mom to take care of me, so screw them. Mom was a free spirit, so I could be one too, she told me. Which meant *alternative*. Whatever. At least she was there, which is more than they can say about their son. Or themselves. Big mystery is why it took them this long to interfere, if they were so concerned about my welfare. Maybe it's because they're old and they want to square things up. They don't want to have me on their conscience. Or maybe they did try but Mom wouldn't co-operate. Well, they can put their minds at ease. They tried this time, but it just didn't work out. I'm thinking, maybe I'll go all the way to the west coast, to the Pacific Ocean. Guess I'm not too different from my mom, always headed for the water.

It's late afternoon when we get off the highway again, and I'm getting pretty hungry. One of Rita's empanadas would go down well right about now. Plus, I think I can feel my period starting, so I need to find a drugstore or something. Guess I wasn't thinking ahead this time, but hey, I left in a hurry. Callum said they were about to take off on a road trip, so I went straight back to the house and grabbed a few clothes and a washbag.

On my way past the study I saw that file, the one they had with them when they came to the marina with their lawyer, so I took that too. But there was no time to think about food. I'd kill for a Clif Bar right now, chocolate chip – no, peanut butter. Mom never let us run out of those things. She figured if we missed meals here and there, at least we were getting our protein and fibre and stuff. Organic, too. Who says we lived off of junk food. That's the other thing they told the social worker. Assholes.

We're pulling into some abandoned parking lot with a squat grey rectangular building, and nothing much else. It does not look promising. *Th Fu l Moo*, the neon sign says above the door. A bar, I guess. I sure hope they have dispensers. If they let me in, and if they even have a Ladies.

—I need the restroom, I tell Callum. He's screwing around with locks and stuff.

—Go ahead.

—What if they ID me?

He shrugs.

Loser. Guess I'm on my own.

—Okay. Got any quarters?

—What do you need quarters for? You can use my phone, dude.

I tell him Tampax; that shuts him up.

He rummages in his pockets and comes up with a handful.

I wait until most of them have gone inside, Callum too – guess he has fake ID – then I follow, scanning like crazy for the Ladies, and I spot it. Awesome. It's down the passage, so I won't need to go into the bar and get thrown out. It's not like I care. I don't even want to drink. But I don't want these guys thinking I'm some kind of kid because then they might not want me tagging along, and I need the ride.

It's not gross. I guess they don't get that many ladies in to mess it up. And thank fuck, they actually have dispensers. I slot in my quarters then I'm good to go, for now, but I'm going to need a drugstore pretty soon. I grab an armful of tissue paper from the stall and stuff it into the pockets of Callum's jacket, for emergencies, then I figure I'll go wait in the parking lot. As I pass by the door to the bar, one of Callum's cousins, the one with the squint and the greasy ponytail, looks up and spots me, and he's waving me over. As if.

When I emerge from the dank cave that is the so-called Full Moon, the actual sun has turned into a huge neon peach, and it's streaking the sky pink like a Disney sunset. It's going down fast behind some industrial buildings and I have, like, about half a minute before it's gone. I'm starting to look for my phone to take a picture, then I remember I don't have it, which sucks.

A couple of minutes later, the last of the purples are grey, and the shadows are getting darker. The dumpster beside me is rank so I move and rest against the nearest Harley. I don't feel like going back in. Bunch of morons, talking moron shit. No one's out here but me, and I like it that way.

But just when I'm starting to relax, here comes the cousin – the brains behind the outfit, not. It's Darren, I think. Or Danny.

—Getting a breather, eh? is his lame opener. I ignore him. He comes closer. He has a beer in one hand and a joint in the other, which he holds out. In the fading light it's just a grey shape with an orange tip.

—Getting a breather myself. Want some?

—No.

—No?

—No thanks.

He gives a dry-sounding *Ha* that I guess is supposed to pass for a laugh.

—Beer?

As if I'd put that to my lips after it's been near yours.

—No.

—Is that all you got to say, no?

I shrug. That's the kind of question you can't answer without getting picked up wrong. I wish he would just go back inside and leave me alone. He looks like he's about to, but he changes his mind and leans over and lurches towards me, like he's going to kiss me.

—What the fuck? I pull away.

Only now he looks like he wants to, I don't know, strangle me or something, but he changes his mind, or maybe he can't because his two hands are already full.

—I don't want you leaning on my bike.

What a baby.

—Fine. I'll move.

—You'd better.

He turns and goes back inside.

I move, like it makes any difference. There's not a single car in the lot, and I don't know why but this makes me uneasy. I'm sorry now I didn't take a hit. Then I'm not. Half the time the stuff just makes me paranoid. It was the same for my mom. She smoked when she was nervous, only it just made her more nervous, but she went ahead and did it anyway. *Carpe diem*, she liked to say when she lit up, like, here's a perfectly good joint, it's a pretty day with the sun up there in the sky, what else is there to do?

Man, it hurts thinking about her. Sometimes, like now, it feels like I won't be able to get through it. The school counsellor wrote my grandparents that I should make an appointment, but I refused because I didn't want to have to tell some shrink how much I miss my mom. Plus, I didn't want to talk about how fucking furious I am with her. Not that I'd admit that, have them going back to my grandparents, giving them more ammunition. *But what would you expect?* was the other thing they said to the social worker. They were talking about how Mom died. *Fell off the goddamn boat*, the old man said, holding an imaginary glass and twisting his wrist a couple of times to imply that she was drinking. Only he was wrong, my mom didn't hardly drink, she fell off the boat during an asthma attack. But it doesn't mean I can't be mad at her. Grandparents.

And a lawyer. Everyone just turning up, everyone knowing what's best for me. So much for all that living outside the loop shit. *Carpe diem*, my ass.

I'm back by the dumpster, slumped on Callum's bike, not too sure what my plan is, if you want to know, when Callum comes out.

—Hey.

—Hey.

—Danny says you're not acting nice. Thought I'd come see what the problem is.

That doesn't merit a response so I don't give one. Instead, I start tugging at the saddlebag.

—What are you doing?

—Nothing. Just getting my stuff.

—It's safer in there.

—Says who?

—Says me.

—Oh yeah, what if I don't agree?

Callum sighs.

—All right, have it your way.

He produces his key and opens the saddlebag. I didn't know it was locked. I reach in and pull out my backpack, which contains pretty much everything I own. I pull it over my shoulder.

—Done?

I nod.

—So what's the deal with Danny?

—There's no deal.

—Look, Ali. It wouldn't hurt to be a little nicer. These guys are letting you tag along and you're acting ungrateful. I don't want you blowing it for me.

I see where he's coming from. Give, take. Only it feels like the rules are stacked in their favour. But it's not like I have a choice.

—I'll try, I tell him.

24

He looks relieved.

—Let's go back inside then. You don't want to be out here on your own.

I do. But that's not being nice. Reluctantly, I follow him into the dingy bar. There's sawdust on the floor, and plastic chairs. I sit on one as far from the rest as I can without looking *ungrateful* while Callum goes to get beers. Danny is at the bar, and he's looking at me, and even from here I can tell he's not happy. I pretend to get busy searching for something in my bag until Callum gets back. He's holding two Bud Lites.

—These are on Danny, he says, putting them down.

—For fuck—

—Save it, Ali. Just pick up your beer and wave thank you to the nice man who bought it for you.

I'm trying to think of some way not to do this as I reach slowly for the bottle and wrap my fingers around it. My mind goes shooting off all over, looking for a plan, but it doesn't come up with anything. I lift the beer.

—Maybe smile? Callum says between his teeth.

I twist my lips and raise the bottle in the direction of the bar.

—Now drink.

—Can you quit telling me what to do? I snap.

—Jeez.

But I drink anyway because my mouth is dry.

He goes back to the bar and starts talking to Danny. They're both looking my way. This is not feeling like a good situation. Next thing, they're standing, and Danny's putting on his jacket. I guess we're leaving. The others are knocking back their beers, like they know by osmosis or something. I wait at my table for Callum, but Danny gets to me first. *Be nice*, I remember, so I mumble thanks for the beer, but he acts like he doesn't hear me.

—You're with me, he says, and keeps walking.

Shit shit shit. Where the hell is Callum? But he's nowhere. Again I can't think my way out, so I pick up my jacket and follow Danny.

When we get to the parking lot, I try telling him that Callum will be wondering where I am, but he gives a short laugh.

—Get on.

That's when I notice it's just me and Danny in the deserted lot. Where are the rest of the bikers? It's like there's a conspiracy, so I do what I don't want to do for the third time, and get on. I take care not to let any part of me touch him, not even my backpack, and I turn my face to one side to avoid inhaling the unwashed smell of his greasy mane.

—Shouldn't we wait for the others? I shout over the noise of the engine.

No response. I'm starting to get it. I figure there's no point in asking where we're going.

He manoeuvres free of the parked bikes then revs up and takes off so fast across the tarmac that wherever we're going, I'll be happy just to get there safe. But we're only getting up to speed when he turns into some kind of industrial park. He stops the bike in an alley between rows of what look like garages. Self-storage units. I've been to plenty. Lots of the houseboat folk have one. Always far from everything, deserted. I can make out the units either side of us, but it's too dark to see any further.

There's a sudden silence, which doesn't feel right. Instinctively, I start feeling in my backpack for my pocket knife. My mom taught me how to gut a fish or cut a rope real quick if one needed cutting, only my hands are shaking so much I can't find it, and then it's too late. In one quick movement he's off the bike, tosses my backpack away, then pulls me off and slams me up against the nearest shutters.

That's when I separate out into parts. It's like, part of me is watching as my body struggles and twists, trying to escape, but another part of me knows I can't escape; this is actually happening and I have to deal with it, and another part refuses to deal and concentrates instead on the rhythmic clatter of the aluminum door reverberating out into the deserted industrial park, and the harsh, speeded-up breaths near my ear.

Then his weight moves off of me, but I stay very still. The bike cranks up and roars off, until there's silence again. I stay a long time like that, how long I don't know, because there's no more past and future, no more *I lived on a houseboat with my mom in Maryland and then my mom died and then I went to live with my grandparents and then* . . . No more *and then*. It's like, before, I had a story about myself, now I have none. The narrative has fractured and stalled, and all the parts of my brain are floundering around trying to hook up with each other to make just enough sense to get me away from this aluminum.

Dublin, 2012

She's glad to shut out the clatter of the downpour and the prematurely dark evening. She shrugs off her backpack and leaves it where it lands, then, with one hand on the wall for balance, tugs off her soaking runners. A long, hot shower and a glass of wine. And maybe something to eat, which invariably means a toasted cheese sandwich, with a tomato if she's lucky. From the living room she can hear the TV. It's an old habit she developed years ago to give the impression that someone is home, to fool any potential burglars. To fool herself.

It would – *will*, she corrects – be nice to come home to someone. Jeffrey is retired and spends his days in his study working on his talks and papers. He's in demand for keynotes and panels, so at least she'll have the place to herself sometimes. She is well aware of the contradiction of wanting Jeffrey to be there, but also wanting him gone, and that it isn't reasonable to expect people to materialise and de-materialise at her whim; a string of failed relationships proved this, and after the last she determined to stay by herself. In her forties, it wasn't hard.

But Jeffrey proved himself to be tenacious. She met him at a conference. He was kind and attentive, and he didn't expect her to tell him all about herself. In return, she didn't ask about his three previous marriages, or his six children – two from each – who did not seem to keep in touch. Because the truth was she wasn't really curious. Life had happened – he was seventy-two, so how could it not? – and it didn't matter to her how he had made and broken those other families. She has no expectations of a life with Jeffrey other than his company, preferably when she wants it.

Her run hasn't settled anything in her mind. Instead of falling to the bottom, the silt keeps on swirling. She tries to separate out the factors. She applied for the master's job because of Jeffrey. No. It was more complicated than that. Jeffrey thought she should apply because she was perfect for the job, and because it would mean moving to London, to him. That part was simple. But she'd hesitated. There was her mother to consider: she was settled in the home that she had chosen so carefully, and moving her would be destabilising and upsetting. But nothing was a problem for Jeffrey. Move her to London's finest nursing home – he would smooth the way – or leave her where she was, and fly back on weekends. But Jeffrey didn't know the difficult history between them, because she hadn't told him. *It's complicated*, she fobbed him off, and he allowed himself to be fobbed. Complicated didn't even come close to covering it.

Then there was the other reason she hesitated. She had lived in London before, and it hadn't ended well.

So Jeffrey leaped to the only conclusion that seemed to be available to him: she didn't want to apply for the job because she was a woman. Once he worked this out, he fell over himself with reassurances. *You mustn't be intimidated, you are perfectly suited*, etcetera, until she wanted to scream. She knew she could do the job, probably better than a man, *because* she was a woman; it was a bloody maternity hospital. So she applied to prove a point, to win an argument that hadn't actually happened other than in her head. But now the job is hers, and she can't prevaricate for much longer.

Dublin, London, 1982

Jasmine moved past the teary couple who wanted to believe that they would be together again some day, and boarded the ferry. She went to the deck and waited, impatient to leave. Already, smells of salt and rust, and the drizzle on her face, were waking her from her Rathlowney stupor.

All the way across the sea she faced forward, towards the grey horizon, wondering what awaited her there. Nerves only hit when they began to pull in to Holyhead. She had arrived, but she hadn't planned this far. She was in no rush to disembark. She'd take her time, wait until the other passengers got off. She'd be fine.

—Excuse me, love?

It was a woman she had spoken to earlier, Ann. She was with her family, on their way to France. Like her, Ann had stayed out on deck most of the time, claiming she felt unwell when she went inside. Jasmine had made only short replies to her friendly questions, afraid of giving something away.

—We were wondering . . . My husband . . . She waved at a grumpy-looking man with a moustache, who was trying to rein in two over-excited boys – James and Ronan, Jasmine knew from the woman's chatter. Six and eight. Pair of live wires. She had wondered at the time if being seasick was an excuse to get a break from them, and watching them now as they grabbed chunks of each other's hair, she felt sure it was.

—We wondered if you'd like a lift? We're driving to London ourselves, well, near, on our way to Dover.

Jasmine's alternative was hitching, because she couldn't afford the train. But she'd never hitched. The thought of walking over to the side of the road and sticking out her thumb was terrifying, never mind all the stories about axe murderers and rapists. Besides, she didn't even know which direction London was. She took a last look at the two boys, who were now trying to push each other over the rails.

—Are you sure?

Ann looked relieved.

—Of course I'm sure. We were worried about you, to tell you the truth. Come on, let's go down to the car deck.

The husband spoke to her only once, to tell her she was foolhardy to have thought she'd hitchhike, did she not know how dangerous it was, but Ann told him to *shush*, and for the rest of the journey he did. They stopped a couple of times, and whatever snacks and drinks they bought for the kids, they bought for her too. She was embarrassed, and the second time it happened she tried to pay, but Ann wouldn't hear of it.

—Isn't it only what I'd like someone to do for this pair, when their time comes?

It was nice to think about it like that. She ruffled Ronan's hair.

—You can send him over to me. I'll be rich and famous by then.

Ann gave her a worried look, but she didn't mind; she was feeling optimistic. She sang songs and played I Spy with the boys until they fell asleep. When the car came to a stop, she realised that she had fallen asleep too.

—This is the best we can do, Jasmine, love, Ann was saying. —Dick doesn't want to drive in to London with the traffic, but you can get buses from here. Are you sure you know where you're going?

Jasmine felt groggy and disoriented. She had a flashback to when she was about Ronan's age, being carried out of the car by her mother and straight up to bed, and in that moment she could think of nothing she would like more. She thought of begging to go to France with them; she could be their au pair or something. But she forced herself to sit up straighter, told them she was grand, thanked them for everything, and asked them to say goodbye to the boys for her. Then she was standing on the path with her rucksack beside her, watching as their car disappeared down the road.

London, she told herself.

Snap out of it, she told herself.

It's what you wanted, she told herself.

Evening was fading and the streetlamps were flickering on. A red double-decker appeared around a corner, but she didn't know what she should do to get it to stop. There was so much she didn't know. The bus indicated and pulled in, and two men got off.

—Well, you getting in or not? the driver asked.

She picked up her bag and stepped on, and he pulled back into traffic. He ignored her as she fumbled with the coins. She had managed to change her money on the boat, but she hadn't worked out what was what yet.

—Where to? he asked.

—Um . . . She dropped one of the coins, the one that looked like fifty pence only smaller, and he mumbled something under his breath. She could feel herself blushing, but then she was annoyed. People made mistakes. People dropped things. Not everyone knew everything about London. She found her coin and straightened up and glared at him.

—Look, mister, I'm doing my fecking best here.

He laughed.

—All right, darlin'. Point taken. Irish, is it?

She nodded, her small burst of audacity already spent.

—Where are you staying?

She had nothing to gain by pretending at this stage. She shrugged that she didn't know. He sighed.

—I know a hostel, it's on the route. Any use?

She nodded.

—Thank you.

He took her fare and told her he'd let her know when they got there.

The hostel slept eighteen to a room, and though no alcohol was permitted, there was evidence from the noise and to-ing and fro-ing that plenty had been consumed. Jasmine was relieved to have a bed, but she lay awake the whole night listening to the shouting and laughing outside, then just shouting, then, when she was right on the edge of sleep, a shrill and terrifying scream. She wondered if she should call the guards – the police, whatever they were called – but she didn't know what the number was, and she hadn't noticed a payphone downstairs. There might be a murderer on the loose, breaking into the hostel at that very moment. What if he picked her bed out of the other seventeen? Why not? She had nothing to defend herself with, and she hadn't a clue what to do.

She hugged her rucksack to her for protection the whole, never-ending night, and as soon as daylight penetrated the filthy windowpane, she was up and out. The footpath was an obstacle course of black plastic bags, and the street stank. Bin day. She stepped carefully over spilt contents, and tributaries of vomit that leaked across the path from piles she was careful not to look at. But at least there was no body, dead or alive. The streets were deserted, which meant she could try to get her bearings without drawing attention to herself. But after walking for nearly an hour she realised that you didn't just *get your bearings* in London. She needed a proper map.

First, she needed tea, and food; she hadn't eaten anything since the batter sausage and chips they'd stopped for yesterday afternoon. There was no shortage of open cafés, though it wasn't even seven o'clock. Tentatively, she pushed a door and went to sit at one of the small, chequered tables. She had never ordered food in a restaurant before; Rathlowney stretched to a chipper and the hotel, and she'd never been in either on her own. The old man came out from behind the counter with his notebook. Anxious not to repeat her experience with the bus driver, she asked immediately for a full English breakfast. As far as she could make out, it was exactly the same as a full Irish breakfast, which would keep her going for a while.

—Tea and toast with that?

She nodded, and he went back to the kitchen. It felt like an achievement.

—Where're you from?

She turned to the table beside her where two lads were horsing into platefuls of rashers and sausages. The accent was familiar.

—Ireland, she said, but as she said it she realised that they were Irish too. She felt like an eejit.

—What part?

She was too flustered to think of a lie, so she told them. What were the odds they'd even know it. Rathlowney was a backwater even by Irish Midlands standards. But it turned out they were from Edenderry, twenty miles away. They were over working on the buildings, they told her. Her relief was matched by her disappointment. She wanted excitement, not culchies from up the road. But they were friendly and seemed glad to talk to someone from home. And when she asked casually what area the café was in, one of them pulled out a battered paperback called *A–Z* and showed her. It was very detailed.

—And where are we on my map? she asked, producing the illustrated one she'd picked up on the boat: Big Ben, Buckingham Palace, the Natural History Museum were all there, in cartoon form. He laughed and pointed to somewhere near her saucer.

—About here.

He hesitated, glanced at his companion.

—Look, if you're stuck for somewhere to stay . . . Just till you get yourself sorted, like. It's only a squat, but . . .

When she looked unsure, he took a napkin out of the steel holder and wrote an address on it, then found the page in the A–Z and stuck it in as a bookmark. He put a couple of pounds on the table and they both stood up.

—It's there if you want it. Keep the A–Z. I have another. Mind yourself. I'm Rob, by the way, and this here is John Boy.

They went out, leaving her to imagine the slagging you'd get in Edenderry for being called John Boy. And why he hadn't changed it when he came over here.

After a few hours of walking London's streets, the scrap of paper in the A–Z started to look like her only possibility. She couldn't bear to go back to the hostel, and even dumps like that cost money. A squat didn't sound appealing, but it was free. Maybe she could come to find the Edenderry accents reassuring. So she made her way there, checking the A–Z every two minutes, and discovered that she had been walking in circles; Keever Estate was only around the corner from the café.

There were no flats in Rathlowney, or if there were, they were just normal houses that had been divided up. These flats, though, stretched out before her in row after row of concrete rectangles with long, shared balconies, and a boarded-up window and door at the front of each. She could still make out some of the graffiti on the nearest gable end. *The queen is a moron. Shaz is a cunt.*

She picked her way across an open area of weeds and plastic bags and broken, faded toys. With every tired step, she worried about what might jump out at her from the undergrowth, but by now her rucksack was really starting to dig into her shoulders and she'd be glad to put it down, even in a dump like this.

Number 118 was in Block A, according to Rob's piece of paper. She stepped on to the first concrete stair, and an unmistakable smell hit her: human shit. What was she thinking? She couldn't live here. But she held her nose and kept climbing, because she didn't have any choice.

—Hi, I'm Jasmine. Rob and John Boy said I could stay here for a while.

She'd rehearsed it all the way, and now she was saying it aloud to a tall girl with a pierced lip. The girl nodded and walked back inside. Jasmine stepped in to the hallway and slid the bag off her back, dropping it gratefully on to the floor. When the girl didn't return, she closed the door and made her way cautiously down the hall. She found her in the front room, sitting cross-legged on a cushion. The room was empty of furniture, except for a large cage in one corner, and the floor was strewn with discarded clothes, dirty cups, empty beer bottles and overflowing ashtrays.

—Smoke?

She held out the packet, and Jasmine reached over and took one. She wasn't really a smoker, but she sometimes joined in at the back of the shed in school, to keep in with the smoking gang. It was all about sending out the right message.

—Thanks.

—Pull up a cushion.

She found one that looked as if it had come out of a skip, covered with cigarette burns and stains that she preferred not to identify.

—Jasmine, is it? the girl said after a long drag. She said it on the exhale, punctuating the words with smoke rings. —I'm Cat.

—Mm hm. Jasmine was holding her own smoke in. She certainly wasn't going to compete with rings.

Cat probably wasn't much older than her, but she seemed older, and if Jasmine was going to make it in London, she resolved to learn what she could from her. The first thing she found out was that the cage in the corner, and the six-foot boa constrictor it contained, belonged to Cat's boyfriend, and she gave slow, deliberate instructions on the likes and dislikes of Jake the Snake. He didn't like being stared at, for example. She also told her that the Tupperware on the mantelpiece sometimes contained a rat.

—Or sometimes I just take him down to the green. Keeps the numbers down.

Jasmine was careful to keep her expression neutral, though it occurred to her that maybe the information was intended to be practical. She awaited further information about the flat, like who else lived here, or if there were bills, or for Cat to ask her about herself, but Cat lay back against the wall as if the talk had exhausted her. Jasmine would have liked to do the same, because she really was exhausted, from the journey and the horrible night in the hostel, and from walking all day, but she forced herself to get up.

—I have to make a phone call.

—Not the one on the corner, Cat said, without opening her eyes. —That one's fucked. You'll have to go down the street, past the old factory, if you want one that works. Or you could go to the one near the green, but it's quite far. Sometimes it's jammed, but if you're lucky it lets you make a call for free. Handy for long distance.

It was useful to know, but she was too tired for the free phone, so she left the flat, crossed the wasteland again, and turned down by the factory until she found the nearest one. She'd reverse the charges.

—Is it home you're calling? the operator asked. It was hard to hear because she had to keep the door propped open with her foot because of the stench of piss and shit. She was starting to think it was how all of London smelled.

—Yes, she replied, thinking that Cat would probably have told her to mind her own fucking business.

—Hold please, caller, and I'll put you through.

With each beep her nerves got worse. *Answer*, she willed her mother. *Answer so we can get this over with*. She felt sick. She needed the toilet. Maybe lots of people in London made these kinds of phone call. Maybe this was why it stank. She couldn't understand why her mother wasn't answering. Surely even someone as out of it as her mother would be waiting beside the phone if her only child was missing.

At last she did answer, and Jasmine could hear the operator ask if she was willing to accept reverse charges from England. There was a fraction of a pause, which felt like infinity.

—You're through. Thank you, caller.

There was a shocking sound, which took a moment to process: her mother, screaming down the phone.

—You little rip. I'm beside myself with worry. Did you ever think about me, with your big plans? Staying with a friend indeed. What friend?

Jasmine imagined the operator, eavesdropping. Well, she wasn't about to provide entertainment for that nosy cow. Besides, there was nothing she could say when Mam was in one of her sober, judgemental furies. She should have expected it. She cut in to her mother's tirade without waiting for her to pause.

—Mam, I'm okay. I'll ring next week. Then, carefully, quietly, she put the phone down and made her way back along the grimy street and across the wasteland to the shitty, half-derelict block of concrete which was, for now, home. She found a corner, as far from Jake the Snake as possible, where she slept surprisingly well.

When she woke, Cat was still curled up, and there were two others who had come in during the night. She'd only risked peeing in the gross bathroom so far, when she discovered too late that there was no toilet paper, but if she was going to live here, she would have to cop on. She decided to brave the shower. It was just a trickle, and it was cold, but it was better than nothing.

—Take up swimming, Cat advised when she emerged, shivering. —Specially if you need to wash your hair.

She duly took note.

Cat's morning routine seemed to involve stripping off to her knickers and stretching out her long limbs. Jasmine was fascinated. She had never stood topless in front of anyone other than her mother, and even then, not since she was about three. Cat had a couple of tattoos, one at the back of her waist, another on her ankle, and other marks on her arms, but Jasmine didn't want to stare to see what any of them were. Instead, she got busy with her make-up. She had a plan, and she wasn't going anywhere without her face.

—How do I get to the BBC Television Centre? she asked Cat as casually as she could, disguising her shyness with an extra coat of mascara.

Cat barely perceptibly arched an eyebrow, but didn't ask.

—That's west London. You'll want to take the Tube. Wood Lane station. She folded her torso on to a raised leg.

Jasmine tried to commit it to memory.

—You look fantastic, she blurted.

Cat gave a short smile.

—So I'm told.

Cat was all cryptic clues, but Jasmine had west London to worry about, and it was off her small, tourist map. As she left, Cat stretched her arms overhead and dropped backwards to the floor in a graceful arch.

Rather than let Cat know how ignorant she was, she decided to take her *A–Z* to the café to figure out her route. Several cups of tea, two Tubes, lots of walking and a few wrong turns later, she stepped into the revolving doors of BBC Television Centre. She forced her wobbly legs to cross the floor to the reception desk, which seemed miles away, and unnaturally high. The receptionist gave her the most fleeting of looks.

—May I help you?

She did not sound as if she wanted to help.

—Yes, please. I . . . Where can I find *Top of the Pops*?

—I'm afraid that's a ticketed show.

She said the word syllable by syllable. *Tic-Et-Ed.*

—Em, I meant . . . Jasmine wished her syllables were clipped and definite. She heard her own accent for the first time, and hated it.

—I want to perform. On *Top of the Pops*.

The receptionist's eyebrows lifted, and a twist appeared at one corner of her mouth.

—Dance, I mean, Jasmine added. —With Legs & Co.

The receptionist's mouth twisted another fraction. She turned to the security guard who was standing nearby.

—She wants to be in Legs & Co.

Now she was laughing openly. The security guard smiled, though more kindly.

—Can you dance, love?

Jasmine shook her head. She could dance – everyone at home said how good she was – but she'd never had a single lesson. She was an idiot to come here. What was she thinking?

—Why don't you try some of the dance studios? he suggested. —Come back to us then, eh?

She was beetroot, and on the brink of tears as she turned and half ran out the door. But once she was outside, swallowed up in crowds of people who all seemed to know where they were going, she remembered again how few choices she had. She had to be practical if she was going to survive. And to prove she could, she went into the nearest shop and bought a twin-pack of their cheapest toilet paper. She pulled the plastic open, carefully tore off three sheets, and blew her nose. She balled them and threw them in the bin. There.

It was easy for John Boy and Rob – lads could always get work on building sites – but what were girls supposed to do? What did Cat do? She supposed she could ask. She trudged back to Keever Estate and up the stinking stairs to 118. Walking around the city seemed to exhaust her in a completely unfamiliar way.

The smell of vinegar and grease drew her down to the kitchen,

40

where she found the two lads, up to their elbows in packages of fish and chips. She hadn't realised how hungry she was.

—It's yourself, one of them said. —Pull up a chair.

She didn't need to be asked twice. There was a greasy mountain of food, with rivers of mushy peas flooding down the sides, the remains of a white sliced pan, and a mauled pound of butter.

—There's a good lot of vinegar, the other one said apologetically.

—No, it's lovely, Jasmine said with her mouth full.

—There's tea in the pot. Grab yourself a mug. They're up there.

She opened the press. There was a single cardboard box on the shelf. *Property of John B Flynn and Robert O'Shea. Fuck off the rest of ye.*

—Yeah, that's it, in there.

Sure enough, there were some cleanish mugs and plates and cutlery. Jasmine took one out and poured herself some tea. She was parched. London was thirsty work.

—How're you gettin' on? asked the one who was slathering an inch of butter on to a slice of bread which he then put into his mouth, whole. —And what's your name anyway? he asked, through it.

—Jasmine.

—Jasmine, bejaysus. Can't say as I know any Jasmines. Where did you say you were from again?

—Which one of you is John Boy? she asked, to change the direction of the conversation. She didn't want to be rude, but.

—You're grand. He's John Boy, I'm Rob. Lots is like that when they come over here. Leave the past where it is.

—Actually, she began, but the word sounded foolish, English. Already. She tried again.

—The thing is, I haven't got much money and I was wondering if you knew of anywhere I could go looking for work.

John Boy washed his wad of bread down with a gulp of tea.

—What can you do?

—Um . . .

—Typing or . . .?

—No.

—Some of the girls goes waitressing, Rob said. Only . . . Well . . . you might have to dress a bit different.

—This is the way I look. They can take me or leave me.

He pushed his chair back.

—You're dead right, Jasmine, dead right. Well, I'm away down for a pint before bed. Are you comin', John Boy?

John Boy stood up.

—I'll have the one.

Then something occurred to him.

—I heard the barman say he was looking for floor staff, someone to collect glasses and take orders, that sort of thing. I'd say he wouldn't mind the hair and that.

Jasmine took a last mouthful of tea and stood.

—Brilliant. Let's go.

The pub was drab. There were a few middle-aged couples dotted around, and a few men at the bar, adding more smoke to the grey cloud that hung near the ceiling.

—What'll you have? Rob asked.

She'd never tried alcohol. At home she couldn't get served, and she wasn't keen on the cider-in-the-park gang. Besides, her mother was enough to put anyone off.

—Vodka, she said. She wanted to seem older, but she could feel the colour rise to her cheeks.

—Ah here, you don't drink, do you? Will you have a Coke or . . .?

—Actually, I'm here on business. I won't have anything. She picked up a couple of empty glasses from a nearby table and flounced up to the bar, where a surly-looking man was polishing glasses.

—How old are you, love? he asked, before she could open her mouth.

—Old enough to collect empties.

He looked her up and down.

—Do you have a name?

—Do you?

He laughed.

—All right. You can try out. Basic wage, but your tips are your own. I'm Ronnie.

She nodded, and walked away to clear a table someone had just vacated. It only took her a couple of minutes to collect the empties and give the tables a wipe with the dubious-looking rag he tossed at her. Then she didn't know what she should be doing. She was tempted to gravitate towards the two boys, where she could at least feel comfortable, but they were as good as their word, and after just one beer they gave her a wave and left. They had an early start, she supposed, but nevertheless she felt a bit abandoned. It occurred to her that she hadn't paid attention to how they'd got here, either. She had no idea how late she'd be, and it was starting to get dark already. She hadn't really thought it through. She made an attempt to look busy, wiping down clean tables, but Ronnie called her over and put a drink by her elbow, something clear with ice and a slice of lemon. It looked sophisticated.

—It's on the house. Put a smile on that pretty puss, eh?

Whatever it was made her mouth pucker, but she was determined to finish it. She couldn't have him thinking she was under age or he might fire her. She drank it back quickly so she wouldn't have to taste it.

—Steady on there, he said, laughing. —Bit of a thirst on you, eh?

—I'm fine, she managed, though her breath was on fire and her eyes were watering.

He gave her a wink and went back to serving. The pub had started to fill up, and soon she was running around trying to keep up. But the drink, and the second one he slipped her, put a buzz into her and she was able to laugh and joke with the customers as if she had been there for ever. In a way, it felt as if she had. The two boys were brilliant, 118 was brilliant, London was brilliant, and it wouldn't be long before she was dancing on *TOTP*. The more the customers drank, the more often they told her to keep the change, and her pockets were starting to feel heavy. One oul' lad actually put in a fiver, and when he pinched her bum the next time she passed she just laughed it off. It was harmless. When the customers began to thin out, she cleared the tables for closing, exhausted but pleased with her evening.

—Toilet break, she called to Ronnie, and headed down the dimly lit corridor. The Ladies was outside, across the small back yard, presumably because ladies didn't go to bars before proper plumbing was invented. The overloud calls of the last few drunk customers sounded far away, and even with the underlying scent of urine, it was good to get a few breaths of smoke-free air.

The outside lightbulb was blown. Typical. She'd have a word with Ronnie. Maybe she'd tell him her name, or some name, anyway. She made her way carefully, afraid of stumbling over unseen obstacles. As she reached the Ladies she heard a noise behind her, and when she turned, she found herself facing her generous customer. But he was standing too near, and her speeded-up heartbeat told her something was wrong. She tried to say something, but it came out in an indistinct *Oh* . . .

—'ello love. Fancy meeting you here.

He stank of beer and bad breath. She took a step back, and another, but he followed each time, and her next step brought her hard up against the wall. His knee was against her thigh, pinning her there. Then his mouth was on hers and he was trying to push his tongue between her teeth. He grabbed at her bum and to her horror she could feel his fingers groping their way in between her legs, but she couldn't move. So this was it. Her adventure would end here, raped and murdered by a stranger in the dark back yard of a pub.

But some part of her wasn't resigned to such a fate. Adrenalin must have kicked in, because with a force she didn't know she was capable of, she got her two hands to his chest and pushed him so hard that he stumbled and fell right back.

—No you bloody don't, she said, as she ran back towards the pub.

—Bitch, she heard him shout after her.

The taste of his tongue was still in her mouth, and she felt like she was going to get sick.

Ronnie looked up at her entrance.

—You all right, love? You look like you've seen a ghost.

—That man out there, he tried to . . . He . . .

The barman raised an eyebrow.

—Did someone hurt you, love?

—Yes. I mean, no. But he could have . . . He had his hands . . .

—But you're all right, I mean . . .

His eyes flickered downwards. She coloured.

—Yes.

—Well, that's all right then. Here, let me get you a drink.

A drink wouldn't make it better, but she didn't know how to explain that, so she stood wordlessly by the bar while he measured her vodka. When the customer came back in, he looked furious, and she bolted behind the bar and hid behind Ronnie, but he walked straight through the lounge and spat another *Bitch* over his shoulder as he left.

—See, you're all right. He didn't mean nothing. Just had a bit too much, is all.

She had begun to shake uncontrollably. She didn't want to hear *He didn't mean nothing*. She didn't want a drink. She wanted someone to carry her to a warm car, then into a house and straight to bed.

—Can you pay me, please?

Her voice sounding stronger than she felt. Good. He looked surprised, but went to the till and extracted the notes, which she counted carefully.

—All in order, love? he asked, winking.

Bastard. They were all bastards.

—Can I get a taxi?

—Be my guest. He indicated the payphone on the wall, and the business cards sellotaped up around it.

She fumbled the coins out of her pocketful and managed to get through. She hung up and went to stand by the door.

—Your drink, the barman called after her, but she ignored him. She was able to do only what was necessary, and answering him was not.

—Suit yourself, he said, but he sounded distant, like a voice on a radio in another room.

When the taxi driver poked his head in the door, she walked in a careful straight line to the waiting car. She heard herself say *Keever Estate*, then she repeated the two words silently until the car stopped. When she got up to the flat, there was nobody in the living room, and she stumbled to her corner, where she slept as deeply as she needed to be able to carry on the next day, as if nothing had happened.

Tennessee, 2012

That's where Callum finds me, still frozen in place against the shutters. He pulls up my jeans and fumbles with the button, then gives up. I don't resist when he leads me to his bike and I see him wince when I wince as I put my leg over the saddle. He zips up my jacket – his jacket – and asks if I'm okay. That's a dumb question so I don't answer, but I don't think I could, even if I wanted to. Hold on, he tells me. I hold on. We're out on the road. We pick up speed. The wind snaps and slices at my hair and cuts my face. Or maybe the cuts were already there. The bike forges through layer after layer of darkness and I don't ever want it to stop.

But too soon we're slowing down and Callum exits on to a dirt track. The ride is bumpy and I am dimly aware that it's hurting me. There is a clearing. The rest of the bikers are there, drinking beer. It's like I'm somewhere else and this whole scene has nothing to do with me, because surely Callum hasn't brought me back to these guys and to Danny? I try to focus on what he's saying. Bivvy, I finally understand, but I don't know what that is. He stops trying to explain, and goes instead towards his saddlebags. That's when I remember my backpack. I start to panic.

—This? Callum asks quickly.

I snatch it and put it on my front, holding it tightly to me like it could keep me in one piece.

—Okay, he says. —Now, this way.

He's speaking softly, trying to help me off the bike without drawing attention to the fact that he's doing it. He's trying to hush me. It occurs to me that he doesn't want to draw attention to me, period, so I co-operate. We walk in the opposite direction to the rowdy bikers, and when he decides we have created enough distance, he pulls something out of a bag and unrolls it. Then he moves about, spreading it out – a long bag. Bivvy. The word repeats on a loop. Bivvy, bivvy, bivvy. If I keep saying it, it will keep me safe.

—Wait here, he tells me, though he doesn't have to.

When he comes back, he has a bed roll and a sleeping bag. He holds them out to me, and when I don't take them he unrolls them himself. He puts the sleeping bag into the first, thin bag, and puts it on to the bed roll.

—Go ahead, try to get some sleep.

It's like a cocoon and I get in, still keeping hold of my back-pack. I cover my head. I want to wrap myself up in the dark until I disappear.

—So, you're okay then, huh?

I had forgotten about him. I lift the fabric a fraction, and I see him standing awkwardly nearby. I guess he's feeling uneasy, like, *sorry about what happened but hey*. For the first time since moving away from the aluminum door, I can feel something: I hate him.

—Leave me, I say.

I hear him walk away.

Their voices are too loud and too harsh, and every sound is a footstep in my direction, but no one comes near me. Minutes become hours and the voices grow fewer, until there are none. When it's been quiet for a long time, I inch out of my sheath and creep behind the bushes, because, as scared as I am, I need to pee, and change Tampax.

It's a real mess down there, and it's sore, and there's a smell I can't place, only then I can, and it's him. I start retching, and I can't stop, and I hear my choking and gagging disturbing the night, and I'm real scared I'll wake them up, but my body wants to be empty. I'm sweating and crying, and even when there's nothing left to throw up, I can't stop. Until at last I do. I can feel the sweat drying on me and I'm cold. I listen for a while before moving, but there's no sound from across the clearing, so I finish cleaning up with toilet tissue, then I crawl back and lie, sleepless and shivering, in my bag.

Only I must have slept, because I can remember my dream. I'm a little kid, all cosied up, watching TV on the boat with my mom and my dad. What's weird is, I can still see my dad's face, but I don't remember him in real life, and my mom didn't keep pictures of him around. That's when I notice that I'm still gripping my backpack to my chest. I release it and undo the clasp. Slowly, I take out the file and open it for the first time, but in the darkness I can't make anything out. One by one, I go through pages I can't see, until I get to the photographs I must have known were there. I can make out shapes, but I don't need light to know it's my father. I trace his outline with my fingertip over and over until I realise that I can make out features; it's getting light out.

I return the papers to the file and shove it back in my bag. It's not my deadbeat dad I need to be thinking about right now. If anyone, it should be my mom, who took care of me when he bailed. But she's gone, and I need to take care of myself. I need to get out of here.

I push Callum's sleeping bag into my pack, then I start unzipping the bivvy, one metal tooth at a time, for what seems like for ever, but rushing it could be the difference between getting away and getting caught. At last it's wide enough for me to take a peek. In the pre-dawn all I can make out is the dark lumps of crashed-out bodies. I figure I have two choices. Steal away on to the road and take my chances hiking, or . . .

Guess I'm not in the mood for depending on strangers. I'm on my own from now on. That gives me pause for, like, a second, but I don't have time for self-pity, so I get back to business. Like my mom taught me, the first rule is be prepared, so I pull the last of the toilet roll out of my pocket and stuff it into my knickers; it'll have to do. Then I rummage in the bottom of my pack until I find my pocket knife. I select the biggest blade and crawl out of my cocoon. My legs feel real wobbly when I stand up, so I'm super-careful when I walk. It's dead quiet, and I want to keep it that way.

As I get closer to the party fall-out, I'm hardly breathing, but with the amount of cans everywhere, these losers are not even close to waking up. Still, I move like a thief. I guess I am one, or I'm about to be. And right here's the victim of my crime. Callum, sleeping like a baby. He's draped his jacket over himself, poor boy, I guess because I had his sleeping bag. Makes it easy to slip my hand into the pocket and extract his keys. He doesn't even twitch.

I'm moving slowly towards the bikes, because I don't want to blow it now, when I spot Danny. He's face-down in the dirt, near the remnants of their campfire. Too bad he didn't fall in; all that greasy hair would've gone up in a blaze. I'm about to go past, then I change my mind. Don't do anything stupid was more of my mom's advice, that and how to use my knife, and here I am, putting the two together. I just hope they don't cancel each other out. Though the truth is, I don't really know what I'm about to do until I'm doing it. I squat down next to him. The stench of beer, or maybe just of him, makes me want to gag again. But I hold my nerve and reach out and carefully lift the ponytail. Gross. I hold it where it's tied with a gnarly-looking elastic band, then I touch the blade to the first hairs. Yup, it's sharp. I'm tensed up, ready to run at the first sign of movement, but he's totally out of it. Before I can change my mind, I slice clean through.

It's crazy, but looking at it, like a dead animal in my hand, makes me feel calm. I toss it on to the last of the embers. There

50

you go, Samson, I'm thinking, and I'm strolling, not terrified any more.

Callum's bike is apart from the rest, nearest the road. It creaks when I heave it off the stand, and someone stirs. I freeze, but he sighs and settles again. I start pushing it down the track. I don't even want to think about getting it started. All I know is that I want to be far away when those guys wake up.

It's properly light and cars are starting to whizz by every couple of minutes, and I'm getting more and more nervous about starting the bike up, but I need to get going. Those guys might be out of it, but they won't be once the day starts heating up, so I need to put as many miles between us as I can. It's now or never. I throw my leg over. Every part of me hurts, but I can't think about that stuff now, so I ignore the pain and concentrate on figuring out where everything is. I put a hand tentatively on the throttle, scared to twist it even though the bike's not switched on yet. I try out the clutch a few times. Okay. The key is in the ignition. I've seen Callum flip a red switch, so I flip it. I turn the key, hit start, and the engine roars to life.

It's loud, but I guess the time for keeping quiet is over. I give the throttle a tiny twist and it answers with a gratifying rev. Okay. But now I have to, like, ride it. I remember the foot rest and kick it, the way I've seen the others do. I check the mirror for traffic, pull the clutch lever, and shift down to first. So, if I let go the clutch . . . I brace myself for a jolt, but the shift is smooth and the bike is moving. The engine sputters and instinctively I turn the throttle and it levels out. Awesome. I put my feet up on the pegs and pull out.

I need to get up some speed so I shift up, but I over-do it and it's rough, so I try again, slower with the clutch, and this time it works; I'm actually riding this thing. A truck overtakes me and I wobble in the draught, but I remember how to lean and I get my balance back. I'm even starting to get comfortable with it after a while, but it doesn't change that there's a bike gang behind me, and at least two of them are going to be mad as hell. Callum knew I was trying to get to the Pacific, so if they come after me they'll probably keep going west. That's why, when the 81 splits for St Louis, I keep south. It's not too hot yet, and it's kind of nice to have the wind in my ears and the countryside flashing past. It looks like I'm headed for Birmingham, Alabama. I wonder if I've seen the last of Maryland. It would've been nice to see the marina one more time, say goodbye to the old-timers. But it does no good to start thinking like that. Before you know it, I'll be back to my mom again, back to how everything was okay when she was around, and how nothing is okay now. But as bad as things are, they could get a whole lot worse if Danny and company catch up with me. I go back to concentrating on the road.

I'm starting to get hungry. I didn't think I'd ever want to eat again last night, feeling the way I did, but right now I could murder a stack of banana pancakes drowning in syrup. I'm not about to pull over at any of the rest stops, though. I'll wait until I need gas, pick up something at the deli. I don't know how much gas the bike uses, but I figure since Callum filled up not far back I should be okay for a while. I let the miles whizz past, hoping south was the right decision.

When the tank finally gets low, I get off at the exit for Johnson City. It's a few miles off the highway, on the way to nowhere, so I figure it should be safe. There's a gas station almost right away, but I don't want to go to the first one. I ride down main street, but bikes are so damn noisy, and Johnson City seems like a pretty quiet place, so I keep going to the edge of town until I find another gas station and pull in. I have to fumble a bit to get the tank open, but then it goes okay. I'm paying cash so I can't be traced, and I'm counting out ten-dollar bills, thinking I might grab a couple of their donuts, when I remember I saw an IHOP on my way through town. I go back outside and get on the bike, and I'm actually feeling kind of proud when it starts up smoothly. I flip the stand and start to move off. Only I guess I mess up the turn, or maybe there was gas spilt, because the next thing I'm on the concrete and the bike is off somewhere else, revving and spluttering like a wounded animal.

London, 1982

When you wake in a freezing room with the window darkened by a nailed-on blanket, and it's freezing everywhere but inside your nylon bag, it's easier to go back to sleep than to get up. Plus, it's free – but even with free rent you need to eat.

Cat told her she could use the word processor down at the job centre to write her CV. *Make stuff up*, she had added, guessing correctly that Jasmine's work experience was non-existent. She was full of enthusiasm at first, making herself as presentable as she could before heading out, CV in hand, to shops and restaurants, a kebab place, even a garage, but there was never anything going. As days turned into weeks, it got harder to stay motivated, and easier just to stay in her sleeping bag. She got up later and spent longer getting ready. She could make a cup of tea last half an hour. She even washed the disgusting, mould-covered dishes that had been sitting in the sink since before she arrived; anything to delay going out.

One morning when she was barely awake, Cat passed her the Tupperware from the mantelpiece and told her she could feed Jake. She wasn't sure if it was meant to be an honour, or if it was some kind of test. Even while she was peeling back the lid she knew what she would find. She thrust the tub with its fat and stiffened rat back at Cat, who took it calmly, extracted the rat, and dangled it by the tail over the top of the cage. He rose up to meet it with a slow yawn and swallowed it whole. Jasmine could see it move down the length of his body beneath his skin. She shuddered.

—Not a rat person?

—I suppose not. Em, I better get going.

—You found a job?

She shook her head.

—Not yet. But I have a dance class.

She had decided to spend money she didn't have giving herself something to look forward to, because she couldn't give up hope yet. Cat looked up.

—Dance?

—I'm not very good.

—No, no, I'm sure you're good.

—Uh, thanks. But I won't be able to go any more unless I get a job. I'm nearly broke.

But Cat had already gone back to stroking the snake and was no longer listening.

It was Jasmine's third class, paid for from her night in the pub, but if she didn't get a job soon, it would be her last. She wasn't even sure she was sorry. As much as she wanted to dance, her body wasn't co-operating. She got tired quickly, and the warm-up stretches were torture. It felt like her hamstrings were about to snap. She didn't have a great memory for the routines either; the others saw the teacher do it once, twice at most, and off they went – they'd all been doing it since they were three or four years old – whereas she'd start out okay, then she'd forget, but the teacher would keep going, leaving her further and further behind.

She liked the end of the class, though, where the teacher blasted out world music and everyone got to move whatever way they wanted. That was when she remembered how much she liked dancing.

—You're good, the teacher had said the previous week. — You just need to put in the groundwork.

In school, this sort of advice from a teacher would have just pissed her off, but now that she was all washed up in London, she could see that it was meant to be encouraging. She was happy to do the groundwork. But she needed a job.

That evening, Cat came in very late. Jasmine couldn't be sure, but she thought she heard her crying. By morning, however, she was her usual cool, unapproachable self, so Jasmine didn't mention it. She was getting ready to go out on another hopeless round of job hunting.

—Dance class? Cat asked.

—Nope. Next class is a week away, but I'm out of funds. Maybe today will be my lucky day.

When she looked up, Cat was petting that stinking snake again, and Jasmine could see marks on her arm. This time she didn't turn away. It was Cat who finally broke the silence.

—There's work, if you want it.

—I'll take it. I'm completely desperate. Well, maybe not completely . . . She was remembering the pub. After all, what were the odds of something like that happening again?

—This is for completely.

—You mean, there's a job going?

—I know someone.

Her glance went to her arm.

—What sort of work? This might be her last chance to make a go of London. Last night, after her once-a-week phone call, after her mother had raged again and she had hung up again, she'd been sorely tempted to ring back and ask her to send over money. She had to force herself to walk away from the phone box.

—Corrigan, Cat said. — There's work. If you're desperate.

She slept late the next day, then hung around the flat all afternoon to meet this Corrigan, who didn't seem to have a first name. She sprayed and back-combed until her hair stood in black spikes. She spent ages on her eyes, and with her black skirt and high-necked black blouse, and her piercings in, she was ready. Cat nodded her approval as she went to answer the door. When Corrigan came in with her, Jasmine stared. This was Cat's boyfriend? His head sat like a block on his shoulders, with no neck separating the two, and all of him appeared bound up in slackening muscle, so that his eyes and mouth appeared to have retracted into the flesh. Cat was draped over his arm, looking up at him as if he was some sort of prize she had won.

—So what can you do then? he asked.

—She's a dancer, Cat said quickly.

—Dancing, is it? He looked her up and down.

She nodded. He released himself from Cat and went to the cage. He took Jake out and brought him towards Cat, and for a moment Jasmine thought he was going to hurt her. But in a sudden movement the snake surged forward on to her shoulder where it swelled slowly around her neck and below her arm, before turning back on itself towards Corrigan, binding them in its reptilian embrace. Jasmine was revolted by the strangely intimate bond, but she held her gaze.

—Bring her along, he told Cat after a moment.

It took a moment to register that he meant right away. She scrambled to grab her bag, then the three of them went outside to a black BMW. Jasmine was in the back seat, feeling like a child, while Cat snuggled up against Corrigan's meaty arm as he drove.

Soon, they pulled up outside a run-down-looking pub. There was no one inside except the barman – not surprising for early evening, she supposed. Corrigan nodded at him, then led them through to the back, down a corridor, and up a stairs, where she could hear music coming from somewhere. They went through a door and when her eyes adjusted she could see that they were in a sort of mini-theatre, with seats placed in rows around a low platform, some of them occupied. The curtain swung back, and a woman came out, dressed in leather, and stiletto boots up to her thighs. She moved to a pole Jasmine hadn't noticed, and began some sort of swaying, squatting dance.

Abruptly, Corrigan turned and said something to Cat, then left. The relief was like the sun suddenly coming out, but it was short-lived.

—This is the gig. Only if you're desperate. Pay is good.

—I'll do it.

—There are costumes backstage.

—You mean, now?

—It's not going to get any easier.

By now, the woman was down to her leather bra and thong.

—Do I have to . . .

—Strip? No. Just get up there, move about a bit. And don't worry about Corrigan. He's the business end.

It was pitch-black backstage and every sound she made behind the makeshift screen – a blanket strung across a wire – echoed around her. She struggled into a tight-fitting dress, which strangled her ribcage and pushed up her boobs, making her pant, and sweat was already trickling down her cleavage. Her confidence was faltering by the second, and she was seriously beginning to think she might faint, when the curtains began to part.

—Go, Cat hissed from somewhere.

She stepped forward on legs that didn't feel like they even belonged to her. Dancing felt out of the question.

—Open your eyes.

Cat again. Jasmine was starting to wish she had never met her.

The bright lights made her squint, but they also made her audience disappear, which helped. She reached for the pole. It was cool and reassuring to her clammy touch. She pulled herself towards it, and stood with her back to the lights, and the audience. The music was pulsing, with lots of percussion the way she liked, egging her on. She slid against the pole to a squat, the way she had seen the other woman do. Her dress was slit all the way up to her backside, which meant that at least she had room to move. Tentatively, she extended one leg, then pulled it slowly in and stood up. She leaned, worried that the pole would come crashing out of its moorings, but it stayed put, and gradually she began to trust it. She tried to remember some of the routines

58

from her classes, then she repeated them with variations until the music faded and the lights went up. There was a smattering of applause.

—Here you go, love, a man said, from the front row. He was holding up a five-pound note.

Jasmine looked at it in confusion.

—I'll make it twenty for a lap dance.

She looked around for Cat, but the curtains had closed behind her. She turned back to her . . . customer? He could be her maths teacher, or her next-door neighbour. Prick. She ran back through the curtains to where Cat was already in character, eyes closed, dancing slowly by herself, wearing the tiniest hot-pants Jasmine had ever seen, and a floaty see-through top and red bra.

—Just sit on his knee until he comes, she said without opening her eyes.

Fuck. Fuck. Fuck.

—You don't have to if you don't want to.

Fuck. She marched back out through the curtains, forcing herself to find the rhythm of Cat's song. A cheer went up as Cat came on stage behind her. Two steps down and across the chasm. She didn't know how to lap dance. She didn't even know how to get herself from standing to sitting, which was presumably what she was supposed to do. But there she was, somehow, with a drink in her hand, and a hand on her leg. She downed the syrupy liquid and let her leg be stroked, willing the song to end. At least there seemed to be rules, because he didn't go any further than that.

She kept focused on Cat, who was seducing her audience without seeming to try. As the music began to fade, Cat opened her top lazily, and the hot breaths on Jasmine's neck became a moan. As Cat stepped forward to take her tips, Jasmine snatched her promised twenty and went behind the stage. Methodically, she got out of her dress and into her own things. She thought about her few minutes' work – sex work, if that was what it was – expecting to feel dirty, or guilty, but she just felt pleased with herself. Twenty quid for ten minutes' work, and from what Cat said she'd get more just for being on Corrigan's *books*. And she had liked it, sort of, the feeling of power it gave her.

She didn't feel like waiting around for Cat, so she swung her bag on to her shoulder and went back out through the pub. She didn't know where she was, exactly, but she fell in with the pedestrians who she thought were going in the right direction. She could always take out her *A–Z*, but for now it felt good just being out in daylight, and out of that dress, with cash in her pocket. She felt taller, and not remotely like a sinner.

She waited up for ages, hoping to chat to Cat, but when she got in, she ignored Jasmine's *Hello* and went straight to her sleeping bag. Jasmine was getting fed up with Cat's unpredictable humours. She decided to try to talk to her the next morning.

It was nearly 1 p.m. before there was any movement from Cat, and Jasmine was already on her fifth cup of tea.

—Want one? she asked.

Cat looked puzzled.

—I thought we could talk, Jasmine pushed on, her nerve faltering.

—You know, about yesterday . . .

No response.

—I mean, was I all right, on the stage?

Cat shrugged.

—Fine. Considering.

—Considering it was my first time?

—Considering you were straight. You can't tell me you don't know what this means, what Corrigan is?

She got out of the sleeping bag and started to move through her limbering-up routine.

Jasmine didn't know what to say. She had known, but she hadn't wanted to spell it out for herself. Corrigan was Cat's

60

drug dealer; that was the hold he had over her, and now she was getting caught up in his world too. But there was a difference between her and Cat. For all Cat's poise, or whatever she had that made people want to please her – the less she gave a damn, the harder they tried to get her attention, just as she was doing now – there was something vulnerable about her. She would not end up like Cat.

She was suddenly impatient to get away. Besides, she had a class to get to, now that she had money again. She left without bothering to answer.

Over the next few weeks, though the steps and routines still eluded her, she improved. She worked as often as Corrigan wanted her to. She even looked forward to it; the pole was solid and dependable, and allowed her to push the boundaries of what her body was capable of. It was easy money. Her Legs & Co. ambitions seemed laughable to her now. What mattered was getting up on stage, any stage, and moving her body, and, unlike Cat, she didn't need to get drunk or stoned to do it. She could make the shift easily into becoming someone else. Even when Cat reported that Corrigan wanted her to start stripping, she was able to do it as if she were undressing a doll, not herself. And when the lights went down, and they wanted to pay extra – she was as much in demand now as Cat – she kept the switch flipped in her head, so that although she might be physically sitting on some old fucker's knee while he jerked off, it wasn't really her. She didn't come back into herself until they produced the pound notes.

Corrigan came to the flat one day when Cat wasn't there. The lads, who were hardly ever there anyway, were gone to work, and there was only Jasmine, bleary from a long night's work. She rarely saw Corrigan, and then only ever accompanied by Cat, and she panicked at the sight of him on the doorstep. He gave her the creeps.

—Aw' right, Jasmine? he asked, as he followed her back in to the front room.

—Em, yeah, grand.

She tried to concentrate on her eyeliner, but her hand wasn't steady.

—Need some help with that?

She looked up. Was he offering to do her make-up? He was. He got down on his hunkers and took the eyeliner. She had never been this close to him before, and she had to force herself not to recoil.

—Lots you don't know about me, love, he said with a chuckle. —Like my short career as a make-up artist. For TV, like.

He was surprisingly deft, and a few moments later he handed her the pen and drew back to admire his handiwork.

—There. Lovely. Punters are liking it too, I hear.

She mumbled *thanks*.

—I think you can do better than that, love, he said, still smiling as he pulled her face nearer and put his mouth to hers.

She pulled away.

—But you're Cat's . . .

But he wasn't interested in what she had to say. He grabbed her arm so hard that she cried out, and pushed his mouth to hers again, this time sucking on her tongue and biting her lip. When he flung her away from him, still keeping hold of her wrist, she could taste blood.

—Remember this, bitch, he snarled.—You're. On. My. Books. Know what that means?

She shook her head.

—It means . . . He paused to pull something from the inside pocket of his jacket, something metal. He pressed a button on the side and a blade shot out. He lifted her arm and pressed the point of the blade to the delicate blue-white skin of her inner elbow.

—It means that, to all intents and purposes, I own you. Just like Cat, just like the others. Do I make myself clear?

She nodded and he released her roughly and left, leaving her staring in shock at the thin trickle of blood running down her arm.

When Cat came home, she was in one of her better moods.

—Corrigan has a job for you this evening, she announced.
—Boxing.

There was no point in trying to talk about what had happened. They both knew where they stood: on Corrigan's books. She tried to take in what Cat was saying.

—Come again . . .?

—Boxing. You know, ring girl.

—What?

—Ring girl, stupid. You hold up a card with a number on it. Piece of piss. It's an important fight and Corrigan wants his best girl. She rubbed fingers and thumb together to imply lots of money.

—Which would be you, Jasmine pointed out.

—Yeah, well. He wants *his girl* by his side for this one. She smiled ironically. —Fat Bobby will be there too.

There's a bet on, lots at stake.

She had heard about Fat Bobby from Cat and the other women at the club. Everyone was scared of him. He had stakes in the club, and several others. The rumour was that they were a cover for prostitution rings. Fat Bobby was Corrigan's role model, and he was not to be crossed. The girls told her stories. When Corrigan caught one of them going home with a punter, he brought her to his office where Fat Bobby was waiting, eating a sandwich, and when Corrigan pushed the girl across the desk, Fat Bobby calmly slashed her face with a flick-knife, then sat back and continued eating.

—Corrigan will pick you up before five.

She was glad to have Cat in the car, but once she showed her where to get changed, she disappeared. Jasmine didn't see her again until it was time to go on, when she spotted her in the cordoned-off VIP section, wedged in between Corrigan and, she presumed, Fat Bobby. She looked out of it, but Jasmine hadn't time to worry about Cat. The stadium was packed, and she was buzzing with nerves. As she waited at the mouth of the corridor for her cue, she repeated Cat's instructions in her head to steady herself. *Walk out, card over your head, circle the ring, back the other way, and out. Repeat between rounds.* It didn't matter how many rounds there were. If there's a knock out, *a KO*, she'd get paid the same amount.

She watched as they punched each other senseless. Eejits. She could nearly feel the dull slaps of their gloves hitting flesh. But in spite of herself, the smells of sweat and adrenalin and the roaring, rising crowd started to get in on her, causing an unexpected thrill.

Then a bell rang; the round was over. The boxers, wet with sweat, returned to their corners. The one in the blue shorts was so close she could touch him if she reached out her hand. Coaches were towelling him, taking out a mouthguard, watering him, giving him instructions, but throughout it all he maintained a kind of focus she had never seen before. He was nodding to their instructions, taking them in, but his eyes never lost their steady inward gaze. Someone gave Jasmine a push. Showtime. She put her nerves on hold, tugged her sequined leotard out of her crotch one last time, raised her card, and strutted out into the crowd.

There were whistles and whoops as she went past, and she heard *I'd do you in a heartbeat, love.* She imagined putting down her card and punching him like one of the boxers, but instead she kept her eyes straight ahead, widened her smile, and finished her circuit. On her third outing, she was calm enough to notice that Corrigan looked pleased with her. But Cat looked even more miserable, sunk down low in her seat between the two men.

As she returned to the corridor, replaced card number three, and lined up the next one, she could hear the commentator getting louder and more excited by the moment. The boxer in blue was going after his opponent with his single-minded expression, pursuing him back towards the ropes and into a corner. Red tried to force his way out with a volley of punches, but even to Jasmine's eye he was flailing, and few of his punches reached their target. Blue kept him at arm's length, as if he was playing with him. There was a lull in the commentary. The whole arena seemed to hold its breath, as if it could sense what was coming, and then it came. One well-aimed punch to Red's temple and he was down. The referee began to count down from ten. At three, Red pulled himself on to an elbow, but then fell back to the canvas. It was over.

Blue's arm was raised – the victor. Red's team had gathered around him so Jasmine couldn't see if he was going to be okay. The crowd was roaring, spilling from their seats, pouring down the aisles, and doing all they could to get into the ring – Blue's fans, Jasmine presumed – until, right in front of her, one of them drew out and punched another in the gut. They were Red's fans, and they weren't happy. Something wasn't right about the knock out. Within seconds it was mayhem, and this time there were no rules. Someone beside her smashed a bottle against a seat, spilling foamy beer over the upholstery and creating a jagged weapon. Nearby, a knife was pulled. She watched, fascinated, as it sliced through a raised arm, making a clean line at first, which then began to seep red, until it was a full-blown gash. She was right in the eye of the fight, and she stood there, frozen. There were sirens over the shouting, then police, with their falling batons.

Then she was grabbed from behind.

—Hurry it.

It was Corrigan, and he half dragged her towards the tunnel as she stumbled on her heels. The noise of the rioting fans was receding as they got further into the backstage area, and at last they reached a door. Outside a car and driver were waiting, and Cat and Fat Bobby were already inside. Corrigan pushed her into the back beside Fat Bobby, and got into the front himself. They sped off down alleys and side streets to avoid the police barriers and the crowds who were starting to emerge, still looking for action.

—Enough excitement for you? Corrigan asked over his shoulder.

—Yeah. Thanks, she added.

—We look after our girls; she heard Fat Bobby's gravelly voice for the first time. —Don't we, Corrigan? He slapped Jasmine's thigh and left his hand there. His other was on Cat's, but Cat just stared out her window, as if she hadn't noticed.

—We do, Robert, we do, Corrigan said, sounding satisfied with himself.

They pulled up outside the club. She couldn't wait to get out of her uncomfortable leotard. But instead of escaping out the back to the storeroom, where she kept some spare clothes, she was ushered directly upstairs. Corrigan called to the barman to bring a bottle of champagne from the basement; they were celebrating. Then he patted Jasmine's bum and handed her a fat envelope. She cringed at his touch, but it felt like a lot of money. He must be in very good humour.

—Slip that into your coat, love.

There was no one on the stage, and just a handful of customers. Corrigan led them to the front table. He made sure Fat Bobby got the best seat, then he steered Jasmine to the seat beside him, where his flesh oozed and swelled over on to her. She could smell curry under the cologne he must have sprayed himself with recently – when had he had a chance to do that? – and the combination was making her sick.

—This is nice, Fat Bobby said.

His *nice* sent a chill through her, but she told herself she could handle it. Once the champagne arrived, they'd drink it, and she'd be allowed to go home. After all, she had done a good job.

—Come on. Give us a few spins while we're waiting, Corrigan said.

She tried to make eye contact with Cat. Surely he didn't expect her to dance? But Cat wouldn't meet her eye, so she got up, partly relieved to get away from Fat Bobby, and walked to the stage. Still in her coat, she reached for the pole, her steadfast friend. The barman arrived with the tray and a bucket and she watched from the stage as Corrigan grabbed the bottle and slopped champagne into the glasses and they clinked, ignoring her. To hell with them. She leaned away from the pole until she found the rhythm, and she began to move.

The spotlight came on, and she arched back, letting her coat fall away from her. Slowly, she extended her shimmery stockinged leg until she was in standing splits. She wrapped the top leg around the pole and drew herself in, then, still holding on with her leg, she released her hand and arched further back until her hair brushed the floor and her coat covered her face. She couldn't see, but she knew they weren't ignoring her now. Snakelike, she pulled her body back up and released the lone button that held her coat on. Looking directly at Corrigan, she slid the strap of her leotard over one shoulder and slowly caressed her nipple, then she let her hand glide downwards. She had their attention, all right.

It was just a nipple, just a cunt. Just words. *Shaz is a cunt*. She hoped Shaz, whoever she was, had managed to pull herself out of the flats, one way or another, and that every once in a while she drove by in a fancy car and gave the finger to whoever had sprayed her name there like that. Screw them, all of them, scrabbling down their trousers in their dark little corners. She was in charge here, and she was getting paid.

But as the lights went up, a little drama was unfolding in the front row. Fat Bobby said something to Corrigan. Corrigan said something to Cat. Cat shook her head. Corrigan raised his hand. Cat drew back. Corrigan grabbed her wrist and twisted her arm behind her. Cat nodded. Corrigan nodded, grimly. Fat Bobby nodded, grinning. What the fuck was going on?

At last, Cat got up and came towards the stage.

—Bobby wants to party a bit longer. She added in a whisper, —Just give him a blow job. That way he won't hurt you.

She walked back to the table, where Corrigan was already standing and Bobby was struggling to haul his bulk out of the chair. There wasn't even time to take in what Cat had said. She left her leotard where it had landed in its shameful little pile, put her coat on and buttoned it fully. Never had she wanted her clothes more, to disappear in their layers.

She followed the others behind the stage down the corridor and into Corrigan's office. He ushered Fat Bobby and Cat through an inner door, marked *Private*, with instructions to Cat to make him comfortable. Jasmine had never been inside this inner room. Cat often disappeared in there after work, only to return to the flat hours later, stoned and uncommunicative. The very sight of the black door, with its tacky red sticker, gave her a shiver. She went to the office window and looked out over the sheds and extensions that mushroomed at the backs of the buildings on the next street. She could almost see into the windows of the flats across the way. She tried to imagine another version of herself looking back at her, from a nicer room, with nicer people in it.

—Have a seat. Corrigan indicated the chair opposite his, where she sat once a week while he peeled notes from a roll he took from the drawer. Cat told her that he kept a gun in there too, but she didn't believe her.

—I'm not really what Bobby is after, she tried.

He raised an eyebrow.

—Bobby has asked most especially for the pleasure of your company, he said, *sotto voce*.

—But I don't—

—Bobby asked for you. Especially, he repeated, and his tone told her there was no way out. He reached into the drawer, and she froze. But he withdrew a glass and a bottle of fancy-looking whiskey, and poured a large measure, which he drank back in one.

—Where are my manners? he said, pouring another. —We are celebrating after all. Big win, Jasmine. Big win.

—The fight?

She could at least stall.

—The fight? Yes, you could call it that. A lot of money riding on our boy. He slid the glass across to her. —Of course, precautions were taken. It was, as I said, a lot of money – Bobby's money, and Bobby doesn't like it when money goes bad. Drink, drink.

He glanced at the *Private* door. She didn't want whiskey, and she definitely didn't want to drink it out of the same glass as Corrigan, but as with everything concerning Corrigan, she had no choice.

—Lovely, lovely, Corrigan said. He adjusted his crotch and sat back, watching her drink.

She couldn't bear it, so she downed the rest in one go. It felt as if she had pointed a Bunsen burner down her throat, but even though her eyes watered, she managed to suppress the fit of coughing that threatened.

—Lovely. Let's get you in there then, before Bobby thinks I'm keeping you for myself. And Jasmine?

—Yes? she managed.

—Play your cards right and you could be moving up the ladder, like Cat.

Like Cat, living in a squat with a cold-blooded reptile for a friend. Funny, she felt as if she was about to move a good bit lower down that particular ladder. She stood carefully, wary of the effect of the whiskey, and he ushered her into a dimly lit room. Bobby had settled his layers of fat in among the cushions on the velour couch, and Cat was by his side. She unfurled and moved to join Corrigan by the door.

—We'll leave you two love birds, he said with a leer, and they left, pulling the door behind them.

Jasmine could hear the outer door close too, and Cat's heels clipping down the corridor until they disappeared She was completely alone with Fat Bobby. He had a big stupid smile on his big, stupid face, but she knew not to mess with him.

—Come on, love, don't be shy. Take the weight off your legs. He patted his huge thighs.

—I was hoping we could get to know each other, she tried. She was not going through with this, she just hadn't figured out how to get out of it. Fat Bobby pressed his head back into the upholstery to appraise her, which had the unsettling effect of multiplying his many chins.

—Well go on, then. Get yourself a drinkie. And pour one for me while you're at it.

There was a bottle on a side table, put there by Corrigan. Or Cat. Not the fancy stuff from the office, either. She unscrewed the lid and placed it on the table beside the glass. Every tiny action felt loaded with significance, as if it might be her last. She lifted the bottle, tilted it, and slowly poured.

—Make it a large.

She kept pouring until the glass was nearly full, and brought it over with a shaking hand.

—And the same for yourself, lovie. I know how hard you've been working. I didn't miss a minute, he said with a wink, and a nod in the direction of his crotch.

She poured another and brought it over too, and sat on the arm of the couch.

—Bottoms up. He clinked her glass, splashing whiskey on her coat, and she obediently put the glass to her mouth and drank hers down in one go. If it didn't make her puke, at least it might anaesthetise her.

—Gagging for it, eh? He pulled her down into his lap and began fumbling with her buttons. —Here, get this off. Let's have a proper look at that beautiful body.

He had just given her an idea.

She pulled away, wagging her finger at him.

—That's my job, Bobby.

She was reversing as she spoke. A minute was all it would take. She just had to brazen it out. She slipped the first button free, then another and another in quick succession, until she was baring her breasts. Hold your nerve, she told herself.

—You want it, Bobby, don't you? Me too. I can't wait to see what you've got for me.

She could make a run for it. But what if the outer door was locked? Bobby would kill her. Simple as that. She couldn't risk it. Without any more preamble, she took off her coat and moved, naked and business-like, towards Bobby, where he had his trousers open. Somewhere, under rolls of fat, his prick was hidden. Jesus. But it had to be done. She knelt and lifted a flabby wad out of the way, and Bobby gave a sort of gurgle and settled deeper into the couch. He probably wouldn't be able to get out of there in a hurry, but she couldn't take that chance either. She grabbed his sweaty balls, and he groaned.

—Good girl, good girl.

There it was, unfurling like a fat little slug. She was right about the whiskey making it easier, but she just hoped she wouldn't be sick. He put his hand on her head and pushed it down. So he was asking for it. What was she waiting for? She put her mouth over his penis and bit down until her teeth met.

The moments that followed stretched and distorted normal time. She picked up her coat, pulled it on, and moved to the office. She must have pulled it on then, because when she landed . . . No, because at some stage she must have opened Corrigan's drawer, because his wad of notes was in her pocket. She must have decided to jump . . . She didn't remember making the decision, and she didn't remember jumping. Only when she landed awkwardly in the alleyway below did she realise that she had chosen to escape through the window, rather than the door. When she stood up, and realised that she had jumped, and that she was not hurt, and that she was wearing her coat and there was a wad of notes in the pocket, only then did she hear the scream.

She hailed a passing taxi as she emerged from the alleyway and gave the Keever address.

—Wait here, she instructed the driver when the flats came into view. She half ran, half stumbled across the wasteland and up the steps. No one was home except Jake. She pulled on as many of her clothes as she could, one layer over the other. There wasn't much more to stuff into her rucksack when she had finished, except her sleeping bag and its hidden savings. She took a last look around the room – it had been home for a while, after all – and it looked almost peaceful in the late evening light. Fuck that for an illusion.

—And fuck you too, she said to the cage in the corner. — And fuck Corrigan, and Bobby and Cat.

They were names she never wanted to hear again, and faces she never wanted to see.

She got the taxi to leave her at Euston station, where she spent a fretful hour looking over her shoulder waiting for the Holyhead train. Even when the train had pulled out and the journey was well under way, she couldn't relax. The middle-aged woman opposite, with a Midlands Irish accent very like her own, soon gave up on her attempts to chat. Her companion, a pale girl about Jasmine's age, was silent the entire time. When, once, they caught each other's eye in the window's reflection, the girl was the first to look away.

When the ferry had pulled out, it hit her. She began to tremble and sweat. Then her body heaved, again and again. Even when her stomach was well and truly emptied, it kept spasming, as if to purge itself of every last trace of London.

Dublin, 2012

A cheer goes up from the living room. *Katie Taylor is digging deep to catch up with Russia's Sofya Ochigava.* She's recording it to watch later, after she's had her shower, and rid herself of her day, but she finds that she has drifted to the doorway, her wet runners still in her hand. It's the third round, and Katie's concentration is absolute. She is taking nothing for granted. In a fight like this, every point counts. Olympic Gold is at stake, Women's Boxing Olympic Gold.

She wanted to watch frame by frame from the beginning, all the hype and the build-up. She wanted the commentary, the slow motion, the close-ups. She wanted to concentrate on technique as intensely as Katie is concentrating. But now she's started watching, she can't tear herself away. Katie is taking this round, no question. No, damn, they've stopped the clock. Some problem with Ochigava's equipment. Idiots. They wouldn't stop a sprinter halfway through the 100 metres for one of them to tie a lace. Get a move on. She'll lose the momentum. But no, Katie has adjusted. She's going strong. She should still . . . At last, there's the bell. And here's the scorecard. Katie is leading 7–5.

Jeffrey would have bought front row seats if he'd had any idea. He already has tickets to dozens of events, gifted to Friends of the Hospital – not that he is remotely interested in the Olympics – but her interest in boxing just hasn't come up in conversation. Or she has been careful not to let it come up because it might lead in directions she doesn't care to follow.

He wouldn't understand the contradiction of wanting to live every moment of the fight as if she were there in the ExCel Arena, but not actually wanting to be there. Or maybe she just doesn't feel like sharing her private interests with him, any more than she cares to share her past. Christ, that should tell her something.

Ochigava is behind and she is going for it in the fourth round, but Katie is coming back hard. Now the referee is breaking it up. Now they're going at it again. Katie stumbles. It's unbearable to watch, yet impossible to turn away. Ochigava is getting the punches in, and some of them are landing. Nothing is certain about this fight. The closing bell sounds. The tension in the arena is audible. Her own breath is suspended. Katie's anxious question to her father and trainer – *Have I done it?* – hangs.

Dublin, 1982

Jasmine was sheltering under a tree in Trinity College, wondering which way to go when the three young men strolled past. She had tried to take a short cut in an attempt to get home before the rain, but the first wet plops started before she was halfway down Dawson Street, and now it was pouring. She didn't mind. She'd spent her day off admiring the window displays on Grafton Street, trying a sticky bun in Bewley's, and exploring Stephen's Green. She'd stared curiously at the protesters outside the Dáil who were handing out pro-life leaflets, and she took one, only to hand it back, telling them she couldn't vote. It was all very exciting. She'd only been to Dublin a handful of times before, and always to the same places – Arnotts, Easons, Hector Grey's – but she lived here now, and she wanted to get to know it better.

London had been a mistake. It had never felt like home, and now it never could. But it was behind her, and she planned never to talk about it or think about it again. Dublin was her second chance, and she was determined to make the most of it. Only, she hadn't a clue how to get out of Trinity. She could have asked them, the three tall, well-built men, all wearing tracksuits and carrying gym bags. But they were talking and laughing and sure of themselves, so much the opposite to her that they might as well have been from another planet, and by the time she decided she should, it was too late.

She didn't intend to follow them, but the rain had eased off and she found herself going the same way they were, keeping enough distance between them so they wouldn't notice. She followed them to the gym, and when they went inside, she spied through a window, fascinated, as they did stretching exercises. Then they began to skip. She was yard champ in primary school, but these lads were good. It was annoying when they moved out of view, but as she emerged from the shrubbery, shivering from her earlier drenching, she could feel that hum you get when you're at the start of something brilliant.

She went back as soon as she could. There was usually some-one there, but always, after lots of stretching and skipping, they moved out of view. It was maddening. When she couldn't stand it any more, she mustered up her courage and crept around to the grey door. She pushed it lightly, testing, and to her horror it opened, releasing a waft of Deep Heat and sweaty socks. She slipped inside and pressed herself against the wall, but the men were too engrossed in what they were doing to notice her. She finally saw where they moved after the warm-ups: into a ring, where they practised boxing with each other. Their coach – an Olympic medallist, George told her later – moved from pair to pair, and they followed his instructions. There was something about their controlled yet free movements that grabbed her, something that she wanted for herself. She had felt it when she got into the ring in London, holding up her card, and before that, watching Legs & Co. She hadn't even considered going to a dance class since getting back to Dublin because it was too bound up with all the other stuff that had happened. But boxing was something else, the same but different. If she could learn to do what they were doing, she could have their kind of confi-dence, plus she would finally know how to protect herself.

It was a few days before she was able to come back, but as she was slipping in to her customary place the coach spotted her.

—YOU, he called. —You can't be in here.

One or two of the boxers glanced over to see what was happening. She blushed beetroot, picked up her bag, and rushed out, mortified. She wouldn't be going back there again in a hurry.

But the next day after work, even though it was getting dark, she was once again at the window. She couldn't stay away. But the stretching and skipping wasn't enough now that she'd seen them actually box. She crept towards the door. She'd be really quiet, she told herself, she'd stay right back in the shadows where the coach wouldn't see her. But as she stood hesitating, the door opened, and she stumbled into the man who was coming out.

—You again? he said, steadying her.

She twisted around and found herself looking at a very black face. It wasn't that she'd never seen a black man, of course she had. London was full of them. But she hadn't fallen into the arms of one, or talked to one, or looked at one up close. He looked worried.

—Are you okay?

She seemed to have gone mute.

—I have given you a shock. You must sit for a moment.

She allowed herself to be guided towards a nearby bench. He was looking at her so intently that he made her prickle all over in embarrassment, as if she wasn't already mortified enough.

—I am sorry. Allow me to introduce myself. My name is George, and I am a medical student.

He indicated the buildings behind them; medical buildings, she presumed.

—I am checking to make sure you are okay.

—I'm okay, she said. —You can stop staring at me.

He grinned, showing very white teeth.

—If I may say, he said, —you are also staring.

Jesus. She looked at her feet. They both began to speak at the same time.

—Well, I . . .

—Well, if . . .

—I should get going, she said.

—Of course. Before you leave, may I ask a question?

—I suppose . . .

—Why do you come? I have seen you watching, in the gym until you were ejected, and at the window . . .

She felt like such an eejit. Watching. Getting caught. And now, falling in the door. Why did she come? She didn't know how to answer.

—Usually people start out with *what's your name*, she said sulkily.

—You are sassy, for so young a girl. Okay then, what's your name?

—It's Sassy.

—Really?

—No.

—You are a handful, young lady. Come. Let me escort you. Which way are you going?

—The main door, arch, whatever it's called, she said, getting to her feet. —And it's Jasmine.

—Really?

—Maybe.

—Pleased to meet you, Jasmine.

—Pleased to meet you, George.

She wished she'd gone by herself. He was much taller than her, and she either had to scurry like a child beside him or take giant steps to try to match his.

—You are from Dublin, Jasmine?

—Yes. I mean, no, not originally.

—I did not mean to ask another difficult question.

She laughed.

—Well, I could ask you where you're from instead. Because it's not Dublin.

—You are so sure?

But he was smiling. Dublin just didn't have black men.

—I am from Kenya.

—Hmm. She knew nothing about Kenya.

—I suppose it would be a step too far to ask how old you are, Jasmine?

—Twenty-one, she told him. That was an easy one. She'd had enough practice.

—Hmm, he imitated her perfectly.

She lifted her head defiantly and walked as fast as she could over the cobbles, which only meant she was finally able to keep up with him.

—Then perhaps I could persuade you, as you are of age, to join me in a beverage?

—Jesus, do you always talk like that? I mean, like you're in a black and white film?

—Do you always talk like that, taking the Lord's name in vain?

She sucked in her breath. Who did he think he was? She could hold her own in most situations, as she'd found out. She didn't have to take any shit from this fella. But he was the nearest she had come to that boxing ring, if she didn't count her stint as ring girl. She could put up with him a bit longer.

—Right, George. You're on.

They stood in the first pub for ten minutes before the barman came near them, and when he finally did, he said he was sorry, but he couldn't serve them.

—May I ask why? George asked quietly.

The barman indicated Jasmine.

—Yer one is under age.

—I beg your pardon, Jasmine began, rooting for her fake ID.

—We will go somewhere else, George said, taking her arm.

—But—

—Shh.

She pulled away from his grip when they got outside.

—Don't *shh* me. He wouldn't serve us because you're black. You know that's why. He's a racist. You're a boxer. You should have punched him.

—That's okay, Jasmine. Perhaps he really did think you were under age. I cannot imagine why. We will go elsewhere.

—It's not okay, Jasmine persisted. —You know what your problem is? You're all mouth and no trousers.

He laughed, which only made Jasmine more indignant, and all the way to the Palace Bar she harangued him, and he ignored her. They were already getting the hang of each other.

The Palace was lovely. The floor was a checkerboard of worn red and black tiles, and there was stained glass in a skylight overhead which, with the evening light coming through it, turned the whole place orange and red. Jasmine hadn't been inside many pubs, though she wasn't going to tell George that, specially since he seemed to be completely at home there. He went to the fancy-looking wooden bar and ordered two Britvik Oranges, and a pint of water. The barman offered to bring them over.

—See, George said as he sat down. —It was you.

Jasmine narrowed her eyes, but she knew he was winding her up.

—You could've asked me what I wanted to drink. Isn't that the gentlemanly thing to do?

—I guessed, with your sporting ambitions, that you would choose the non-alcoholic option.

Sporting ambitions. She couldn't hide her pleasure.

The ice rattled against the glasses as the barman set down their drinks. George took a long, steady draught from the water, draining it.

—Good job it's not alcohol, Jasmine observed.

—Boxing is thirsty work.

—I wouldn't know.

—But you want to?

—Yes.

—The club is men only.

—You don't say.

She took a swig from the cold, viscous juice.

80

—Is there no gymnasium in your school, Jasmine?

She shot him a look, but decided against bothering with the *I'm twenty-one* line again.

—I work.

He looked surprised. She couldn't blame him. On her way back from London, she'd thought about brushing out her hair, losing the piercings, toning down the warpaint, and generally reinventing herself as a nice girl, but her boss hadn't objected to her look so she forgot about it. George was probably dying to ask her what she did.

—In a bookies, she said finally, when he didn't ask.

He nodded, like he met girls who worked in bookies all the time.

—And your family? Do you live with them here in Dublin?

—No way, she said, too quickly.

—That is a pity, George said. —Family is important. You did not attend university?

—It'd be fairly sad if I did, wouldn't it? Nope, so far you don't need a degree to work in a bookies.

—Do you regret leaving education?

—No way. I couldn't wait to get out.

—You mean, you did not finish even your secondary education?

He had leaned very far forward, his eyes bulging out of his head, as if she'd just told him she robbed old ladies for a living. She shook her head.

—But education, it is so important. You are a smart girl—

—How do you know? You don't even know me.

—It is in your expression, in your eyes, in your words.

—What if I happen to believe there's more to life than books, George?

—Education gives you opportunities.

—I have opportunities.

—That is why you work in this . . . bookies?

She shrugged. He sat back and looked thoughtfully at her.

—I will tell you what . . .

—Don't bother.

—You go back to school . . .

—No.

He put his hands up to stop her protest.

—First, listen. You go back to school, and I will train you when the gymnasium is quiet. I will investigate suitable times. But first, you must enrol in school. You are too young to be out in the world. I would not like to think of one of my own children in your situation.

Jesus. It sounded like an offer she couldn't refuse. But like it or not, she was out in the world, and she had rent to pay. She had found the job before she had even set foot in Dublin through an ad in an *Evening Herald* someone had left on a bench on the ferry: *Cashier wanted. Experienced applicants only.* Jock Rooney Bookmakers was a good walk from the boat, especially with a rucksack, but every step away from the port and London was a step in the right direction, as far as she was concerned. She knew her odds from her evens because she had helped her uncle in his bookies a few times when she was small. She got the job on the spot, and she was very glad to have it; she'd passed the queues snaking down the street outside the dole office on her way there.

—I have to work, George, she said, all her attitude gone.

But he was undeterred.

—There are evening courses, special colleges.

Jasmine rubbed her thumb and two fingers together: money.

—Go back to school and I will train you. You will find a way. He pushed his chair back and stood. —You know where to find me. Now, I must go to the library. Would you like me to escort you home?

—No, you're grand, Jasmine said with a sigh. —I'll head in a few minutes. I'll just finish . . . She rattled what remained of her ice and her watered-down juice.

George nodded.

—You know where to find me.

There had to be some way around this stupid deal. But something told her George was not the yielding kind. If she wanted to box, she was going to have to find some bloody school that would take her. Or at least convince this George that she had.

The barman came down to collect the empties.

—Can I get you anything else, love?

She shook her head. Then she changed her mind.

—Do you know where I could find out about evening courses?

—You could try the papers. Or the ILAC Shopping Centre. There's a library in there, a grand place, I hear.

She found it, hidden on the first floor of a cheapo shopping centre; she'd never have guessed it was there if the barman hadn't told her about it. The librarian was far too enthusiastic about her returning to school, and gave her directions to a college in Ringsend which she had no intention of going near. She wandered through the shelves for a while just to humour her.

Next day, she waited nervously for George beside the gym.

—Hello, Jasmine, he said when he spotted her. He kept walking, and she had to trot to keep up again.

—When can we start?

—Start?

He seemed to look straight into her soul when he said it. She swallowed.

—Training. I'm doing the Leaving Cert. Evening classes in Ringsend. Her voice was shaky. She'd have to do better, or there'd be no boxing, so she lifted her chin defiantly and recited the subjects the librarian had suggested: Irish, English, maths, because they were the core subjects, biology, geography and French, because she had done them in Rathlowney. —You'd better not have been messing, mister, she warned, and she sounded convincing even to herself.

He nodded. No smile, no messing. It was a serious business, a serious deal.

—Can you be here at six?

She'd have to be up at five. Jesus.

—Six is fine. See you then.

She spent a restless night, afraid that she wouldn't wake up in time and she'd blow her chance before she even got started. When the alarm went off it jarred her out of some kind of terror she couldn't remember, but she could guess at: they were following her, they would track her down, they would find her. But as the weeks passed, it was getting easier to tell herself that it was just a dream. She tied her hair up, and pulled on the grey sweatshirt and pyjama bottoms that would have to pass for a tracksuit, and crept downstairs, runners in hand, because she'd never hear the end of it if she woke the other residents.

There were a couple of people at the bus stop on Dorset Street, people who actually got up at this mad hour every day, but she set off at a brisk walk because buses in Dublin seemed to have a fear of crossing the river and she'd still have to walk at the other end. She had a feeling George wouldn't tolerate lateness, so she had worked up a sweat by the time she got there, and she was dying for a cup of tea. George was already outside the gym, stretching out his legs.

—It loosens the hamstrings. We do not want injury.

—Grand, Jasmine agreed.

She set down her bag to watch. George threw her a look without pausing in his bouncing.

—What are you waiting for?

—Oh.

She felt foolish doing exercises outside, even with no one around. Why not do them inside the way the others did, before they moved on to the ring? She couldn't wait to try the punch-bag. She would give it hell.

George interrupted her thoughts.

—Let's go.

He took off at a run towards the back gate, leaving her no choice but to follow, at a sprint. She was panting too much to ask what was going on when she caught up with him on Westland Row. Besides, it was obvious: they were jogging. She'd only seen it in London, and on the telly of course, but not in Dublin and definitely not where she came from. You'd be the laughing stock. If you wanted exercise you worked, on the farms and the bogs, even in the garden. No one jogged.

Her heart was pounding, and before they even got to the river she had to stop, clutching her side where it felt like a knife was sticking into her. When George noticed, he circled back.

—Stitch?

He kept running on the spot.

She nodded.

—Walk until it goes.

And he was off running again. And so they proceeded, Jasmine doubled over every few hundred yards, George way ahead, coming back, running on the bloody spot until she was able to go again. She wouldn't please him to ask if they could stop, so they went all the way to the North Wall Quay, where the river widened.

—Now we turn back.

She felt as if she might throw up, then she did – only a tiny bit, since she'd had nothing to eat. She leaned on the quay wall to recover. Below her, the green water flowed on unconcerned, out into the sea.

—Are you feeling better? George asked, shifting from slave-driver back to medical student.

She lifted her head and looked upriver at how far they'd come. How far she'd come: a job, a flat, a city she could call home. She vowed to look forward from now on.

—Much better, George. What are we waiting for?

She pushed herself away from the wall, and set off running, ahead of George for once.

She hated him every day at about the mid-point of their run. Then, when it ended, her head felt clear and spacious, and she loved him enough to hug him – not that she ever would. The best bit was she was improving. She could run much further, and there were no more stitches. She couldn't keep up with George, but sometimes she came close. She was even thinking about buying a pair of decent runners.

But running wasn't boxing. Every day for weeks she asked the same question: *when can we go to the gym?* Every time he answered: *when you're ready*. She was starting to think he was playing some sort of trick, and she would never be ready. She could run the length of the quays now, and further, past the busy docklands. All this bloody running would turn out to be for nothing.

—Can you make it that far? George asked over his shoulder one morning, pointing.

Feck George. And feck running. With barely a nod, she accelerated until she caught up with him, then she kept on going until she had passed him. For once, he let her. Or maybe she was finally able to outrun him. She ran until it felt more like country than city, and briars were forcing her off the path, until the path disappeared altogether. She passed the Electricity Supply Board and the Pigeon House – what was that fancy old house doing all the way out here? – then, as she rounded a corner, she saw the South Wall, a broad granite pier tipped with the red lighthouse George had pointed at.

A last burst of energy she didn't know she had surged through her, and with a glance back to see where George was – far enough – she turned and sprinted the full length of the wall. By the time he caught up, at his steady pace, she was standing with her back to the lighthouse, panting, looking out over the steel-grey sea.

—When can we go into the gym? she managed, through gasps.

Droplets of sweat flew towards the fluorescent light, forming tiny rainbows. Her Mysterious Musk mingled with the musty smells of the gym as she moved to his rhythm, arm to arm, foot to foot, breath to breath. Their bodies circled, drew apart, then closed in. Everything felt slowed down and distant. Their grunts echoed back at them from far-off ceiling vaults.

Sunday, he had promised, and she couldn't wait for it to arrive. But when she had got into the ring, the extent of her dread took her by surprise. Her mouth was dry and her legs trembled. Not that George was hard on her, at least, not at first; he kept her at arm's length. He wouldn't hurt her, of course he wouldn't; he was a medical student, he was a gentleman. But when his punch connected with her upper arm, it hurt. He ignored her *Ow* and hit her again, right on the same sore spot on her muscle. Pain, her brain informed her, and it was a relief close to pleasure to discover that her body could take it.

Now that she was no longer afraid of being hurt, or of hurting George, she was able to react. He was her opponent, and he had just hit her. She harnessed her strength and pushed away from him, only to come at him again, fists flying. She moved away, then went in, surprising herself with her sure-footedness. It felt like dancing invisible trigonometry on the canvas. She might be a beginner, but her instincts were intact. Her body knew what to do and she felt as if she could keep it up for ever.

But then George came back at her, all arms and gloves. Just before impact she turned slightly and he hit her jaw. He looked as shocked as she was, but he kept going. Then, in what felt like a single moment, there was an impact to her ribs, she was staggering back, knees bent, her hip hit something, she was on her back, her head was bouncing against the canvas, two, three, four times. There was blackness, then there were flashes of light, then she was tracing the angles of the roof beams. There was a puzzling taste in her mouth.

Blood. She must have bitten her lip when she fell. She hadn't fallen since she was small. Damn George. Then she was up and going for him again, her fists pounding into any flesh she could get at. When they fell into each other, she held on, stealing a breather. She could hear his heartbeat, loud and fast. Good, she was making him work. She pushed away, then came back at him. It was brilliant. She gave everything she had, but he kept coming, and she had to keep moving backwards, until the ropes were pressing against her back.

She raised her gloves.

—Okay, okay. You made your point.

Her heart was pounding as she struggled to release her hands from the sweaty gloves. Sweat rolled down her face and into her eyes. She was dripping on to the floor. Jesus, she must look a sight. With her hand finally freed, she pushed a strand of hair out of her eyes.

Then his hand, gloveless, came towards her face. She baulked. What was this? They weren't hitting any more. She wanted to retreat but there was nowhere to go. She leaned into the ropes but his hand followed, and he eased the chunky guard out of her mouth. She was morto.

—Thanks. I forgot that was in there.

He smiled and handed her the mouthguard.

—Towel?

It was small and threadbare, more like a teacloth, so often washed that she couldn't tell what colour it was supposed to be. When she pressed it to her face it smelled old-fashioned – Lux.

—Thanks. She handed it back, embarrassed at the wet imprint she had left on it, like that shroud. —I'll bring my own next time.

He raised an eyebrow.

—Next time?

She was not amused. It was her first time to box, her first time in the ring – properly – and it felt brilliant.

—Next time, she repeated firmly.

—Same time next week, George relented.

—Next week? She was dismayed at having to wait so long.

—Meantime, we shall run.

Jasmine groaned. Bloody running.

—Tuesday, six?

—Fine.

He lifted the rope to allow her to step down out of the ring.

—You did very well in there, Jasmine.

She looked at him suspiciously in case he was teasing again, but he looked dead serious.

—I know, she replied.

They walked in companionable silence through the college.

When they got to the gate he offered to walk her home, as he invariably did.

—No, you're grand, she told him.

It wouldn't do to start depending on him. Or on anyone. She'd manage on her own, even if it was late to be walking through town. She had to. There was no one else.

She emerged from the insulated hush of Trinity expecting the usual wall of noise to hit her – buses and cars roaring past the wall – but for once the streets were quiet. People were probably all relaxing at home with their families, eating Sunday lunch leftovers, getting ready for Monday. She tried to remember what was in her own small fridge. She hoped there was at least a tin of soup, because she was ravenous.

God, it had felt good in there. She felt guilty for deceiving George about school, but when she turned her back on the convent in Rathlowney it was meant to be for the last time, and it would be very hard to go through the doors of this school in

Ringsend – too hard. But for now the adrenalin was enough to cover the guilt. She'd *think about* school because she had promised George, but she wasn't ready yet.

The lights changed at O'Connell Bridge. Lots of pedestrians took their chances and dashed between the cars and lorries, but Jasmine preferred to wait for the green man. Even after London, she wasn't a city girl. Besides, she was in no hurry; she was relishing the moment-by-moment replay of her time in the ring, surprised to remember details she hadn't even been aware of at the time. Instinct was amazing; what the human body knew, and what the human mind was able to deny.

—Rosemary?

She was jolted out of her daydream. She turned to where the voice was coming from, then immediately regretted it. When she saw who it was she wanted to pretend she hadn't, but it was too late. He didn't even bother to hide the triumphant grin.

—So this is where you went. We thought you were in England.

The same puffy face, the same small, mean eyes. She walked away from him, merging with the surge of pedestrians as the lights changed. But he was still there when she looked over her shoulder, still grinning.

—What do you want, Adrian?

—What? Can I not have a chat with my long-lost cousin when I bump into her up in the big smoke? Are you too good for a country cousin? I like the shiner, by the way.

Her hand went to her eye. It hurt to touch. She didn't know she'd taken a punch there, but, for some reason, she was pleased. Maybe because George wasn't as much in control as he liked to think.

—New boyfriend? Adrian asked innocently.

—Actually, Adrian, why don't you fuck off before he sees you. He has a bit of a short fuse, as you can see.

It had always been easy to frighten Adrian when they were kids, even though he was two years older, and he went a bit pale now, but still he continued tagging along as she walked up

O'Connell Street. She ducked down an alley in an effort to lose him, but when she emerged further up, there he was again. Soon, she'd be back at the flat, and the last thing she wanted was for Adrian to know where she lived. Then she remembered Fibbers, where her neighbour, Deano, worked. Please let him be working this evening. He'd told her more than once that he'd see her right if she came in, whatever that meant; she had never been tempted to find out until now. She weaved through the crowded paths, crossed the busy road, turned the corner, and there was the neon sign, glowing like a beacon. She marched up to the bouncer.

—Deano on tonight?

He looked her up and down, then settled on her face, the bruise. Feck. She held his gaze, and he hesitated just long enough for her to push past.

It was a barn of a place, nearly empty, but music was thumping regardless, vibrating up through her feet and clashing with the rhythm of her speeding heart. She could feel herself sway, and it occurred to her that she might fall, for a second time.

Then Deano was there.

—You're all righ', Jazz. I have ya. Sit yerself down a minute, yeah?

He guided her to one of the booths.

—A bit too much to drink, was it? You're all righ' now. He called to the barman for a glass of water.

A bit too much of Adrian's ugly mug, more like. The water arrived, and she took a few sips. She was starting to feel better.

—Thanks, Deano. I just bumped into a blast from the past out there. Got a bit of a fright. I'm grand now.

He caught her quick glance towards the door. Then he noticed her face.

—Wait, did this blast from the past do that to you?

He stood up, fists clenched, ready to pulverise someone.

—Steady on, Deano. No, he didn't do this. I . . . fell, against the edge of a table. Clumsy. No, he's just someone from home I don't want to see.

—Righ'. Deano sounded doubtful.

—Well, I'll make sure he's not hanging around so. Put the frighteners on him if he is. What does he look like?

Mushroom-coloured face, bad skin, ears that stick out, hair that sticks up, teeth crossing over each other in their hurry to get out of his big gob: she nearly felt sorry for him. But it'd do no harm for him to meet Deano.

—About my height. He's wearing a denim jacket and jeans.

—Righ'. Stay here.

She finished her water, figuring she was probably just dehydrated. Deano came back to report that there was no sign of Adrian.

—Come on, I'll walk you up to the flat.

—No, you're grand. I'll be fine.

What was it with men wanting to walk her home? She just wanted to walk home by herself without fear of being attacked, or stalked by a cousin. Couldn't a girl be left alone?

She woke feeling as if she had been run over by a steamroller. Her body didn't seem to work. Her legs wouldn't lift themselves off the bed, and her arms felt the same size as Popeye's. At least she didn't have to run; they were taking a day off. But she did have to go to work. She remembered the ancient, salt- and dust-encrusted Radox box in the bathroom. A hot bath should loosen the muscles.

She coaxed her legs over the edge of the mattress and lifted her arms into the sleeves of her dressing gown, shivering at the cold fabric. Her flat was always cold, even when it was nice out, though she couldn't tell what it was like yet today because her only window was in the roof. Hers was one of the top flats in an old house that had been divided into eleven bedsits. With only two bathrooms.

Radox would be nice all right, but first, from under the

sink, she extracted a bottle of Jif and an old sponge. She shuddered, remembering the first night when, exhausted from her escape from London and relieved to have found somewhere to live so soon, she threw off her clothes, grabbed a towel, and went for a shower. But the avocado and brown bath which was also the shower was vile, worse even than the squat. Grey rings of dirt marked it at various levels like a measuring jug. But she needed a shower badly, so she held her breath and averted her face, and pulled clumps of hair and slime out of the plughole, threw them into the toilet, and flushed. To her horror, the water kept rising, with its tide of shit and slime, until it threatened to overflow, and she could do nothing except watch. Only at the very last second did it began to recede, very slowly.

Feeling sick, she had closed the lid on it and stepped into the filthy bath. The water was freezing and she couldn't get it to warm up, so she squatted down, as there was no curtain, pointed the hose, and doused herself in cold water. Then she scurried back upstairs to discover that, by closing the door behind her, she had locked herself out. It was the last straw in a litany of horrors, and she burst into tears. That was when Deano came out of his flat, the first time they met.

—Locked out, yeah?

She nodded. He put his shoulder to the door and, with the smallest push, it yielded.

—There ya go. You'll have to ring Flanagan-the-fucker to fix that. Tell him you came home and found it that way. Cheap piece of shit.

She didn't know whether he meant the landlord or the lock, but she was in too much of a hurry to get into her flat to ask. She barely remembered to say thanks.

She had learned her lesson though. With the cleaning stuff under one arm, she took the top off a tower of fifty-pence pieces for the meter, and put the coins into her dressing gown pocket, along with the keys of the flat. She patted it to double-check before closing the door. Even that hurt. Every step of the two flights was torture, but after she had slid the money into the slot, she tackled the bath. She was the only one who ever cleaned it, but she was so glad to have her flat that she didn't mind.

Going back up the stairs was even worse than coming down. The backs of her calves, her knees, her thighs, her arse, even her breathing hurt. Some of the soreness was her muscles, some from being hit. George, you bastard.

—Ouch.

—There ya are, Jazz, me oul' flower.

Deano, knight in armour twice now.

—We'll have to stop meeting like this.

—How's the head this morning? He nudged her ribs with his elbow.

She winced.

—I wasn't drinking, remember. But thanks for the water. And everything.

She took a step to go past him, and winced again. Deano pulled back to scrutinise her.

—Are you sure no one's beatin' on ya? You looked wrecked. If you don't mind me sayin'.

—I'm grand. Thanks again, Deano.

She attempted a reassuring smile and hobbled past him. Even smiling hurt.

In the safety of her flat, once she had the kettle on, she took the mottled mirror off its nail and propped it on the kitchen chair. She must look bad if Deano was commenting. She took off the dressing gown and her pyjama top and, with difficulty, stooped to take off her bottoms. She braced herself. Large, irregular shadow on her left hip; reddened fist-sized area of skin over her rib; darkening eye; grazed right jaw. She twisted around with difficulty, and saw darkening blotches on her waist, thighs and right upper arm. They would change from greys to greens and yellows and purples, like an abstract painting. She liked it; her body as a work of art. She pulled on the dressing gown and made her tea.

The bath, with its chunks of solidified salts, had helped, though it made the marks on her body look worse. But who'd know when she was dressed. She pulled on her layers of black, the alternative uniform that had served her for years, and finished the look with her well-scuffed Docs.

Next, she appraised her face in the small sections the mirror would allow. She'd have to get started on the bruise on her jawbone and her eye, if she didn't want to be answering questions about them all day down at the bookies. She tipped her tools on to the kitchen table. Concealer first and last. Too-light foundation in between and, ta-da, no more bruise. Expertly she drew a jet-black liquid line around her eyes, and added layers of mascara until she was more eyes than anything else. Done.

Her hair was almost dry, and she backcombed and sprayed until it reached maximum height and volume. Then nose ring, eyebrow ring, and just two studs in each ear. It was a pain taking them in and out, but George was adamant, and she could see his point. Bruises were one thing, strips of flesh were another thing altogether. She peered for a last time into the tiny mirror, and this time she was satisfied.

Ten minutes later she was perched outside the counter on a bar-stool borrowed before her time from the bar next door, chalk in hand. She was keeping one ear on the telly to mark up the board while half listening to Bapty.

—It's a racket, that's all I'm sayin'.

Jasmine had the feeling that wouldn't be all he was saying.

—If it's a racket, Bapty, she asked, all innocence, —why would you keep at it?

They had this conversation at least once a day. She knew it back to front. He ignored the question. He had just lost a tenner on a *sure thing*, and he was feeling sore about it.

—Some of them nags is only good for glue. It's a scandal putting them in a race.

—Better not put anything on them so, Bapty.

—Hush, hush, child. The race has started.

The chat around the bookies tapered off, and all eyes were on the horses.

—Go on, Merry Lad, go on, Bapty whispered. —They're over the first fence. Go on, Merry Lad.

Jasmine chewed the ends of her hair to pass the time. She didn't care who won.

—Go on, Merry Lad.

Bapty was getting more animated as they came around the final bend. —Go on. Move your arse, you fuckin' nag. Go on . . . Ah shite.

Merry Lad came in third. Jasmine reached towards the blackboard to mark up the results.

—Bad luck, Bapty. She gave him her most sympathetic smile, knowing that it wouldn't do any good.

—Bad luck me arse. I'm away from this racket.

Away to the pub next door. He'd be back in ten minutes, reeking of whiskey, full of optimism over a tip gleaned from the barman or the newspaper or another morning pub punter, ready to give it another go.

When she was small, Jasmine asked her uncle why the customers kept coming back to his betting office, even though they lost their money all the time. It was because they won sometimes, he told her, and it was the small wins that kept them going, because every one of them believed that the big win was just around the corner. Then he squatted down and put his hand on her shoulder and told her that she shouldn't worry about the big wins – if they happened, they happened – but life wasn't about the big wins. It was about the small wins, and appreciating them when she got them. She should remember that. It's funny that she did – she can remember how serious he looked even now – because she doesn't remember much else about him. He died when she was still small. Poor Bapty was right. It was a racket. But it kept her in a job. He had been her first customer when she started the job and, as it turned out, he was Jock Rooney's first customer every morning. He was as contrary as a sack of ferrets, but Jasmine was fond of him, and his routines and their bit of banter helped pass the time.

Next day, the rain woke her with its pounding on the roof window. It was never going to be easy getting out of bed at that hour, and it was getting harder now that it was October, and the mornings were darker. But she knew how good she'd feel when she got moving, so she forced herself out from under the covers and got dressed.

The weather was still mild, but she was shivery from waking up, and the want of a hot cup of tea. She broke into a jog and crossed the road towards the North Circular, where she had to dodge leaf-strewn puddles if she didn't want her new runners ruined. As she reached the corner of North Circular and the North Strand, she spied George in his black tracksuit, hood up, coming out from town.

—Good morning, Jasmine.

Always polite. As usual, he didn't stop, and she fell in beside him. They ran through Fairview Park, towards the seafront.

—A beautiful morning, he said, finally glancing at her. But when he saw her face, he broke his rhythm.

—Surely I did not . . . ?

He actually stopped, dismay all over his face. She paused, running on the spot.

—What's up?

—Your face is all bruised. This is terrible. It should not have happened. It must not happen again. Jasmine . . .

She had seen this coming, and she was ready for him.

—Boxing is not for girls. Is that what you want to say, George? Because the way I remember it, we had a deal.

She ran off in long strides so she wouldn't have to look him in the eye. He had asked only a few days before how her studies were going, and she lied and said *fine*. She had actually found the school, and watched as students, some her own age, some older, pushed the doors open and disappeared, but she was just not ready to return to the classroom.

He caught her up, his legs always longer and more powerful than hers.

—We do. We do have a deal. But I do not want to hurt a girl.

She stopped and faced him. Her breathing was hard, and she swiped at the drip at the end of her nose.

—*If* we have a deal, let me worry about getting hurt. It's my body.

The force of her words belied what she was feeling. If George wouldn't train her, it was over. There was no one else who would. Somehow he had understood her need to acquire the speed and strength and power that boxing offered – but not to girls. He was her only hope. She watched as his face moved towards one expression then another, until it settled, finally, in resignation.

—We have a deal. I will be more careful.

Her bravado was almost spent, but she managed a cheeky *I'm glad to hear it.*

They set out again. Soon the sea appeared, and then they were on the seafront. Right beside them the water slurped and sucked against the granite wall, spraying them. She could taste the salt. George picked up the pace and she followed. Up ahead, the Wooden Bridge stretched out to Bull Island like an invitation, but they'd never gone that far. A few weeks before she'd have been panting by now, and wanting to turn back, but today her runners beat rhythmically on the wet path and she felt as if she could run for ever. But as usual, George told her to turn around, and she did. With the sea and the spray, and the rhythm of the run, she didn't even feel like arguing.

Light was breaking through the clouds by the time they got back to Fairview. They were walking now because there were too many pedestrians, and Jasmine noticed one or two funny looks in their direction. It might have been her bruise. But more than one passer-by had looked from her to George, and frowned. Or maybe she had imagined it.

—Thursday? George said, either oblivious or pretending to be.

She took her cue from him, but she didn't like it.

—Thursday.

—You are improving, Jasmine.

She blushed with pleasure.

—Thanks. She tried to sound indifferent.

—Well, goodbye then, Jasmine.

Just as they parted, someone caught her eye across the road, a fella wearing a grey tracksuit top, hood up. Bloody Adrian. Was he watching her, following her? She went back up the North Circular, where wet drops from denuded branches splashed on to her head. She hurried home, her peace all gone.

She was just in the hall door when Deano's face appeared over the banister.

—Howya, Jazz. There was some big pasty-faced culchie here lookin' for you last nigh'.

It could only be Adrian. No one else knew where she was. Now it looked like he knew where she lived too.

—Oh?

—Yeah. Only, he was callin' ya Rosemary. Told him there was no one by that name here. Then he goes on about your hair and that. It was you all right. I told him you were out turning tricks. That's all right, isn't it?

—Deano, how could you, when you know perfectly well I was with my rich fiancé.

Deano's face disappeared with a parting *Ha!* only to reappear when she reached the top of the stairs.

—Ya mad thing, he said, looking at her running shoes and tracksuit. —At this hour?

—Actually, it's brilliant. You should try it. Work off all that unhealthy living.

—Yeah, I might, yeah.

He looked as if he were seriously considering it. Jasmine had a vision of Deano huffing along beside her in the morning, saying God knows what to George. She was sorry she opened her mouth. On the other hand, if she was going to have a stalker, she could do worse than stick with Deano.

—Take care of yerself, Jazz, he said as he went down the stairs.

When she ran, she felt as if no one could hurt her because she wasn't solid flesh any more. The cells of her skin, that boundary between what was you and what was not you, loosened up and the air was able to filter in around them so they could breathe. Especially when there was wind, and there nearly always was, by the sea. Anyone who tried to hurt her would pass right through her. Other runners felt it too. She could see it in their faces, in the occasional glance as they passed. When she ran, she was part of something much bigger than herself.

But there was still the awful guilt of pretending to George that she was back in school. He hadn't asked about it again; he had taken her at her word, she supposed, but she decided to join the local library so that she could at least read something, if only to make her lie more convincing. It was amazing the stuff you could learn just by randomly picking books off the shelves, and browsing through them. She found atlases, African history, bird books, language tapes for every language you could think of, and ones Jasmine had never heard of. There was every kind of music too. She hadn't known you could borrow records and tapes.

When she was small, her mother brought her to the library every week. There were no tapes; there weren't even any good books – a few battered *Victor* annuals and some of the Biggles books, and a yard-long section of Bible storybooks and *Lives of the Saints* – so she went through the motions of taking out two books, then bringing them home and putting them on her dressing table, where they remained until the following week when she returned them. She wondered if her mother had known she didn't read them.

She knew her guilt about George was all mixed up with her guilt about her mother. She hadn't spoken to her since coming back because she didn't want to admit she had failed. But more than that, when she last phoned from London, her mother had sounded as if she didn't care any more. Instead of the usual shouting she had told Jasmine that she could do what she liked, she always did. She was hurt, if she was honest, but she told herself that if her mother didn't care, neither did she.

Behind the music section, Jasmine spotted something she wouldn't even have thought to look for. It was the black and white case of a video. She didn't have a TV, let alone a video player, but she slid it out of its slot on the shelf – *Boxing Through History* – and put it on top of her pile.

Deano could pick her up a video machine for a song.

—Back of a lorry. You know yourself.

—No, you're grand, Deano. Just a lend.

—Suit yourself, Jazz. Your loss, but.

He dropped the portable television and video player in to her that evening and set it all up on the kitchen table.

—There you go, Jazz, me oul' flower. Will I get a takeaway, couple of cans, snuggle up on the . . . He looked around the flat: table, single straight-backed chair, bed. —The bed will be grand.

—The door will be grand, mister. She turned him to face it.

—But thanks, Deano.

—What is it you're watching anyway? he asked from the hall. —Porno, is it?

—You wish.

—Here, did yer man ever come back, you know, the big culchie?

—No. And Deano? It's a boxing video.

She closed the door on his *Wha'*?

As soon as the credits faded she remembered. How old was she? Seven? Eight? She paused the tape and two men in shorts froze on the screen, mid-action. She had completely forgotten. Saturday afternoons, the curtains pulled against the sunlight so as not to cause a glare on the telly, bar of Dairy Milk *and don't tell Mam*. Where was Mam anyway? Squash. She used to play squash, with Maggie O'Brien, the other Margaret. In a short skirt. Dad whistling when she came down the stairs. Mam pleased-looking. *Would you give over, you eejit*. Light steps going out the door. A ruffle of the hair for Jasmine, *Be good now, mind*. It was hard to imagine Mam playing sports, and even harder to imagine her happy.

She reached forward and pressed *Play*, and the two men sprang back into action. With the volume down, the way Deano had left it, she found herself running her own commentary, the way her dad used to. *Isn't the human body something, Rosie*. Her eight-year-old self would sit on the arm of his chair, letting a square of chocolate melt slowly in her mouth, listening, trying to follow his commentary. Wondering what it would be like to be Muhammad Ali, arm held high in the air by the referee. *I am the best. I am the greatest. I am pretty. I am the king*.

In black and white and every shade of grey, Deano's small telly had given her back her dad. A long time ago, when she was still a child, she had made the decision not to think about him because it was so painful, and because it wouldn't bring him back. But now she welcomed it. She wondered what he would think if he could see her holding her own in the ring. Probably, he would say it was not for girls. He was traditional, after all. As for her mam, she wouldn't even register that there was anything unusual about it, she sounded so out of it. This time, though, she was surprised to find that instead of her usual annoyance and defensiveness, she felt a flutter of pity for her mother.

She couldn't wait to see George, and not just to tell him about the video. She'd been poring over her books too, on boxing, and tonnes of other stuff. The next day, he was there in the gym before her, hidden in the shadowy light they made do with. After all, they didn't want college security in on top of them.

—So, is it Turkana you're from or . . .?

She was rewarded with the smile she'd been going out of her way to earn lately.

—Actually, yes. But we are not here to chitter-chatter about me, Jasmine. Let me see what you can do with this skipping rope.

She took the rope and started jumping. She loved it, always had, the feeling in her muscles as they started to warm up, knowing she had created the heat herself, each impact and rebound a confirmation of the power of her own body.

—Bag work, George broke into her rhythm.

—But that wasn't five minutes.

—Yes it was. You have improved.

She flushed, both from pleasure, and because it looked as if she had been fishing for compliments. But the truth was, she could have kept jumping for ages more.

She held out her hands and George wrapped the long bandages until they formed the herringbone hand mitts that stopped her knuckles from splitting. She pushed her bandaged hands into the big clumsy gloves, and held them out again, and George made sure they were good and tight, with no lace left flying about to get her into trouble. Then she headed to the punch-bag. She began to circle it, jabbing at it every couple of steps, with George encouraging her from where he was punching his own bag. Her training was part of his training, and he had a fight coming up. She could hardly wait to see him in action. It would be her first time at a live fight as a proper spectator.

—Cross punch, he called.

Then it was a 1-2, jab, followed by cross. She even loved the language of boxing.

—Now, 1, 2, 3. Jab-cross-hook, George said, and her body responded: jab, cross, then a round punch with her left hand.

They moved to the speed drills, then strength, then stamina. She exploded against the bag, jabbing furiously, giving it everything until her heart was flat out and her body coated in sweat.

—Good, she earned from George.

She went on to arm circles and shoulder stretches to cool down.

It was good, it was better than good.

As she was pulling on her jacket over her sweatshirt to leave she plucked up the courage to ask George something that had been on her mind for a while now.

—In a real fight—?

—No real fights, Jasmine. It is not legal for women.

—Yeah, yeah, I know all that. But just supposing there was a real fight, for women, I mean. Because this is a women's fight question . . .

George gave her the sidelong look that let her know he was only tolerating her now.

—What about your boobs?

—I do not have any, as you say, boobs.

—*My* boobs, I mean, smartarse. Uff.

She wasn't looking where she was going, and she had banged into someone. It was one of the three men she had seen that first evening in Trinity.

—Sorry, she stammered.

He acknowledged her apology with a smile, then nodded to George.

—George.

George nodded back.

—Terry.

They continued their separate ways.

—You know him? Jasmine whispered when they were out of earshot.

—Yes, Terry Christle. He and his brothers, Mel and Joe, are all Trinity boxers.

Of course. The Christles.

—Do you think he heard me talking about my boobs?

—Yes. George kept walking.

—Then he'll know—

—That you were consulting with your doctor about concerns regarding your breasts.

—Of course. That's it. Brilliant.

—You are being silly, Jasmine.

Chastened, she walked in silence with him to the Front Gate, but he had hurt her feelings – she had a serious question – and she still hadn't forgiven him by the time they parted company.

She walked fast with her head down. If he was such a great doctor, shouldn't he have sorted out her boobs already? What if she got punched there? And who was he to say she couldn't box in a real fight? Who was going to stop her?

Dublin, 2012

She remembers that she has to call Jeffrey back. But not just yet. She's waiting for the result, and the waiting is like a physical ache. Come, on, come on, she wills the judges. She remembers her amazement and delight at discovering Katie Taylor, when she won a gold medal in Norway in the '05 European Amateur Championships. Until then, she had no idea that women were competing in boxing. But this was hardly surprising, given the line of work she was in. It was something of a contradiction for a doctor to take pleasure in watching two people inflict deliberate damage on each other's bodies for sport, so she began to follow Taylor's career closely, but in secret. The man she was seeing at the time – the relationship before Jeffrey, which had persuaded her that relationships weren't for her – actually suspected her of having an affair, and she let him think that she was, because it was easier to end it that way.

Before she can learn the verdict, she is startled by her phone ringing. What terrible timing. But it would be very poor form to ignore Jeffrey for a second time, and she is recording the fight after all, so she tears herself away and goes to the hall. But it's not Jeffrey, it's the nursing home. All thoughts of the fight vanish as she slides her finger across the screen.

—Dr McCarthy speaking?

Her mother has developed a temperature, Sheila tells her. It's not raging, but she wasn't herself this evening either. She might want to come back in.

This time she takes the car, reversing carefully out the narrow gates of her terraced house on to the busy street. Dublin traffic at this hour is usually light, but tonight, because of the rain, it's at a crawl. She wills it to move; even a small rise in temperature can be significant in the elderly. She trusts Sheila and the nurses, so when they say she was not herself, she knows something is amiss. The Alzheimer's has taken its toll on her mother's body, which was already weakened from years of drinking and medication, so making it this far is something of a small miracle, one that she has long been grateful for, because it has given her the chance to do the right thing. Still, she is surprised at how shaken she is. Theirs was never an easy relationship, and these last years it has been reduced to a routine, and a sizeable direct debit every month. Yet she is trembling, some involuntary response from her nervous system. Dealing as she does every day with the physical aspect of childbirth, it is easy to forget how closely connected the body is to the mind, and how fragile that can be. Her relationship with her mother might not be much, but it is all she has.

Dublin, 1982

Someone was lacing her into a corset in preparation for a fight, but it was too tight, and she couldn't see who was doing it. She woke terrified, but half elated too at the prospect of fighting for real. She couldn't get back to sleep, so she went for her run early. George was on duty in the hospital, and she was glad to run by herself, because she was still holding a grudge.

After the run she felt better, but she was tired from lack of sleep when she arrived at work. Bapty was there before her.

—Morning, Jasmine, love.

—Morning, Bapty. She stifled a yawn and climbed on to a stool to switch on the TV. She started marking up the board when something occurred to her.

—Have you ever heard of the Christle brothers, Bapty?

—Sure of course I have. Aren't they some of the best boxers we have. The three of them won national titles on the same night a couple of years back. Sure you watched one of them here only the other day, Terry, it was.

So that's where she knew him from. No wonder they were so confident. Terry had KO-ed his opponent too, if she remembered rightly. And she'd bumped into him, literally. She tried to remember how his shoulder had felt. Had he smiled when she apologised? More than once during the day she caught herself daydreaming about these Christle brothers, or this Christle brother in particular.

*

When they met up the next day, George was oblivious to her coolness, so she stopped bothering. It was hard to stay annoyed when it was one of those gorgeous November days, with blue skies and the sun sparkling on the bay. They beat a steady rhythm on the path, saying little. George's gaze was off towards the horizon. She wondered what he was thinking about. Maybe his wife and his children, who were living with her parents in Kenya until he finished his studies. But she wanted his thoughts to be somewhere else.

—So, how well do you know Terry Christle?

He gave her a look, *Silly*, so she decided to leave the subject alone. She let herself enjoy the run, and the day, and they reached the Wooden Bridge without her noticing. As usual, they leaned into the wall and stretched out their calves.

—I might be sparring with Terry tonight. You could watch, George said casually.

Sparring with Terry Christle tonight. She jumped around, and could have kissed him. As if he suspected as much he drew away and faced back towards town for their run back.

—I said *might*. If it is possible to smuggle you in. If you can behave, he finished drily.

The thrill of knowing she would soon be watching Terry Christle fight buzzed inside her for the rest of the day. Her excitement was purely professional, she told herself. Still, it was a bummer to have to tone down her look after work: no make-up, no visible piercings; she needed to be as inconspicuous as possible. In her grey tracksuit and runners, and grey wool hat, she hoped to pass as a student – a male student.

She was amazed at how busy the gym was; she was only ever there when no one was around. Tonight, there were men still skipping and working with the bags, but the excitement was building around the ring where George and Terry Christle were warming up. They danced around each other, throwing an occasional punch, sussing each other out. Then, without any signal, it was on for real. They were making each other work, matching punch for punch. And they were well matched, Jasmine saw with pride. Even if she was a bit infatuated with Terry – okay, she could admit it – she wasn't about to overlook the skill and power of her own coach.

She sat, riveted, by the grace and beauty of them both. The other boxers had given up any pretence of training and had gathered near the ring in twos and threes. Jasmine was the only one there on her own, and as much as she wanted to move closer, she didn't dare in case one of them said something and exposed her. She didn't really mind; she was just glad to be there.

When someone sat down beside her, she was startled, but she kept her eyes firmly on the fight.

—So this is what you're up to. Watching the boyfriend, is it?

Jasmine turned sharply to see her cousin's fat backside settling on to the bench.

—Jesus, Adrian, she hissed. —What are you doing here?

—What are you doing here, more to the point? he replied.

—None of your business, she snapped. She turned back to the fight.

—I wonder what Aunty Margaret would think of your boyfriend, he mused, following her gaze. —Your *black* boyfriend.

—Shh. And he's not my boyfriend. He's married, for Christ's sake.

—Then what are you doing here?

Jasmine looked around to check that no one was listening to them. Everyone was still engrossed, but it looked like they were winding down. There was a coach in the ring, instructing Terry to do something – she couldn't see with the spectators – and some of them had started to drift back to their own training.

—If you must know, I'm a boxer, she said.

—A boxer?

Adrian laughed loudly, and a couple of the lads looked over. Out of the corner of her eye, Jasmine could see George climbing out of the ring, and he looked as if he was coming their way. She didn't know whether she should be worried, though Adrian certainly looked less sure of himself as George came and towered over him.

—Jasmine. Is there a problem? he asked, over Adrian's head.

She was embarrassed, and unsure how to explain Adrian.

—He doesn't believe I'm a boxer.

George looked from her to Adrian.

—And *he* is?

Adrian looked even more uncomfortable.

—My cousin, Jasmine mumbled.

—Then, cousin, you should know that she is a boxer. A good one. I am her coach. Now if you will excuse me.

With a nod to Jasmine, he returned to the knot of men surrounding Terry Christle and his coach. Someone's arm drew him in, and another hand patted him on the back. Even Adrian couldn't spoil how proud she was. And he had said she was a good boxer. She couldn't have got that out of George in a million years by herself. It shut Adrian up too, but not for long.

—Your coach, is it? So you are a boxer? he said loudly.

—Shut up, Adrian, you creep. Look, I'm sick of you following me. Tell me what you want from me, then leave me alone. But not here.

She got up and left, without checking to see if he was following. Once she got outside the gym she made her way to the nearest gate, then across the road to Mahaffey's Pub.

—You're in a rush to get out of there, Adrian said breathlessly when he caught up with her.

—I'm in a rush to get rid of you.

There were just two couples in Mahaffey's and it was very quiet. Too quiet, depending on what Adrian wanted. But it would have to do. She was determined to get rid of him once and for all. She walked to the bar and asked for two orange juices. She was a sportswoman, after all. Adrian sat opposite.

—What do you want, Adrian?

—Hey, cuz. He threw his hands up. —We're all worried about you. No one knows if you're alive or dead.

—I rang Mam, she said, folding her arms.

—Not recently, from what I hear. She doesn't know where you are. Or what you're doing. His eyes narrowed. —And she doesn't know you're a boxer, or about your black . . . coach.

—So?

—So maybe she'd be interested.

Jasmine sighed.

—Fine. Tell her whatever you want. Just leave me. And Adrian?

—Cuz?

—Stop following me or I'll report you to the guards.

He made a pretend-shocked face.

—You wouldn't. Your own cousin.

Jasmine looked at a corner of the ceiling, wishing he would just evaporate. She was not especially afraid of him, or what he might tell anyone. He was just a gobshite. She'd always felt sorry for him when they were growing up, given who he had for a father; Uncle Adrian was no picnic. In his school, he took so much care not to favour Adrian that he went too far in the opposite direction. No child in that school had a harder time, and when the master's son didn't seem to be amounting to much, Jasmine wasn't surprised.

—Look, Adrian. I'm doing nothing wrong. I have a job. No doubt you followed me there too . . .

—Jock Rooney, Bookmakers. Yes, I saw that you decided to stick with *that* side of the family.

Uncle Adrian always let it be understood that her mam had married beneath her when she married a bookmaker, so it was no surprise that Adrian had absorbed the same bias. *The Murphys were always a cut above buttermilk.* She was pleased when her dad's words came to her. It was how he teased Mam if she showed a preference for curtains with pelmets, or lemon sole over a plate of rashers. But she wasn't about to be drawn into those old politics.

112

—What do you care what I do? Why don't you worry about yourself, and leave me alone.

Adrian slumped.

—The thing is . . . he began.

She waited.

—Look, Jasmine. I'm in a bind here. Dad thinks I'm settling into second year teacher training, only I decided to go a different route . . .

—You got kicked out, didn't you?

He nodded.

—I only got in because of him anyway. I hate it. I can't speak Irish to save my life, and I have no interest in teaching.

Jasmine shrugged.

—So I thought . . . When I bumped into you on O'Connell Bridge . . .

—So you weren't following me?

—No. At least, not until then. But then I didn't want to lose track of you. He looked around as if he was expecting someone to be listening. —You were . . . You are my only hope.

—Creeping around after me, jumping out of the shadows, how do you think that felt? Why would I want to do anything to help you? Besides, you're an adult, Adrian. As much as Uncle Adrian mightn't like it, you can do what you want. Just tell him to go shite. Or don't even bother to tell him.

—It's not that easy . . .

—Why isn't it that easy? Just pick up the phone, tell him you're doing something else . . .

—The thing is . . .

His face looked clammy and even paler than she remembered. What had he gone and done?

—Dad paid the fees into my account, and he pays in living expenses every week . . .

—And you spent it? Just tell him . . . I don't know what. She was growing impatient.

—I got into something. I owe money . . .

—Jesus, Adrian.

He looked at his feet.

—For feck's sake, have you no sense? Yeah, you're right. Uncle Adrian will kill you.

—Yeah, well, if he doesn't, the lads I owe money to will.

—What difference does it make so? She started to stand.

—Wait. Rose – Jasmine, I just need a loan . . .

—I haven't got money to spare, Adrian. Cash in hand on Saturday, spent by Tuesday. Rent, food, basics.

He looked at her as if he couldn't decide whether to believe her or not.

—So where did you go? What have you been doing?

—None of your business.

He started to get a sly look. From growing up together, she knew this meant he had an idea, and his ideas usually meant trouble for her.

—And I suppose this boxing is none of my business either?

—That's right.

—Auntie Margaret might think it's her business.

—Tell her whatever you like.

—About the abortion? And the black boyfriend? He forced you to do it, didn't he?

—What?

—Because he was *married*.

Jasmine looked at her cousin through slits of eyes, trying to determine how much he really believed any of this. His expression was triumphant, and slowly she understood; it didn't matter whether he believed it or not. She tried to weigh up what he was saying. She could never go back to Rathlowney if he spread a rumour like this. Not that she cared. She wasn't planning on going back anyway. But if her mother believed him, it meant that things between them could never be patched up. Somewhere in the back of her mind, she had always assumed that some day they would sort out their differences.

—I already told you I have no money. Why would you make up stuff like that, Adrian? What's in it for you?

—Oh but it's not made up, is it, cousin dearest? It's the God's honest truth, isn't it, Rosemary?

She stood. Let him make up whatever he wanted. What did she care what her mother thought, or what anyone thought, when she had her own flat, and a job and friends – George, Deano, maybe even Bapty – and she had boxing. It was enough. More than enough. Adrian could sort out his own mess.

—It's Jasmine. And you can do what you want.

—Wait. Rosemary – I mean, Jasmine. Please.

His blank, empty expression stopped her. He would never have enough. Whatever trouble he was in, and however she might help him, there would always be more trouble. She should be angry with him. She should be furious; the little shit was trying to blackmail her. Abortion. As if she hadn't enough problems.

—What do you want from me, Adrian? Last time. And spare me your threats and your bullshit.

—Just . . . I mean . . . Could I stay with you for a while? Just until I get back on my feet.

All the cockiness was gone, all the bravado. He looked about eleven, after he'd endured yet another tongue-lashing from his father in front of the whole school. But her flat, her own space? The thoughts of sharing it with anyone, let alone Adrian . . .

—But where are you staying now? Surely you have a place. You said Uncle Adrian . . .

—I owe it all to these fellas. Look, you don't want to know. I just haven't got any money, all right? Or any place to stay.

—Where have you been staying?

She was stalling, trying to see some way around it. The thought of Adrian in her flat was intolerable.

—I had a couch for a few nights here and there. Look, Jasmine, you have to believe me, I've run out of options. I'm desperate. It's your place or the streets.

—Jesus, Adrian. Okay, fine.

Her *fine* was little more than an exhalation, and she was already walking away by the time he registered it. He scrabbled to his feet and caught up with her before she reached the door.

She woke to the snuffling, wheezing noises Adrian was making from his sleeping bag on the far side of the room. It was too early for the alarm, and the skylight was a black square in the ceiling, but she got out of bed anyway and took her clothes down to the freezing shared bathroom to get dressed. Bloody Adrian.

By the time George arrived, she had already spent twenty minutes stretching against a railing in the dark. She told him what had happened.

—Looks like I'm stuck with him, she finished ruefully.

—He is family. You are doing what you must do.

There was no point in even trying to contradict George on the question of family, so she pushed the image of the big pasty lump, still tucked up warm and snug in her flat, out of her mind.

—Let's run.

George set their pace, as usual. Beside her, his breath was unlaboured and steady, and she found herself falling in with it. Following his lead had not let her down yet, this complete stranger who had decided to help her when she needed it. He had patiently taught her about running and boxing, and some-how, at the same time, he was teaching her how to be a better person. It wouldn't cost her much to let Adrian stay a few nights on her floor. As soon as she had thought it, her frustra-tions vanished, and there was just the run.

—Ready to go to the end? George asked. They had reached the Wooden Bridge, the point where they usually turned around. She nodded.

The sun-bleached wood was more yielding than the concrete and their runners landed with soft thuds. Between the planks she could see slivers of blue. The sea spread out either side of them, sparkling in the low winter sun, and up ahead it was blue to the horizon. They were running out to the very edge of the world – or that was how it felt, with the water so close. George met her glance, and, reading each other's minds, they broke into a sprint. With his long legs and all his training, he flew away ahead, but she wasn't bothered. She could feel the power in her legs and the satisfying cold as she pushed her face into the east wind. She was gulping for air by the time she got to the end, where George waited. He was leaning against one of the concrete stilts that held up the bizarre Virgin Mary statue – elevated so she could keep a good watch over sailors or something.

—It's just because you've had more training, she managed between gasps.

—You did well, Jasmine. Ready?

Her lungs were burning and the muscles in her legs were twitched madly from their exertion. She nodded. But instead of sprinting, or even jogging, George started walking, and she fell into place beside him. Now that the sun was on their backs, and the wind was behind them, she could appreciate the beach and the dunes, and the sand-green grasses.

—How are your studies progressing? he asked.

His tone was pleasant, conversational, but she was on the alert.

—Fine.

—No problems?

—Nope.

—And your plans?

She looked at him in surprise.

—What do you mean?

—For your education.

—Oh, I'll probably do the Leaving in June, she said casually. He didn't have to know which June. School – if she ever went back – wasn't even enough, it seemed. It all had to add up to something.

—That is wonderful, Jasmine, he said. —As your coach, I am very proud.

She blushed out of both pleasure and shame, and punched him on the arm to hide her confusion.

—Ah give over, would you, George.

They walked on. Overhead, a flock of birds flew in formation, honking as they passed.

—Brent geese, Jasmine said, pleased to be able to identify them.

—Indeed. George sounded suitably impressed.

—Of course, you're used to much more exciting wildlife back in Kenya. Lions and tigers and bears.

—Actually, there are no bears in Kenya.

—It's from the *Wizard of Oz*, she explained, before she realised that he had been teasing again.

—When will you be going back?

—When I qualify.

—But don't you miss your family?

His look told her it was a redundant question, and she was mad with herself for making him sad.

—I might apply to do medicine myself, she said. He'd be sure to lecture her on realistic goals or knowing her limitations or something like that, but at least it would take his mind off his family.

—You would make a fine doctor, Jasmine. Let me know if I can be of any help.

Her strategy had worked, though his response certainly surprised her. She hadn't known such a thought existed in her head, even for purposes of distraction, but the more she thought about it, the more she liked it. Stranger things had happened. It wasn't so long ago that she was in a brown sack of a uniform, listening to shite from the nuns, and now here she was, living in Dublin, hanging around with a Kenyan, and boxing. Why not study medicine? She just had to take the plunge and go through those doors in Ringsend, back to school.

*

When she got back to Dorset Street and let herself in, she was met with the sight of Deano pressing Adrian up against the banisters. Adrian's head was at an odd angle, his eyes bulging.

—Ah Jazz, me oul' flower. I found this scumbag coming ourra your flat. What d'you want me to do to him?

A strangled sound emerged from Adrian. Well, he deserved it, for following her and threatening her, and just for being Adrian. She went over and gave Deano a peck on the cheek.

—Go way ourra tha', leadin' fellas on.

—Dean, this is my cousin, Adrian. Adrian, Dean.

—You're havin' me on, Deano said, without adjusting the arrangement of Adrian's shirt in his fist.

—No, I'm afraid I'm not. So I suppose you'd better let him go.

—It's the same muppet was sniffing around for you before, but.

—Yep, same muppet. Still. He is my cousin, so . . .

Deano prolonged his hold a little longer, then he let go suddenly and Adrian collapsed in a heap, gasping and pawing at his throat.

—Aw righ' so, Jazz. He's all yours. You know where I am if he starts givin' ya gyp.

—Thanks, Deano, I appreciate it, Jasmine said sweetly. She looked down at Adrian. He really had had a scare. —I suppose we'd better get you a cup of tea or something.

She was lost in her new plans as she put on the kettle. Adrian was moaning away, how he thought they'd come for him, how he was done for, and what kind of a place was she living in anyway, but she didn't pay him any attention. She didn't even mind about him being there. Once she got down to her studies, on top of work and training, she probably wouldn't see much of him anyway.

—And as for the company you keep, he finished indignantly, meaning Deano.

—You're one to talk, she replied. Deano was good to her, always looking out for her, and she liked knowing that he was just down the hall. She gathered up her clothes for work and left Adrian looking deep into his milky tea.

It was nearly ten o'clock when she got home, and there was no sign of Adrian. Good. She collapsed on to her bed, fully clothed. It had been a long day. She'd gone to the school in Ringsend after work, determined to go through with it this time, but there was nobody there. Then she remembered it was a bank holiday. Never mind. Tomorrow. She'd put her name down for six subjects tomorrow.

Right now, she just wanted to sleep, but she couldn't because bloody Adrian wasn't here yet. Where was he anyway? He was supposed to be broke and desperate. She had imagined him holed up in the flat keeping himself busy while she was out at work, though admittedly she had no idea what Adrian did with his spare time. She went over their conversations. He hadn't answered her when she asked him about drugs; maybe he was an addict. Though he didn't look like one. An unbidden image of the marks on Cat's long white arms flashed through her mind, but that was London, and she didn't think about London. Besides, Adrian was definitely not scrawny. He had plenty of spare flesh. Maybe this was some sort of drug thing too. But then she remembered that he had always looked that way.

Damn, she was wide awake now. She wondered if it was too late to ask Deano if he had seen him. She decided it was either too late or too early, depending on whether he was working or not.

If Adrian was a drug addict, she definitely didn't want him in her flat. She should send him home to Uncle Adrian. But how would she do this without alerting her mother of her own whereabouts. She imagined the scene, stuffing him into a taxi while he shouted all sorts of lies about her. Of course, she didn't know for sure that he was into drugs. But if not drugs, then what? He said he owed someone money, that he'd spent all

Uncle Adrian's. Good. She liked the thought of Uncle Adrian's bank account haemorrhaging into his son's. But he did seem to be genuinely scared, and as nasty as Uncle Adrian could get, it wasn't that kind of scared. He must have been desperate, to come following her the way he did. So who was after him then? And what if they found out where he was staying; was she in danger too? She shivered, remembering how easy it was to break in to her flat.

As if she had conjured the sound herself, she heard footsteps on the stairs. By the time they reached her door her heart was racing as if she had been sprinting, then they went past. Deano, probably.

She got up and put on the kettle. Tea would warm her up while she decided what to do about Adrian. It was past bloody midnight now. She made the tea and brought it to bed, and tried to read a book, but she was too tired and kept catching herself dozing off, cup still in hand until, inevitably, she spilled some onto her pillow. Damn him anyway. She was wide awake now. She got back up to dab at the spill with the tea towel. She was rinsing the cup when she heard the front door slam, followed by more steps on the stairs, and a bang on the door.

—Rose – I mean, Jasmine, are you there?

He was loud enough to wake everyone in the building. Did he like being manhandled by Deano? She rushed to the door to try to minimise the noise he was making, and his fist was lifted for another assault as she swung it open. She pulled him inside, but she was so relieved that it was just him that she had to work at sounding angry.

—Shh, you fecking gobshite. Do you want to wake the whole house?

He was grinning ear to ear, his normally pale face bright red and shiny. She wondered if he was drunk, but there was no smell of alcohol.

—Jesus, Adrian, have some consideration. It's half two in the morning. I've been sitting waiting.

—Thanks, Mammy, he said, attempting to hug her.

She pushed him away.

—Where the hell were you anyway? I thought you were supposed to be broke.

—Just out making ends meet, he told her, settling himself in at the table. —Any chance of a cuppa?

—Make it yourself, she said, climbing into her bed. —Some of us have to work.

He clattered and banged around, but somehow she managed to fall asleep in the middle of it all.

When she woke it was after eight and Adrian was snoring in his sleeping bag, his clothes neatly folded on the chair beside him. She put on the kettle and went to put money in the meter for a shower. He still hadn't moved when she came back up. On an impulse she lifted his jeans off the pile of clothes and shook them out. She didn't know what she was expecting to find, but it was certainly not the splatter of what looked like blood on one leg. It had to be ketchup, she reassured herself. He must have gone for a late night burger. She was folding them up when something fell out. She stooped to pick it up. It was a sizeable roll of ten-pound notes.

—Broke, my arse.

She badly wanted to interrogate him there and then, but she didn't have time. She didn't want to be late because she needed her job, because unlike *some* she had rent to pay. She restrained herself from giving Adrian a kick, and instead refolded the jeans and replaced them. He gave a spluttering exhalation in his sleep and turned over as she left.

It was grey and drizzly when she got to work, and a disgruntled Bapty was waiting outside.

—Third time this week. You could catch your death, waiting to give that fecker your money. He coughed deeply and wetly, then expelled what he had excavated on to the path.

Jasmine hugged her coat around her and tried not to look

at the green jellyfish-like blob that lay on the ground between them.

—Do you think the rain will clear up, Bapty?

—Hmm, he said in disgust, at the weather, or her attempt to distract him, or most likely at Jock. —Here he is now, the fecker.

Jock's black Mercedes pulled up on the path beside them, with his usual disregard for double yellow lines.

—There you are, Bapty, he said when he got out.

—I'm freezin' me bollocks off out here, Joxer. With apologies to the lady.

—Traffic was bad, he said, looking distracted.

He set about unlocking the shutters, then the door. He was breathing heavily by the time he turned off the alarm. When at last he let them in, Bapty hawked up another phlegmy jewel and looked as if he was about to spit on the floor, but he aimed it out the door at the last minute.

—You'll have to watch out for that traffic, Jock, or your best customers will have to take their custom elsewhere, he said ominously.

Jasmine heard Jock sigh as he turned towards the counter. Bapty could get on your nerves, all right, but usually Jock paid no attention to him. She was too busy getting set up to give it any more thought. The heaters needed to go on quickly, before Bapty could start complaining again, then the lights and the TV. She wiped the board from yesterday and marked up results that had come in overnight. The place was starting to warm up by then so she took off her coat and went into the back to hang it up. Jock was leaning against his desk. He had gone a funny purplish colour.

—Jesus. Jock . . . Are you all right? She stood, paralysed, as he struggled to breathe. She didn't even know first aid. Some doctor she'd make. She tried to think what George would do.

—Do you want me to ring for an ambulance? Jock? I'll ring for an ambulance, okay?

He didn't seem to hear.

—What? What should I do? Jesus. Was he going to drop dead in front of her?

But whatever it was seemed to pass, because he straightened out a bit, and his face began to look more normal.

—I'm . . . okay.

But she was not convinced. He really had looked as if he was dying. George would make him sit down, and he'd get that ambulance.

—Sit down, Jock, she said with an authority she wouldn't have thought possible a few months ago. Even a few minutes ago. She put a hand to his shoulder and guided him to the chair which, to her surprise, he seemed glad of. She picked up the receiver and dialled, then the calm voice at the other end took over: was he breathing, was he conscious, what symptoms was he displaying? She answered as best she could, then hung up and waited for the ambulance.

—They're on their way, she told Jock, who was alarmingly pale now. —You'll be grand.

He nodded. He could be a right prick – rude, late opening up, mean with her wages – but at that moment she felt sorry for him. He looked like a little boy sitting there, obediently doing what he was told. She remembered his wife.

—Do you want me to ring Vivienne for you?

Vivienne was plump and well-dressed, and she was very fond of Jock's money, if not his business. It wasn't obvious that she liked Jock much either. Jasmine had only seen them together two or three times, usually when Vivienne popped in to pick up a wad of banknotes, and all they had done was snipe at each other. But now he was nodding, and he looked like he might cry. Jesus, where was that ambulance?

She picked up the phone again and asked Jock the number. He croaked the digits as if each one was costing him dearly. Vivienne, when she answered, didn't sound much better. She must have been asleep. It was well for some.

—Yes? It's who? Do you know what time . . . Oh. Oh, all right . . . You called the ambulance . . .?

—He's going to be fine, Vivienne, Jasmine said, glancing at the waxy-skinned Jock. —But you might want to come down and go to the hospital with him. And the car will need to be moved.

She'd be there in a jiffy, she said, and hung up.

—She'll be here in a jiffy, Jasmine repeated to Jock.

Today was going to be the day she asked Jock if she could work a four-day week. It was to be the start of her new plan. She had decided at some stage last night that there must be something in George's emphasis on education, and Adrian, scrounging around after dropping out of college with dodgy cash and blood on his jeans, was the evidence. But if she was serious about going back to school, she would need study time. If she made it official at work, and put arrangements in place, there was more of a chance that she might actually do it. Now it was out of the question. As if he was reading her mind, Jock pulled his keyring from his pocket with effort and dropped it on the desk.

—Open? he managed, then collapsed again, just as the ambulance men arrived at the door.

Jasmine told them as much as she could while they got him on to a stretcher, then, when the commotion was over, she sat on in the office for a moment, letting the quiet of the windowless room wash over her. At last, with a sigh, she slid the overloaded keyring across the desk. She took off the car key first, then put the rest into her coat pocket, figuring it was probably better not to leave Vivienne in charge of the shop.

When Vivienne finally arrived, she had on a full face of make-up and her hair was freshly blow-dried. Wordlessly, Jasmine handed her the key of the car.

—The Mater Hospital, is it? Vivienne snapped, as if it was Jasmine's fault that she was being inconvenienced.

Jasmine nodded, and she left.

—A rip-roarin' bitch, if ever there was one, Bapty commented from behind his newspaper before the door had fully closed.

Instead of the shorter working week she had imagined, with days spent at the library bettering herself, Jasmine was at work at nine thirty every morning, lifting shutters, pressing alarm buttons, and listening to Bapty.

—Is there any word?

—Of Jock? Apparently he needs a triple bypass. I rang Vivienne yesterday after we closed.

She tipped an overflowing ashtray into the bin bag Bapty was holding open for her.

—Triple, no less, he mused, as if he was questioning the diagnosis.

—According to Vivienne, he should be out in a week.

Bapty chuckled.

—I bet herself is disgusted.

—She didn't sound thrilled. I am though, I can tell you. This place won't survive much longer without him. I haven't a clue about the accounts and that. Even keeping it clean is hard enough.

She took the bag from him and knotted it.

—Allow me, young lady.

Bapty took the bag and carried it outside to the kerb.

He was an old softie, and he was doing his best, but the place needed a manager. Jasmine didn't even dare extract her own wages out of the till in case she messed up the system. Money was getting tight as a result, and the rent was due again. Her thoughts turned to lumpen Adrian, asleep as usual while she went out to work, and the wad of cash she had found. It was time they had a talk. And, as much as she didn't want to see Jock in his pyjamas, she would go to see him as soon as he was well enough for visitors.

*

She had only just poked her head around the curtain when Jock told her that no one had been in all day. He looked very sorry for himself. Jasmine plonked her bag of grapes on the locker and pulled out the visitor's chair. He looked thinner, and old, and at the V of his pyjama top she could see a Frankenstein-like scar. She could have done a better job with the stitching herself.

—You're looking better, she lied.

—How are you managing? Are you making the deposits?

Ah, a glimpse of the old Jock. She was in more comfortable territory now. She told him she was there every day to open, and still there to close in the evenings, and that she made the deposits into the night deposit box every two days, the way she'd seen him do it. But though she didn't want to worry him, she was barely managing on her own.

—Is there anyone who could help out? she finished.

—On your own? he spluttered, his outrage practically lifting him off the bed, drips and tubes and all. —Bloody Vivienne is supposed to be down there to relieve you every day. You mean to tell me . . .

—Jock, calm down. She looked around for a nurse. She was sure he was not supposed to be getting himself into a state like this.

—Look, I'm managing. We'll be glad when you're back though.

Jock nodded, somewhat appeased, but she suspected Vivienne would be getting an earful later. Well, good, she deserved it. But now she didn't know how to approach the four-day week. It wouldn't be fair to put him under pressure. She sighed.

But to her surprise, it was Jock who brought it up.

—How're things otherwise, school and that? He sounded gruff. They didn't usually discuss anything not work-related. He only knew she was thinking about going back to school because Bapty had blabbed about it the day she had first run to

Ringsend to enrol, and she hadn't had the nerve to tell them she'd bottled it. They knew she often went to the library, and she had let them think she was studying away for her exams.

—Grand, grand, she started, but her eye kept coming back to his wound, which pricked her guilty conscience. Feck it, she had to try.

—Actually, not too good, she told him. —I can't get time . . .
At least this wasn't a lie.

—You're working too hard.

—I was going to ask you before. The day, you know, when you came in here. I mean, it'd be a bit tight, the money, but I was going to ask if I could go down to four days. To give me time . . .

Jock was nodding as she spoke.

—I never did it myself. Left at fourteen. Always regretted it. The teachers used to say I had brains to burn but . . .

Jasmine was embarrassed at the new intimacy, and she didn't know what to say.

—You could always—

He brushed away whatever she was going to suggest.

—Too late, too late. He waved his arm around at the equipment he was hooked up to, and the whole ward, as if he was weighing up his own mortality.

—But not too late for you. Leave it with me, love.

She blinked hard at the endearment. It was a real Dublin thing, and she'd had to get used to being called love by all kinds of strangers, but Jock never used it. This whole heart business must have really shaken him.

—Em, thanks. But you should take your time and get better first. I'll manage. Sure haven't I Bapty.

They both smiled, but Jock repeated that she was to leave the problem with him.

He came through the very next day, in the form of a sullen-looking Vivienne, who turned up at lunchtime to take over.

—For lunch?

—For the rest of the day. Vivienne enunciated each word as if she'd like to shake Jasmine in time to each syllable.

For a moment, Jasmine was too surprised to move. Then she gathered her wits and dashed into the back for her coat in case Vivienne might change her mind, or disappear, or melt into a puddle like the Wicked Witch. She was on her way out the door when she remembered that she'd need the keys to open up the next day.

—Em, Vivienne, do you want me to meet you here to get the keys later?

Vivienne rounded on her.

—I will keep the keys. I, it seems, will open up. You have been given . . .

She paused and swallowed down what appeared to be a very unpleasant taste from her mouth.

—. . . study leave.

Adrian was still asleep when she got back. He had his own key now, which she had got cut for him, and which she had paid for. She still hadn't broached the matter of the money she'd found, mainly because she'd been working so much she barely saw him. She accidentally on purpose gave him a dig with her foot as she went past to get her library books, but he didn't stir. Lazy slob.

The librarian knew her by now and smiled when she came in.

—More boxing, Jasmine?

She couldn't get enough of books on boxing, biographies of the great fighters, instruction books, novels about boxing, whatever she could lay her hands on.

—Studying this time, Jasmine told her. She was embarrassed, though she didn't know why. She wondered if it was pride, if going back to school was proof that her big adventures had come to nothing. Not that the librarian knew. She smiled her encouragement, and pointed her to the study room.

The air was warm and still, and the carrels were perfect for concentrating. At last she could really get down to work. She took out an A4 notebook. Her first task would be to figure out what she needed to do and how to fit it into the time she had. To her surprise, she actually got absorbed in her task, and stayed on until hunger finally drove her out, pink-cheeked and happy. Any day now, she would get back to school.

She got home to find Adrian rolled up on the floor in his sleeping bag, again. Did he ever move? She tugged the end of his bag until he was awake.

—What? What?

—It's just me. Your flatmate. Your cousin. Remember? I live here?

—Uh. He pulled his sleeping bag back up over his shoulders.

Jasmine tugged it down again.

—Don't you ever get up, Adrian?

He mumbled something. She pulled even harder, exposing a grey vest stretched over Adrian's flabby chest. She averted her eyes. He needed a seriously good workout.

—Okay, fine, fine. He lifted himself on to his elbows and looked around, bleary-eyed, for his clothes.

He was easier to look at when he put his shirt on, but when he reached for his jeans, Jasmine got there first. Holding them by the waist she let them unfold. Adrian tried to grab at them, but she stepped away, leaving him sitting, half dressed and only half awake, with his warm sleeping bag puddled around him, at a distinct disadvantage.

—Give them, he tried in an imperative tone.

—Why have they got blood on them, Adrian? Are you some sort of serial killer now or what? She knew it was never ketchup.

He began to protest, but gave up almost as soon as he started. He sighed.

—And the money, she pressed on. —I saw. A big roll. You're supposed to be broke.

He sighed again.

—It's gone. Won it on the Friday, lost it on Saturday. You win some you lose some, I suppose, he said, as if he was some wise old man.

—What do you mean, won? Gambling? Is that what you've been doing with Uncle Adrian's money? Adrian, Adrian, Adrian. He answered before she asked again.

—Dogs.

She was more puzzled than before. Harold's Cross, Shelbourne Park – she knew the greyhounds well. Bapty was very fond of them. When he wasn't in the bookies or the pub next door, he was down at the track with a couple of his buddies, drinking pints and talking form. He often regaled Jasmine the next morning. But blood? Adrian looked so uncomfortable that she almost understood. She looked away.

It came flowing out of him as if he'd been waiting to get it off his chest for a long time. It was just cocks at first, he said, down home. The Moroneys – do you remember them? – they used to set it up, in a derelict cottage up near the bog. Just a bit of sport, like. Something to do. But you could make a tidy bit of cash once you got in the know. And it went on from there, cocks, ferrets, American mink . . .

—What? Jasmine didn't even know what an American mink was, let alone how you might keep one, or get it to fight.

But Adrian was very knowledgeable. They were farmed, but lots escaped into the wild, so you'd find them around the rivers and the canals. But these fellas were reared specially.

—To fight?

He nodded. There was silence in the flat. She focused on the traffic outside so she wouldn't have to think about what he was describing.

—It's a skill. Breeding them, rearing them. Training them up. They're well treated.

Jasmine walked over to her bed, wishing there was another room she could go into to get away from Adrian. In a small voice, she asked —Dogs?

He didn't reply.

There was a damp stain on the wallpaper, up near the ceiling, that looked like an amoeba. It was on her biology curriculum. She had listed it only this morning. Unicellular. One of the lower forms of life. Like Adrian.

—And this is where your money goes?

She presumed he was nodding but she couldn't bear to look at him yet.

He cleared his throat.

—Em, actually . . . I'm a bit short . . .

—You're a bit short? She swung around and stormed over to where he was still sitting on the floor. She leaned down over him to repeat her question. Some of her spit landed on his face but he didn't dare wipe it off.

—You are a slug, a waster, a waste of space. A waste of my space. You need to get your act together and get out.

The more she ranted, the more pointless she knew it was. They were back where they started out, him with no money and nowhere to stay. He lifted his hands helplessly, as if he was thinking the same thing.

—Jesus, Adrian.

She finally ran out of steam and went and sat heavily on her bed.

—I know, he agreed in the whiny voice he used when he wanted her, or anyone, to solve all his problems. Well, not this time. He wasn't ten years old any more. This time he'd have to help himself.

—You know, Adrian, she said, in a normal voice. —You know what other people do when they have no money and nowhere to stay?

—What? His expression lifted.

—They get a job.

His face collapsed, like a child who'd been tricked. She persisted.

—I happen to know somewhere that might take you on. Somewhere very convenient, in fact.

132

He still hadn't cottoned on, the dope.

—Somewhere you can put all your knowledge of gambling to good use.

Vivienne was not happy. Instead of lying around the house, or whatever it was she usually did, she had to turn up at the bookies every day. It didn't suit her at all to have to get up for work – and on time, too, if she wasn't to be on the receiving end of Bapty's sharp tongue. For some reason she was nervous of Bapty. Jasmine put it down to his knack for seeing things exactly as they were. When Jasmine first started working there, some of the older customers had complained about the way she looked, but Bapty had put a frayed-tweed arm around her and told them she was *a grand young wan*, to go back to giving out about the cost of living and the state of the nation and leave her be. Good old Bapty. Though since she'd started training, she hardly had time for her appearance. She still put her face on, but she often left her hair in its shoulder-length layers instead of the old back-combed spikes. Come to think of it, she'd been out of hair-spray for ages and hadn't bothered to stock up. Well, she had more important things to worry about, Adrian being one. But she just might have the answer to everyone's problems now. Vivienne was already on the phone to one of her friends, where she spent most of her 'working' day when she got there.

—Morning, Vivienne.

Vivienne didn't even glance in her direction. But then it dawned on her that Jasmine wasn't supposed to be on today, so she said a hasty goodbye and hung up, her face lifting at the thought that maybe she could leave.

—A word? Jasmine mouthed through the glass, indicating the back room.

Vivienne frowned and began to shuffle the few bits of paper that were in front of her, implying that she was far too busy for whatever Jasmine could possibly want. Yesterday's dockets, Jasmine could see at a glance; in other words, rubbish. She pressed the buzzer, and Vivienne had no choice but to let her in.

—You're in today?

Jasmine grinned and shook her head.

—Well, what is it then? I have work to do.

—How is Jock? Jasmine asked, just to aggravate her.

—Fine. Jock is fine. What do you want? I'm busy here. She already had a hand on the phone, ready to resume her endless gossip session.

—It's just, I can see how busy you are . . .

Vivienne looked at her suspiciously, but Jasmine kept her face deadpan.

—And since I can't take on any extra hours because of my studies, I thought you might like a bit of help around here. If it's all right with Jock, that is.

Vivienne's hand slid away from the phone and a glimmer of hope appeared in her well-fleshed face.

—Well, we could certainly do with . . .

—My cousin can do a couple of days a week. He has tonnes of experience with the business. I can send him round later. Just thought you might want to okay it with Jock.

Then she went back around the corner to the flat to break the news to Adrian, and to lay down the law: before he even got his wages, she was taking out his share of the rent, and putting aside money towards the debts he owed. She figured if he started paying something back they might leave him alone. He didn't look convinced, but he didn't have any better suggestions. His other condition, she warned, was to stay away from the damn dog fights. And cock fights, and ferret fights and any other fights he had in mind. He nodded, convincing neither of them, but it was the best she could do.

There were posters on the door of the gym when they arrived to train: a club trip to the National Stadium for Nash v Ryan.

The two boxers were pictured, face to face, one in green shorts and one in red. The fight was all the talk at work; it would be the biggest match the country had seen. Tickets were like gold dust, but the club had an allocation, and for over a week Jasmine had been dreaming of getting one for herself.

—I'd learn so much. Pleeeease, George.

He shook his head.

—They are keeping them for the more senior members.

—But I'll never have a chance like this again, George. You have to try. It's a once in a lifetime.

—You are young, Jasmine. You will have other chances, other fights.

—Easy for you to say, you're not a woman. What club is going to sell me tickets?

She tried not to think about the fact that George was nearing the end of his time in Dublin, and that when he left she would have no gym to train in, and no one to train her. Tickets would be the least of her problems. But when he hesitated, she jumped in.

—Come on, George. There's nowhere for me to get a ticket. You know there won't be a woman in the place, unless she's strutting around in heels with a number over her head. And that's bullshit. You know it is. Inexplicably, she felt tears welling up. She pushed the door open.

—Well, are you coming or . . .?

Her words fell away when she saw what was delaying him. His big George grin was spread across his face behind the two tickets he was holding. She flung herself at him, which he tolerated for a moment before gently removing her and replacing her at arm's length.

—You sly dog. You had them all along. How did you manage? Two?

—I called in a favour. Some private tuition I have been giving to a pre-med, who happens to be the son of our treasurer.

He was doing his best to appear modest, unruffled, but Jasmine could tell that he was pleased with himself.

—You mean? Spell it out for me here, George. I can't bear . . .

There were those tears again, which she tried to blink away so he wouldn't notice. He had taken on more work, when he was already under so much pressure with his own studies, and keeping up his training, not to mention training her too. He patted her on the arm.

—Come, Jasmine. We have work to do. Do you need help with your bandages?

—I can manage.

He went to the dressing room, and by the time he came out, she was already on her bag work, stepping, jabbing, stepping away.

—Good. Now, jab and cross.

He gave the signals and her body responded, as if nothing transpired between the two actions: no thought, no process, just signal, action, signal, action. No matter what he called, her feet were taking her there, and her arms were already in motion. When they sparred, she had to make the calls herself, but still it felt like a single action because she knew George by now, knew the way his body moved and reacted. It was like a choreographed dance, timed to perfection.

—That was good, Jasmine.

As usual he called a halt long before she felt spent. A tingle of pleasure ran through her at the compliment.

—And Jasmine? I agree. It is too bad that women cannot box freely.

The tingle turned into a full body glow.

It was too close to Christmas to start school. Somehow the days had just slipped away from her and still she hadn't managed to enrol. But as soon as term started up again in January, she'd be over to Ringsend like a greyhound out of a trap. Besides, she had been studying. Every morning she was there waiting when the janitors came to open up the library. The librarian asked if she was working towards her 'mock'

Leaving Cert, which was something she hadn't thought of. She found out that these mocks were usually in February. Plus, there were bound to be registration dates and college applications. Maybe she wasn't being realistic and it might take another year, but the mocks would be a good opportunity for her to find out.

Between studying and training and work, she was like a one-woman military operation.

—It's all about being organised, she told Bapty. —And focused, and determined.

She barely saw Adrian, but Bapty said he was getting on all right. He turned up more or less on time, and he seemed to know what he was doing.

—That's good enough for me, Bapty, she replied. —After all, I'm not his mother.

—No, that you're not, that you're not, Bapty had replied thoughtfully. —A mother would be worried, to be sure.

He had asked only once about her family, when he learned that she lived on her own. She'd told him there was only her mother, down the country. *And does your mother know where you washed up?* he had enquired. *Sort of,* she had replied, getting busy sweeping up the dockets on the floor. She didn't want to talk about it, and she didn't want to think about it, but the guilt crept up on her every so often, and Bapty's comment had stirred it again. After the mocks, she told herself. That was when she'd ring, when she'd be able to tell her mother something that she would approve of.

Some sixth sense told her Adrian was home, even before she climbed the stairs. It was only when she got to her door that she realised it hadn't been premonition; she had subconsciously been following a trail of blood splots from the hall to the flat. Shit, now what? She hesitated, her key hovering near the lock. What if she didn't go in? Ever. She could find another flat, another job. Or maybe she wouldn't bother. She imagined

137

staying in rooms in Trinity, like George, just studying and boxing, everything else all taken care of. Yeah, right. By who? Who was going to pay for fancy rooms? Come to think of it, who was going to pay for college? Stupid girl. She hadn't even thought of that. She jabbed the key in and turned it, not remotely in the mood for Adrian's bullshit.

He was there all right, but this time he hadn't managed to make it into his sleeping bag. He was lying on her bed, with his head thrown back, holding her one and only tea towel to his face. It was soaked in blood.

—Shit, Adrian. What happened?

—Id by dose, he said from behind the bloodied cloth. —I think id'th broken.

—What happened?

He sat up and took the cloth down so she could get the full benefit of his indignant expression.

—I told you they were after me.

The blood was dripping from his nose on to her bed.

—Put the bloody cloth back, she snapped. —I thought you were supposed to be paying them back. I thought that was the Whole. Bloody. Point. Of you sponging off me. Of me giving you somewhere to stay. Getting you a job. She felt her muscles tense, her fingers curling into fists. If Adrian's nose wasn't already broken, she would have broken it for him. She folded her arms to give them something to do, then took a deep breath and expelled it slowly.

—Who are they, Adrian? Isn't it about time you got the Gardaí involved? Or at least Uncle Adrian?

—No, he squealed. It came out *Doh*.

—Where did this happen, at least?

He looked furtive.

—Adrian, she threatened, reaching for the cloth.

—Okay, okay, it was at a meet.

—A meet? She knew where this was going, and, sure enough, he confessed that he'd been going to dog fights, betting every penny he could *to try to clear my debts*, and instead losing hand over fist. She caught his guilty eye as it wandered involuntarily to the Lyon's tea tin on the shelf. She took it down and pulled off the lid, knowing what she would find. A dusting of tea on the bottom still gave off its woody scent, but her hard-earned pound notes were gone.

—Adrian, you little shit. The rent is due tomorrow. Where am I going to get it in time?

—I had to, he said sullenly, not meeting her eye. —It wasn't enough, what I was giving them. I knew it wouldn't be.

As if it was her fault. She was at a loss.

—There is one thing, he began, that sly look appearing over the top of the cloth.

—One thing my eye. The way you make money is, you work. Only I'm doing that. You're even doing that. And there's no money. What one bloody thing, other than handing you over to the guards?

—Your boxing.

—What do you mean, my boxing? What are you talking about now, Adrian?

—One fight. You'd be rent-free for the year, and I'd have these fellas off my back.

She could see the idea gaining traction in his porridgy brain. He even sat up again and, after checking to see if the bleeding had stopped, took the cloth down.

—One fight, and you wouldn't have to work. You could go back to school.

He inclined his head towards the books on her shelf. So he'd figured out what she was planning.

—How can you make money from a fight, I mean, when nobody's ever heard of you? she asked despite herself.

His eyes narrowed to slits.

—But you're not nobody. You're a girl.

—A . . . ?

—Girl fight, Jasmine. Everyone loves a girl fight. Three

weeks, no, two, and I can put together the biggest fight this side of the National Stadium. Nothing fancy, mind. Can't be attracting the Gardaí . . .

—Wait . . .

—Jasmine, Jasmine. He looked at her with an expression somewhere between pity and exasperation. —You know better than I do that it's illegal. Girls boxing. Getting their pretty faces all messed up.

—No.

He looked bewildered.

—But it's the perfect solution. You get to fight – you do want to fight, don't you Jasmine? And I know someone else who wants to, a Chinese woman who works . . . Well, I'm not going to tell you where she works. She might be a bit bigger, but it's not like there are many choices. You both get what you want, a bit of roughing each other up, whatever turns you on, eh Jasmine? Me and my crowd get the best night's entertainment of the year, and we all make a bit of money. What's your problem?

How was it possible to have such a bag of shit for a relative? Her eye fell to the blood on the floor, Adrian's blood, same as hers. She could get an advance from Jock for the rent, but no matter how far away she went, how many times she changed her name or even her whole identity, she could never get away from the fact that Adrian was bound to her for ever, as immutable as her fingerprints.

She curled her fingers into fists; fists which, if Adrian was to be believed, could solve all her problems. She would give anything to be able to fight this Chinese woman, but privately, away from Adrian and his heavies and their money and their leching; Adrian's big fight didn't feel too far from carrying a number into the ring wearing a sparkly leotard.

—The problem is, my flat is covered with your blood. My tea towel is ruined. My rent is gone, and so is my patience. I'm going out, and you're going to clean this place up. Then you're going to figure out your own problems, Adrian.

140

She gathered up a few items and pushed them into her rucksack.

—And Adrian? If I were you, I'd start at the hall door. Deano won't like it.

She needed to get away from him, and since she couldn't throw him out – family – she planned to stay in Deano's for a while. Only when the door had closed behind her did it occur to her that Deano mightn't be in. She would be really annoyed if she had to skulk back to her own flat. She rapped on Deano's door.

—It's Jasmine.

He never answered to just a knock, he had told her, explaining that it was inner-city DNA. He came out holding a towel to wet hair, wearing only his jeans.

—It's yerself, Jazz. What's the story?

—Can I come in?

He stepped aside.

—Be my guest. To what do I owe the honour?

My cousin is bleeding in my flat and wants me to cat-fight a Chinese woman for money, and he's spent my rent and his debtors are still unhappy, she could have told him. But it didn't really answer his question: what was she doing there? So she shrugged, walked past him and plonked down on to his couch. It was the first time she'd ever seen Deano flustered. He was searching around for his shirt, which he pulled on quickly. Then he sat awkwardly beside her, all damp and smelling of soap, not a trace of the hard man in sight. Without thinking, she touched his hair. It was much softer than she expected, like a child's.

—Jazz?

She shrugged again. She didn't know what she was doing either. After a moment's hesitation he reached his arm around her shoulder. She turned her face to him before thinking got in the way, then somehow his mouth was on hers. It was nicer than she would have guessed, if she'd ever tried to guess. Which she hadn't. She'd never thought of Deano this way. He was never part of her plan. No man was. But now that she was kissing him, his mouth both rough and gentle and tasting of stale smoke, she wanted it to continue, and she was dismayed when he stopped and pulled back.

—Are you sure, Jazz?

—Course not.

She drew him towards her again. She wasn't sure of anything, but her body was acting like it was. Her hands explored the torso he'd just covered up, and she repositioned herself until she was half reclining. He found her skin under her layers of tops, and when he paused to play with her navel-ring, her back arched, surprising her. Her body had a mind of its own, and it appeared to be after some fun.

—Wait.

She slipped out from under him and switched off the lights so that orange streetlight filled his flat, bathing it in a soft glow. That was better. Because even though she'd taken her clothes off for men before, this was different. She pulled her outer top, a see-through chiffon, over her head. Next was a lacy Victorian blouse with about a hundred little buttons. It was a demure creamy-white when she picked it up in a second-hand shop, but she'd dyed it black. The buttons were taking for ever, and Deano was laughing and helping and getting in the way but at last it was open, and she slipped it over her shoulders. Her last layer was a tight black vest. Still standing over him, she lifted it from the bottom. He released a held breath.

—This is what you were after. She reached for his hand and spiralled his finger around her navel until it rested on the small, titanium ring at the centre.

—Mmm. Always was partial to a bit of metal. He moved in to kiss her where their two fingers lay.

His other hand slid up along her leg.

—Any more surprises?

—Nope. The rest is virgin territory.

His mouth was on her belly, his tongue moving, searching, playing with the ring, and his hand on her thigh, between her thighs, tracing the edge of her knickers. She was sort of losing track of what was where, but it all felt amazing. Jesus, to think this was right on her own doorstep the whole time. But Deano suddenly made the connection and jerked away.

—Jaysus, Jazz. It's not your first time, is it?

She nodded.

—So what?

—So what? So, what age are you, for fuck's sake?

She hesitated. Stopping like that, in the middle . . . She could feel tears threatening.

—Old enough. She scrambled around for her shirt so he wouldn't see her flaming face.

—What's *old enough*, Jazz? he asked more gently.

—Seventeen. She mumbled it. It was embarrassing. A seventeen-year-old virgin. Back in Rathlowney, everyone assumed. Even when she was just fourteen or fifteen. It was the make-up, the hair, the bad attitude they loved complaining about. But they assumed wrong.

—Really?

—Really.

—That's all righ', then. You're legal. He grinned. Then he grew serious again.

—But, are ya sure, Jazz?

—Sure I'm seventeen, or sure I'm a virgin? She spat *virgin* at him so furiously that he drew back again, and his expression was so comical that she couldn't help laughing. Then he was laughing too until they were falling around the couch, unable to stop. There was no more awkwardness as his mouth found hers again, and when he took out a condom, and checked that she was still sure, she was; it was her body, and she was ready to let it do what it wanted to do.

*

143

Deano lit up a cigarette.

—Is that not a cliché? She was flushed and excited. She had liked it. She liked Deano. She couldn't think of anyone better for her first time.

He winked.

—That's me, Jazz. One big cliché. He drew in a lungful of smoke.

—So when will we get married? she asked.

He inhaled when he meant to exhale, or the other way around, and ended up choking and coughing, unable to get his breath. Jasmine lay back on his couch laughing. She punched him on the arm when he managed to breathe again.

—Messing. So you're a shag 'em and leave 'em kind?

He gave a sheepish grin.

—So, what brought you over, anyway?

She raised her eyebrows.

—That wasn't enough?

—On your to-do list, was it? In the ol' Filofax? Virginity: lose. To Deano.

—All right, all right. It's my pain-in-the-arse cousin. You don't want to know. I was hoping you'd give me your couch for the night.

He stubbed out his cigarette.

—Righ'. Off you go and brush your teeth or what have ya. We'll set you up.

When she returned from the bathroom wearing the T-shirt and pyjama bottoms she had brought, with her face well scrubbed and hair brushed, Deano pretended dismay.

—Jaysus, Jazz. Don't tell me, you're really only fourteen.

—That's why I wear make-up, she replied, heading for the couch.

—This way, he corrected her, steering her into the adjoining bedroom. —Your boudoir, madame. Fresh sheets an' all.

The just-stripped sheets were in a pile in the corner. She was touched.

—Thanks, Deano, you're a good guy. She gave him a peck.

He looked embarrassed.

—Ah, go on . . . Sleep well, Jazz. He gave her another wink and turned to leave.

—Wait. Deano?

He stopped.

—This is a one-off, right?

She hadn't room for a complicated relationship with her neighbour. She had let it get complicated enough already.

—Right, Deano agreed. —A one-off.

It was almost Christmas. She'd bumped into Deano a couple of times, and it hadn't been awkward at all. As for Adrian, they stepped around each other on the rare occasions they were both in the flat; she usually managed to time it so that one of them was already asleep when the other got in. The library was closed now for a week, but she had her books lined up for the break. The bookies would be closed for two days, and George was going down to Tipperary with someone from his class who took pity on him, he said, so there'd be no training either.

She didn't know what she'd be doing herself on Christmas Day. It didn't mean much to her anyway. Since her dad died, it had been just her and her mother, sitting at a table covered with far too much food. For the last couple of years they hadn't even bothered forcing themselves to be cheerful. The worst bit was pulling the crackers – first hers, then her mother's – and pretending to find the paper hats and the stupid jokes amusing. After that it was a matter of sticking it out until they could escape from the table to the Christmas films for Jasmine, and the bottle of sherry for her mother.

She should phone. She got as far as the coin box and listened to the dial tone. Then she replaced the receiver quietly and turned to go back upstairs. But when she got inside her flat again, she didn't know what to do with herself. She needed distraction. She needed to get out.

She headed towards town. She had gone a few weeks ago to the newly pedestrianised Grafton Street to see the lights being switched on, and Switzer's window, and it was lovely. There was a real, festive atmosphere. In contrast, Dorset Street was dreary: Reg's Hardware had erected a foot-high artificial tree in the middle of their permanent coal bucket and fire tongs display; Dino's Fish 'n' Chips had sellotaped red tinsel around the sides and top of the window, and sprayed fake snow along the bottom; Maura's Fashions had gone all out with a moving Santa wearing fishnet stockings and high heels. Christ. She thought about buying a cheap string of lights to cheer up her flat, and even got as far as the till in the Pound Shop before she changed her mind – it would look just as sad as the half-hearted attempts in the shop windows. She turned back towards home, empty-handed and distinctly lacking in Christmas cheer.

As she approached the house her pace slowed. Parked outside her front door was a fancy car with a Co. Offaly registration. She had a bad feeling. The front door was ajar, so she pushed it tentatively, and there he was, wearing the familiar camel-hair overcoat and the polished brown brogues: Uncle Adrian. He was standing right in the centre of the hall as if hoping not to come in contact with any surface that might contaminate him, transferring his keys from one hand to the other impatiently. He swung around at the sound of the door.

—Rosemary.

She didn't know why he was bothering to feign surprise. She had already figured out that Adrian must have told him where she was, and probably her mother too, in revenge for her not going along with his stupid sexist fight. On cue, Adrian appeared on the stairs, bag in hand. He lowered his head when he saw her, unwilling to meet her eye. When he reached the hall, Uncle Adrian inclined his head towards the door. Jasmine attempted to pass both of them without saying anything, but Uncle Adrian reached a long arm out and grabbed her hand.

—Not even going to say hello to your uncle, Rosemary?

She leaned away from him.

—What's the matter, cat got your tongue?

—Let me go, Uncle Adrian.

Then there was an echo from behind her.

—Let her go, Uncle Adrian.

Deano.

Uncle Adrian released her and turned, all smiles.

—And who have we here? Is this a boyfriend, Rosemary? Have I a bit of news to bring home to your poor mother? She's worried sick about you, you know. He stuck out his hand like a politician.

—Are you all righ', Jazz? Deano asked, ignoring it.

She tried to tell him with a look that she was anything but.

—Dad, I think we should get going . . .

—I agree, *Dad*, Deano said. —No one wants to get hurt.

—Hurt? Uncle Adrian spluttered. —There's no need for that sort of talk, son. I'm just trying to talk to my niece here.

Deano raised an eyebrow at the *son* and Jasmine could see that he had Uncle Adrian rattled. He gave one last disdainful look around at the damp wallpaper and threadbare carpet before he turned and strode to the door, ushering Adrian out before him.

—Worried sick, he repeated, as Deano pushed the door closed on them.

—Thanks, Deano. Again, Jasmine managed. She was feeling a bit faint, and was holding on to the banisters with both hands.

Deano shrugged.

—Didn't look like you were in the mood for a family reunion.

—I'm not. Him especially.

—Yeah, you're not looking the Mae West, Jazz, if you don't mind me sayin'. Come on, I'll help you up.

Adrian appeared to have cleared out, hopefully for good. Back under Uncle Adrian's thumb; it was the best place for him. Without his stuff, without constantly expecting him, her flat felt more inviting than it had for ages, and the thought of having the place to herself for the evening was very appealing, but she couldn't just throw Deano out, not after all he had done for her.

—You'll have a cuppa?

He shook his head.

—I'm heading back to work in a few. Get yourself a good night's sleep, yeah?

She nodded, relieved.

He looked around the bare flat.

—I see you're all set for the festive season.

—I nearly bought lights . . .

—So you're stayin' put?

—Where else would I go?

—Grand, yeah. Same as meself.

He hesitated.

—Now, it's just an idea, like, and you can say no, but if you fancied a bit of company on the day you could always drop across to mine?

She smiled.

—That'd be nice, Deano. Thanks.

—Grand so, see you then. Maybe. Unless you change your mind. That's grand too.

Deano left, and at last she had the place to herself. Tea in peace, bed in peace. And the comfort of knowing that she wouldn't be on her own for Christmas, unless she wanted to be.

On Christmas Eve she went into town with a vague plan to buy something festive. The last rays of winter sun dropped behind the buildings just as she reached O'Connell Street, and the cold of the early evening made itself felt. Her jacket felt thin and comfortless, but then, it was summer when she left Rathlowney, so she didn't have a winter wardrobe. She shoved her hands deeper into her pockets, wishing she at least had a hat.

The stalls lining Henry Street were heaving with Selection Boxes, tree ornaments, fairy lights and Santas, and last-minute shoppers handed over pound notes as fast as the traders could take them. Carollers were out in force, hoping the Christmas spirit would loosen purses for charity, and she could see their breath on every *Gloria*. She gave them all her loose change. She had to zigzag through the crowds to avoid the pushy pro-lifers with their leaflets; there was something about them that made her uncomfortable, and she wasn't in the mood for them, today or any day. At one of the stalls she chose a Selection Box for Deano, not to be turning up with empty hands, and in a moment of weakness she picked up a box of crackers too. At the last minute, it occurred to her that she should contribute something to the dinner, so she ran into Dunnes and bought their last trifle. She couldn't think of anything else, so she turned for home, looking forward to getting out of the cold.

She put her shopping bag down inside the door of the flat. There was nothing to suggest Christmas, and even less to suggest cheer; it was as cold inside as it was out. She put coins in the meter and switched on the heater, but it'd take ages to warm the place up, so rather than sit there in her bleak flat, shivering, she decided to go for a run. She put on her tracksuit and runners and headed back outside.

The pubs and shops were all closed and the streets were unnaturally quiet; everyone was at home with their families. She wondered how she felt about that. She listened to the beat of her runners for a while, until she concluded that she didn't feel anything at all. There was nothing to miss about those awful, silent Christmases with her mother.

But when she got to the sea, which tonight lay as still as a lake, she remembered another Christmas: unwrapping a book, charms for a bracelet, the longed-for Fuzzy Felt, and the hundred-piece jigsaw they did together after dinner, Mam and Dad and herself. Her pace slowed to a walk at the memory, and she was filled with loneliness and longing. She looked out across the water, as if its scale could somehow dilute the intensity of the feeling, but its pewter surface only seemed to reflect it back to her. She turned back towards home. A lone dog-walker wished her a happy Christmas as he passed.

She was inexplicably nervous the next morning. The plan to have dinner with Deano was very loose, and she didn't know if dinner meant lunchtime or evening. She was dithering in her pyjamas because her flat was warm for once – she had treated herself by leaving the heat on all night – when there was a rap on the door. She opened it as far as the chain allowed.

—Did Santa come? Come up whenever, yeah?

—Great . . .

But he had already vanished down the corridor. She held the door ajar for another moment because, though it might have been her imagination, she thought she could smell cooking, real food, not the cabbage and takeaway that usually pervaded the building.

She spent ages getting ready because she didn't know how to dress because she didn't know what the occasion was. A date? An act of charity? Besides, Deano had already seen her in her running gear and her work gear, and her pyjamas, not to mention in the nip. In the end, she settled on a black skirt and a lacy top, a sort of sexy going-to-Mass outfit. She added a touch of silver eye shadow and a bit of lip gloss, all her piercings, and a last sweep of glitter across her cheekbones. She didn't know what she was at.

Her efforts elicited a whistle when he opened the door. He bowed low and swept his arm wide to admit her.

—*Entrez*, madame.

—Wow, Deano.

His flat was unrecognisable. There were fairy lights everywhere, and he'd draped branches of holly over the fireplace, where he, too, had the electric fire on full blast. He had a mountain of fifty-pence pieces at the ready to keep it going. And there definitely was a smell of real cooking.

—Ya get sick of him fairly quick, Deano said, with a nod towards Santa who was dancing on the hearthstone to a tinny 'Jingle Bells'.

There was even a small tree propped up in the corner.

—It's brilliant, Deano.

—You missed the best bit.

—What's . . .?

He guided her in reverse to the door and planted a kiss on her lips. He laughed at her expression.

—Don't panic. Look up.

Sure enough, there was mistletoe.

—Drink?

—Sure. Oh, your present. She held out the Selection Box.

—What I always wanted. Hang on. There's something under the tree for you too. He nodded at the Santa. —Himself must've left it.

She hoped Deano hadn't got her a serious present; she'd feel stupid about the Selection Box. She put her other offerings on to the counter, too embarrassed to take them out, and picked up the clumsily wrapped ball-shaped gift.

—Go on, open it.

She pulled the paper off nervously while Deano got their drinks. It was soft, woolly . . . a bright pink hat with a bobble on top. She hadn't worn pink since she was about four, but she put it on straight away.

—You're gorgeous, Deano said, handing her a tumbler.

—It's perfect, she said, and she meant it.

—What's this?

—Champagne, of course.

—Champagne?

—I know. You're only twelve and you don't drink? Don't worry, Jazz, I'm not trying to get you drunk.

She grinned.

—I was going to say, I never tasted it before.

—Then bottoms up. He raised his own glass and they clinked.

—To . . .

Their eyes met for a moment. What did she want? What did he want?

—. . . to a happy Christmas, and a brilliant 1983, he finished softly, and they drank to it.

—Right. Deano put down his glass. Sit yourself down. I have some turkey business to attend to.

—Seriously?

Soon his small table was laden with slices of turkey and ham, sprouts, carrots and parsnips, mashed potatoes, roast potatoes and gravy.

—There's even stuffing. He pointed it out proudly where it nestled under the turkey.

—Got it from the carvery at work. Don't worry, it's not leftovers. They did it specially for me when I told them I was having a young lady around. Chef made up a dinner-for-two, with a list of instructions for warming it and all.

—It's delicious, Jasmine said through a forkful. She didn't know when she had last had a proper dinner. —I'm afraid the trifle I brought looks a bit puny now.

—Trifle, good stuff. Chef put in pudding, and even a tub of brandy butter. But there's no trifle. Me ma was a dab hand with the ol' trifle. Too bad she usually finished off the bottle. Herself and the old man, pair of them in it.

—Where are they now? Jasmine ventured.

—Gone. It was the liver with him, cancer with me ma, within a year of each other.

—Sorry. That's sad.

—Yeah. The two brothers went off the rails. Usual inner-city shite. Disappeared years ago. Might be dead themselves, for all I know.

He tapered off, lost in thought for a while.

—What about yerself, Jazz? You're young to be on your own.

Maybe it was the champagne. The fizz seemed to have gone straight into her bloodstream, but for once she didn't mind talking about herself.

—I ran away from home. She half expected him to laugh, and when he didn't, she continued.

—My dad died when I was nine. He was in a crash. Mam and me . . . Mam was on tablets. And she started drinking. It got worse when I got older. I suppose I got worse too.

She didn't know how to explain about the grief and guilt and rows, so she grabbed the bag containing the crackers and took them out.

—This is what I hated most about the Christmases with my mam.

—Wait, you hate these? Deano snatched the red and gold box and read: *Twelve Luxury Christmas Crackers*. —Nice one, Jazz. Will you go first or will I? Joking. Getting you warmed up, like.

He tore the box open, and held one out.

—Together, yeah?

They pulled the flimsy cardboard and there was a small bang and a smell of gunpowder.

—Your prize, Deano said, pulling a sad face.

—We can share. She tipped out the contents: hat, joke and the fish that curled and uncurled in her palm.

Deano grabbed the hat and put it on.

—Read it out, Jazz. The joke's yours.

—What do you get when you cross Santa with a duck?

—Go on, I give up.

—A Christmas quacker.

He groaned.

—Where did you say you got these quality crackers again? The reject shop?

—Let's see you do better.

They pulled another. Jasmine put the paper hat on over her woolly one and Deano got the plastic car.

—Read it, smarty-pants.

He unrolled the tissue-thin paper.

—Righ'. So, what did the inflatable teacher at the inflatable school say to the inflatable child caught holding a pin?

—This better be good.

By the time they got through the box the place was littered with rubbish and junk, and they hadn't stopped laughing since *You let me down, you let your friends down, you let your school down, but most of all, you let yourself down.*

—Come on, let's clear up this tip before dessert.

They were a good team, bagging up rubbish and clearing the mess away.

—Wash or dry? Deano asked.

She washed, and he dried and put away. She was surprised how orderly his kitchen was.

—Thank you, *madame*. His bad French accent was back. — Now please take a seat for the next course.

He brought a whole pudding over to the table, followed by a small saucepan containing brandy, which he poured liberally over the top. With a flick of his lighter there was a *whoosh* and it went up in blue flames.

—Wow, I've never seen anyone do that. You keep on impressing me, Deano. What's next? Will a naked man jump out of it?

—Whatever *madame* wants. After the trifle, all righ'?

The trifle was sloppy and sticky and sweet.

—Sorry, Deano. Dunnes' best. I'm not much of a cook.

—It's fantastic. Look. He stuck his finger in and dragged it right through the middle and held his custardy finger to her mouth. —Taste.

Uh-oh. Where were they headed?

—Not without some *hundreds and thousands*, she retorted.

—Like this?

He draped his finger through the creamy topping, making sure to attach a good number of the multicoloured sprinkles.

—Hmm. She moved to lick it, but he smeared the trifle on to her nose instead.

—Oh, I see, so that's the way it's going to be, is it? She looked at the spoonful of trifle she was about to put in her mouth, and flicked. It landed smack in the middle of his face.

—That's it. Trifle war.

It didn't end well, as far as Deano's orderly flat was concerned. But even the clean-up afterwards was a laugh. They collapsed at last on to the couch.

—Best Christmas ever. Thanks, Deano.

He patted her knee.

—To tell the truth, I wasn't looking forward to spending the day on me own. Here, wha' happened to yer cousin? Gone for good, is he?

—He's not the worst. Harmless, I think. I always end up feeling sorry for him. But . . .

—But you weren't planning on moving him in?

—Exactly. Though now Uncle Adrian has his hands on him I doubt he'll be back.

—An' that's a good thing?

—That's definitely a good thing for me. I don't envy Adrian though, stuck in the sticks with Uncle Adrian on his case. But . . . well, he was in some sort of trouble. He owes someone money. Got beaten up and everything. There was blood . . .

—All over the hall, yeah.

—Yeah. So he's better off away.

—You don't need that shit on your doorstep, Jazz. Any more grief – from anyone – and you come and tell me. All righ'?

—Right.

They lazed for a while, not bothering to talk.

—Film? Deano asked eventually.

They caught the end of *Chitty Chitty Bang Bang*, then it was *The Muppets*. But they were drowsy from the food, and when Jasmine woke up, *Gone with the Wind* was on, and Scarlett was already weeping on the stairs, vowing to win Rhett back. She eased herself off the couch, trying not to disturb Deano, then tiptoed to the door and let herself out.

A knock woke her.

—Jazz?

Deano.

She stumbled out of bed, wondering why she had a headache, then she remembered the champagne. She opened the door and without even looking at him, turned back to put on the kettle. She needed tea. He followed her in.

—You left before I could give you your real present.

Damn.

—But Deano—

He dropped what looked like a toolbox in the middle of her flat, then he went back out to the hall and when he returned, he was dangling a punchbag from his hand.

—Get ya set up here in no time. When Flanagan-the-fucker comes for his rent, just detach it off of the hook and he'll never notice.

He took a drill from the toolbox then climbed on to her chair and got to work, and a few minutes later she had her own punchbag, smack bang in the middle of her own bedsit.

—Deano . . .

—You're dyin' to try it out, aren't you? Give us a demo, there, Jazz, the old one-two. He gave it a few slaps to encourage her.

—Uh, tea? she managed. She felt uncomfortable about the punchbag, but she didn't know how to explain it to Deano.

—Ah, the Christmas hangover, is it? I'll love ya and leave ya so.

—Thanks, Deano, she said, but he was already gone, leaving the punchbag to swing in ever-decreasing arcs as she made her tea.

What was the story with all these men wanting to see her fight? When she left Rathlowney she thought she was finally in charge of her own life, but London taught her to be afraid. And boxing had helped her to rebuild her confidence so that she could go back to figuring out her place in the world. But when they wanted to watch her box – Adrian, and now Deano, maybe even George – it seemed to her that what they were really thinking about was sex. Maybe that was why it was illegal.

She watched as the punchbag grew still. She wouldn't be touching it any time soon. Because Deano, the dozy git, was so anxious to see her flexing her girl muscles that it didn't occur to him that she didn't have any gloves.

Dublin, 2012

1983. That was when it began. She and her mother had fought against each other, and the world, for long enough, and in 1983 they began again, learning to give, learning to take. They learned well, and they have given and taken for so long now that it is impossible for her to consider that some day it will end. But she is a doctor, and she is reminded more often than most that some day, her mother will die, and she will be on her own. She just isn't ready for this to be the day. Would this traffic not move?

She considers the bus lane, but decides against it, because even with her reasonable explanation and medical credentials, being pulled over would only delay her further. She switches on the radio for distraction, then switches it off again; there are already too many frequencies competing for her attention in her brain.

In 1983 she didn't listen to the radio or watch TV. She was too busy feeling her way into this new life with her mother, and too busy with her books, to take any notice of what was going on around her. She failed to pay attention to a referendum, and even though she had turned eighteen by then, she didn't bother to vote. Sometimes it feels as if she has spent her whole life trying to make amends, as if hers was the single vote that would have changed everything. But despite the phone calls, the letters, the meetings, the reports, she and her colleagues have been in the same position since 1983. The law is the law, and none of them wants to go to jail for terminating a pregnancy in order to save a woman's life. *The State acknowledges the right to life of the unborn and, with due regard to the equal right to life of the mother, guarantees in its laws to respect, and, as far as practicable, by its laws to defend and vindicate that right.* It is this – the Eighth Amendment of the Constitution – that dictates their decisions. So despite all their training, and their instinct to save lives, women are still dying unnecessarily.

Yet in other areas changes have come so fast that it makes her head spin. Her thoughts stray back to Katie Taylor, still waiting to see if she has won, and, briefly, the flicker of hope that has kept her motivated this long returns. But just as quickly, darker images intrude. A fourteen-year-old, refused permission to travel to abort her pregnancy, the outcome of statutory rape. A raped and pregnant immigrant to the country, God help her, forced to have the child. And now, the news is full of another tragic, stupid, shameful, perhaps avoidable, death. It's a mess, and she's tired of dealing with it, and tired of trying to change it. Tired enough to apply for a new job in London. But is she tired enough to take it up? And even if she is, could she do so now?

Dublin, 1983

January came at last, bringing biting-cold mornings, when Jasmine's nose wouldn't stop running, and the cold air felt like razorblades as it entered her lungs. On Sundays, as usual, she had her training session in the gym. She was getting stronger and fitter, and her technique was improving all the time. When she sparred with George, she made him work hard; he wasn't faking the sweat he worked up. But for a real fight, she would have to wait for the big match in the Stadium, where she would have to be content to be a spectator. She couldn't wait. She had been counting the days, and finally it was only hours away.

It was also her first day back in work. She'd been taking full advantage of Jock's goodwill trying to prepare for mock exams – or mock-mock exams, as she was beginning to think of them, since she still hadn't enrolled in school – and Vivienne was royally pissed off, especially since Adrian had done his runner, *without so much as a by-your-leave.*

—Are you back in the land of the living? she asked when Jasmine turned up for her shift.

—If that's what you'd call it, Bapty muttered from behind his paper. Vivienne shot him a poisonous look.

—Four days a week. I might have to go back to two coming up to the exams, she added, to annoy her.

Vivienne rolled her eyes and turned her attentions to getting out of there as fast as she could. When the door closed behind her, Jasmine and Bapty sighed their relief in unison.

—A right . . .

—Now, Bapty, Jasmine warned. She was not in the mood for a rant about her employer's wife; it could go on for hours. She had been hoping for a bit of peace, marking up results, taking in and, less frequently, paying out money, and whiling away the last few hours before the fight.

—Who do you fancy for tonight?

He sniffed to let her know he was not that easily fooled, but then he conceded.

—I have my money on Ryan.

Jasmine nodded. So did lots of her other punters; Jock stood to clean up if Nash won, as George expected. But she hoped for Bapty's sake Ryan would come good.

—Right, Bapty said, still a bit huffy. —I'm off to see a man about a dog. Are you coming, lads? He folded up his paper and slid it inside his coat. His two cronies, Leo and Finbar – Jock's second and third best customers respectively – followed suit, down to the pat on the breast pocket to make sure the newspaper was secure; they were diligent students of form, and they conducted their study group next door, over a pint. They'd be in better humour when they got back, and at least she'd have peace while they were gone.

She moved behind the glass partition to take up where Vivienne had left off, and she was just starting to sort out the cash when there was a clatter out front. She looked up, startled, and it took a moment to process the fact that there was a gun pointed at her face. It was held by a man wearing a stocking over his head.

—Give me the money, he growled.

She was paralysed, but his *Hurry up!* frightened her into action.

Automatically, she started to grab the cash from the till with shaking hands. The glass was supposed to be bullet-proof, but she wasn't going to chance it; employee loyalty didn't stretch to dying. But even as she pushed the money down into the safety deposit bag, she knew there was something not right about this robbery. The gun, the voice. There was something familiar about the accent, and the slightly nasal *hurry up*. She stopped what she was doing and looked directly at her robber. The tights were so thin she could actually see his face.

—For fuck's sake, Adrian.

—The money, he tried again, without conviction.

—Take those tights off your head before Bapty comes back in, and before I phone the guards, you feckin' eejit. You do know they're completely see-through?

Adrian lowered the gun, which she could now see was a toy, and pulled off the tights. What the fuck was he thinking? This was going too far.

—Jasmine, I'm desperate.

—I can see that, she said.

—Just a few hundred, Jasmine, please. To get back in the game.

She gave him her dirtiest look. He didn't even have the cop-on to realise that his *game,* pitting two terrified animals against each other in a confined space to bet on them, was never going to earn any sympathy from her.

—You know what he's like. I had to get away from him.

He meant Uncle Adrian. But Adrian was an adult. This was farcical. He was pathetic.

—Could you not think of anything better, Adrian? Like, maybe, get another job, instead of robbing your cousin at your old one?

He hung his head.

—If you would only fight the Chinese . . .

—No.

—Are you going to report me? he asked after a pause.

She looked to the window behind him.

—Did anyone see you?

He shook his head.

—Then I'm not going to report you. I'd be too embarrassed to admit being related to you.

His face brightened.

—Thanks, Jasmine. You're a real mate. Jazz . . .

—Don't call me that, she snapped. —That's reserved for *real* mates. Now can you please piss off. I have work to do here.

—Sorry. Look, Jasmine, I know I'm not your favourite person at this moment, but I am really, really desperate. If I could just stay at your . . .

—No.

—Please?

—Go away, Adrian.

She went back to counting. She heard him shuffle towards the door, heard it open and close again, then there was only the steady stream of results from the television. Finally, peace.

She wasn't surprised when she came downstairs that evening, on her way to the fight, to find him waiting outside the front door. She ignored him. Halfway down O'Connell Street, she asked over her shoulder if he was planning on coming with her to Mass, because that was where she was going, *to pray for all your sins.*

—I thought I'd come with you to the gym. That's where you're really going, I presume.

—Well, you presumed wrong.

—Look, I thought if I could talk to your man, George, your coach, he might get you to see sense. It'd be fantastic. Two girls. Official, like. Proper referee and judges. I already told the lads about you. They promised there'd be nothing seedy. Just honest-to-God fighting, Jasmine. You know you want to.

Maybe she did, but she didn't like the sound of *the lads*, especially if they were the same lads who broke people's noses. But her more immediate concern was shaking Adrian off, within the next five minutes too, or he would, in fact, meet George. And his friends. Which she was already nervous about.

—Get lost, Adrian. I'm meeting people.

—I'll tag along. Maybe they're sensible people who'll persuade you—

—To box some Chinese woman somewhere in the back of beyond, with a few ferrets waiting their turn in the bottom of a barrel? Forget it, Adrian.

They were almost at the Front Gate. There was a cluster of men at the railings, George among them.

—Please. Look, it's just the lads from the gym. We're going to the Stadium—

—Nash v Ryan, Adrian interrupted. —I have money on Ryan. You have tickets?

Jasmine gave a slight nod.

—I'm impressed.

—Yeah, well.

They were almost there.

—So, I'll stroll up with you, take in a bit of the atmosphere. Your friends won't mind that, surely?

By then it was too late to do anything about it, so she tried to pretend he didn't exist, and approached them shyly. George spotted her.

—Jasmine. I'd like you to meet Philip, Robert, Daniel and Keith. You have seen all of them spar.

Jasmine blushed underneath her make-up.

—Hi, she managed, hoping that was it, and now she could fade into the background. But these were well-bred young men, and they insisted on shaking her hand in turn.

—Pleased to meet you, the last one, Keith, said. —I am an admirer of your work.

—Keith has known about you for several weeks, George told her. —He likes your combinations.

Jasmine blushed again. So Keith wasn't actually taking the piss.

—I'm just a beginner. But thanks.

—And your friend? Keith asked politely.

164

Dammit, there he was still, grinning, all ready for his introductions.

—The cousin, George mused.

—Keeps turning up out of the blue, Jasmine said, attempting a light tone of voice. —This is Adrian. He was just leaving.

But the polite young men were doing the hand-shaking all over again, and Adrian, the little shit, was lapping it up.

—Shall we get moving? George said, after the last of the introductions. —It is quite cold.

He was right about that. It was freezing. They moved in a group across the road and up Dame Street. Adrian had managed to get himself into a conversation with one of George's friends, and other than giving her a triumphant glance when he caught her looking, he was engrossed in whatever they were talking about. She dreaded to think. She concentrated on the fight instead. *Amateur boxing at its best*, it was being billed. She couldn't wait.

They took the short cut past Dublin Castle, and she imagined other fans taking other short cuts all across the city at the same time, shoulders raised against the chill, hands plunged deep into pockets, weaving through side streets and alleys, emerging on to the South Circular from every direction, and converging on the Stadium. She couldn't believe she was actually one of them. The only problem was Adrian, but at least they'd be losing him at the turnstile.

By the time they reached Leonard's Corner she didn't have to imagine the fans because they had appeared in their droves. Their own small group merged with the flow, and they were joined by others as they strolled, the jokes and banter flying back and forth between strangers.

—One of these days it'll be your turn, Keith said, smiling at Jasmine. —Women in the National Stadium, can you imagine?

Presumably he meant to be friendly and supportive, but she

could see that he couldn't imagine it in his wildest dreams. George, ever the diplomat, patted her on the arm.

—One step at a time, Jasmine.

These were his last words before it happened. They came from an alley beside a launderette, three or four of them, maybe more; it was hard to know with the crowds. There was a sudden scuffle, a shout . . . *off of her, nigger.* A knife pulled from the folds of a coat. Fists were no match. *Out of the way, bitch.* A push, a shove, a scream – hers – and George slid quietly to the ground.

—Someone phone 999.

Blood was already pooling where he had fallen. Where was the wound? It didn't look like there was one. But there was. There. So neat. She knew not to touch the tear in the fabric, so close to his heart.

—Phone a fucking ambulance.

—The phone box is vandalised.

—Then go into a fucking house before he bleeds to death.

Jasmine found Keith's face.

—I'll go. Stay with George.

As the crowd parted to let her through, she spotted Adrian slipping away down a side street, but she had more pressing concerns.

—Change. I need change . . .

Pockets were emptied, and she took fistfuls and ran. The first door she knocked on had no phone.

—There's one three doors up, the woman told her, peering down the street at the disturbance.

The door opened before she got to it. The ambulance was on the way, the man told her.

Sirens screaming, ambulance and Gardaí. An oxygen mask, a stretcher. They sped away.

The show was over, and the crowd began to disperse. Those who had witnessed it had to stay and make statements to

Gardaí who wrote painfully slowly into notebooks. Jasmine couldn't tell them much. It had happened so fast. She didn't see faces. Or, she did, but no one she knew, and there were so many people around. No, there were no distinguishing marks. How tall? She didn't know. Taller than herself? Yes. Taller than George? No. Maybe the same. She didn't know. She just didn't know. No, no provocation. They came out of nowhere. Nothing said. *Nigger, bitch*, that was all she could remember. Nothing before that. No warning. What had happened in the moments before? Nothing. A comment about women boxing. A hand on her arm. A friend. George was her friend. Yes, a medical student. No, not her boyfriend.

The questions went on and on and didn't seem to be getting anywhere. She knew nothing. She just wanted them to hurry up so she could find George. What hospital . . .? At last, after checking and rechecking her address, they said she could go. Keith put an arm around her.

—You're shaking. Come on—

—I want to go to the hospital.

But George's condition was critical, and only relatives would be allowed in.

—His family . . .

—We're contacting them, though it might take several hours, maybe even days.

Jasmine felt her knees buckle, but he had her before she fell. From what felt like very far away, she heard Keith shout at a passing taxi.

She managed to tell him where she lived, then she closed her eyes, hoping that when she opened them none of this would have happened. They were going to the fight. George touched her arm. Someone stabbed him. In a racist attack? Or was it her they meant to hurt? When she saw the knife, she was sure it was Corrigan, because she had never really believed she would get away with what she had done in London. Then she remembered Adrian's pasty face as it disappeared into the crowd. Had he something to do with it? It didn't make sense. But nothing did. She was sure of only one thing: whoever was behind the attack, it was her fault.

It was a week before they would let her in to see him, when his status was changed from critical to stable. Keith had warned her that he was still very weak from the loss of blood, and was sleeping a lot. His left lung had been perforated and they'd had to operate. They said he was lucky to be alive. The lads in the gym were trying to raise money for his medical expenses, and to help George's family to fly him home when he was well enough to travel. *But his finals?* she had asked, and Keith only shook his head.

He was asleep when she went in, and it was awful to see him hooked up to all those tubes. She had already been warned that she could only stay five minutes, and a nurse hovered nearby, as if waiting to evict her.

—It's Jasmine, she whispered. She had to tell him. It was her fault, and she was so, so sorry. And she would do anything to make up for it. She would go with him to Kenya and make sure he recovered. She'd bring his books and help take care of his children so he could study.

There was no reaction.

—George? Can you hear me? Let me come with you. Please, George.

She was sobbing now. The nurse moved towards her, frowning, but she was waylaid by another patient, and Jasmine was able to compose herself. When she turned back to George, she saw his eyes flicker. Then again. He was waking up. He managed a smile through cracked lips.

—Do you want a drink?

He nodded.

She brought the plastic beaker to his mouth and allowed a couple of drops to fall. He swallowed.

—Thank you, Jasmine.

Polite even in his sickbed. Had he heard her?

—Your life is not in Kenya, Jasmine, he said with a smile.

—It could be, she pleaded. — I have to make up for what happened. It was my fault. And there's nothing for me here when you leave.

—Of course it was not your fault, Jasmine. You must stay here. You have your studies.

That was the other thing she had to tell him. At this stage, there was no point in lying about it.

—I didn't enrol. I was going to but—

—We made a deal.

He closed his eyes again, just as the nurse decided to interrupt.

—That's enough now, your time is up.

—Wait. George, please . . .

With what seemed like a supreme effort, he opened his eyes again and looked directly at her.

—Go home to your mother, Jasmine.

—Yes, off you go, the nurse said, and swished the curtains closed; she was dismissed.

She went to the gym a few times, hoping to see Keith, or the Christles, or anyone she recognised, to hear any news they might have about George. She didn't want to visit him again because she couldn't bear to hear that he didn't want her in his life any more. She knew it wasn't what he meant, that he only wanted what was best for her, but since their boxing relationship was over, it was what it boiled down to. The other reason she was hanging around the gym was to feel part of it again – but there were only strangers there. She trudged home after for a third time, and went to bed feeling defeated. When her alarm went off the next day, she didn't get up to run, and then she didn't get up for work. Everything seemed pointless.

When a knock came on the door it was late afternoon, judging by the darker grey of the skylight. She ignored it but it persisted.

—Come on, Jazz, I know you're there.

Even Deano couldn't fix her problems this time. Unless he had a ticket to Kenya in his arse pocket.

—Bapty sent out a search party. He thinks you've been kidnapped.

By the sound of it, he was going to stay out there shouting through the door until she let him in, so she hauled herself out from the warmth of her bed. For a moment she felt dizzy, probably because she'd had nothing to eat all day. The flat was freezing, so she pulled the blankets around her shoulders and went to the door.

—Jaysus, Jazz, you look like shit.

She shrugged, turned back towards the bed and got in again.

—Look, Jazz. It's fuckin' terrible what happened to your friend George, but you can't just give up.

—I'm tired, Deano, that's all.

—Then take a break. You got a bad shock. You shouldn't be on your own now. Go back home for a bit, recover. Jock will keep your job.

So, Deano too. If he wasn't on her side, then she had nobody. She felt weary. She would think about it, she said, to get rid of him. She was already close to sleep when he closed the door. But snatches of nightmares probed from her subconscious while she slept, half waking her, sweating and terrified, until she'd fall back asleep, only to wake again to some new terror. The night seemed to go on for ever as faces came and went and morphed into each other: George, to Deano, to Corrigan, to Fat Bobby . . .

—No!

Her scream woke her fully and she sat bolt upright. For a long time she stayed that way with the blankets pulled up around her, afraid to go back to sleep, afraid to be on her own, afraid to move.

But as the room lightened, she began to make sense of things. George hadn't spent all this time training her to sit in a pile on her bed afraid of her own shadow. She was a sportswoman, a boxer. She knew what she had to do. She would do it for George.

She threw off the blankets and pulled on her tracksuit and runners and headed out for a run, her first since the accident. But by the time she got to Fairview she had to stop because she thought she might faint. Of course. Food. She could hear George in her head, telling her she was silly to try to run without any fuel. Come to think of it, she hadn't eaten properly in days. Slowly, she made her way back to the flat, pausing for breath as she climbed the stairs. She knew all right, but she'd have to be a bit more patient.

She decided to take another day off work to rest and get organised. Jock wasn't too happy when she told him that she'd be able to make up the hours because she wouldn't be taking any more study leave; she would not be going back to school.

—Ah Jasmine, after all I did for you.

He sounded like a disappointed parent, but too bad, she was a working girl now, and a boxer. She went into town where she stocked up on food, then spent more than she could afford in the martial arts shop on a pair of boxing gloves. She owed it to George.

Every morning, she was out running before it was light, and after her breakfast she pounded the punchbag, talking herself through her routines the way George used to, not stopping until she was spent. She paid attention to what she ate, getting in the proper balance of protein and carbohydrates that George had taught her, and she was in bed by nine every night. On Sundays, when she used to train, she watched boxing videos on Deano's portable TV.

She was running further, skipping faster, punching harder, punching faster, 1-2-3, jab-cross-hook, ticking boxes of her own making. The nervous energy that drove her remained unspent, but for now it was enough. Because it was only a matter of time before Adrian was back, desperate, and begging her to fight, and this time there was no George to tell her what she couldn't do.

She spotted his ugly mug as he passed by the window and she didn't even look up as he entered. Bapty and the lads had gone next door for their medicinal sup, and she was on her own.

—What is it this time, Adrian? Uncle A throw you out again?

—I left.

—And, let me guess, you have nowhere to stay and no money?

—Aunty Margaret is in a bad way.

—A bad way how?

—Drinking.

—I know. So?

—So I thought you'd want to know. She's worse, that's all.

She wondered what had changed. But she forgot all about her mother when she saw Adrian's face.

—Woah.

It was a mess. His eyes were hidden in a puffy, purple swelling, and his nose seemed to have shifted slightly to one side.

—Let me guess. You're back five minutes and you're already in big trouble, and I'm your only hope. If I'd only fight your fantasy girl fight everything would be all squared up and we'd all live happily ever after, right?

He looked at the floor.

—Well, it's your lucky day, Adrian. I'll fight. Three weeks and I'll be ready.

—But I don't have three weeks, he spluttered.

—Then no fight, she said calmly. It might be a sick betting game to him, but she knew the level of fitness she wanted to achieve, and there would be no half-measures.

—You can see what they've done to me. What will they do next?

—Let's see . . . You still have ears. And limbs. They'll find something.

172

—Fuckit, Jasmine, it's not funny.

—Ah, ah. Language, Adrian. She wagged a finger. —What would Uncle Adrian say?

—Fuck him, he said with feeling. —And fuck you too. He turned to leave.

She let him get as far as the door, where she could see Bapty, about to come in.

—Three weeks. If two girls boxing the crap out of each other is the big deal you say, your friends will wait. Besides, it'll give you time to get up a crowd. Now go, and don't come back. Some of us have to work.

He fled.

Tennessee, 2012

—Holy shit, are you okay?

A girl is looking down at me, with her dark hair hanging so I can't see her face, but she sounds worried.

—You really took a spill. Can you stand?

She's holding a hand out to help me up. I try to get my feet under me, but everything hurts, so I stay where I am.

—Oh shit, you're bleeding. Wait. You shouldn't move.

I look to where she's looking, and she's right, my knee is a mess. The jeans are torn, and there's blood soaking through halfway down my shin. Shit.

—Wait here.

She doesn't go anywhere, just takes out her phone.

—No!

She looks surprised, but she stops tapping the screen.

—Well, at least you're conscious. Look, you're bleeding a lot. I was just going to call my mom. She's a nurse. She'll know what to do.

That's when I see the contents of my backpack, strewn all over the place. The clasp must have got broken. I try to sit up, but my wrist goes from under me and I sprawl back down.

—Let me call my mom. If I don't, someone's going to call an ambulance. Or the cops. She looks me straight in the eye, this time pushing her hair behind her ears so I can see she's serious.

I nod.

—Okay, good. Now stay still. And stop worrying about your stuff. I'm on it.

She taps her screen.

—Hello, Mom.

Nice to be able to press some buttons and have your mom answer. I turn my head away.

She's brief, then she listens for a moment before she hangs up. She starts gathering up clothes and papers from my file and fitting them all back into the pack, which she takes over to her car. Then she's back to see if I'm able to try standing again.

—Do you think you can make it to the car?

This time I use my other hand to get to sitting, and she puts her hands under my armpits.

—On three. One, two . . .

And I'm up. I survey the damage, and man, it's not good. My wrist hurts like hell, and there is blood everywhere. It's even in my shoe. Eew.

—Shit.

—What is it?

I don't know how to say it, but I can't just get into this girl's car and bleed all over it. But she figures it out.

—Don't worry, my car's a mess anyway, but I have a blanket you could use.

—Thanks.

Then I remember my next problem, but she's there first again.

—I'll have the store guy lock up your bike. I know him. We went to grade school together. Your bike will be fine.

—Can you do me a favour? I manage, though I hate asking favours from anyone because you always have to pay later.

—Sure.

—Can you ask him to put it round the back, somewhere out of sight? I . . . borrowed it . . .

She gives me that look again, like she knows more than I want her to.

—Sure. I'll explain how you took your brother's bike and how he'll be mad as hell if he finds out. Soon as you're patched up you'll be back to fix the bike. Right?

My attempt at a grateful smile turns into a wince when I try to put weight on my right foot, so she puts an arm around my waist and I'm able to hobble to her car. At last I'm in the passenger seat, with a blanket and Callum's jacket under me, and my backpack at my feet, and she goes to talk to her old classmate.

A few minutes later she's back from the store.

—That's all cool. I'm Kit, by the way.

—I'm Ali.

—I guess you're not from around here?

—I guess not.

Kit laughs.

—Okay, so you don't want to tell me where you're from? That's cool. How about where you're headed?

I look down.

—Hey, don't worry. I'm just making conversation. How about I tell you about me instead, we let my mom look you over, then you decide if you want to talk. And if you don't, that's cool, I can bring you right back here to your bike.

I look over to where the bike is lying, with wheels still spinning, and I know that I don't ever want to see it again. I nod, and she starts up the car and pulls out.

Dublin, 2012

Sheila leads her to the single room where her mother has been transferred. The resident doctor has been in, she tells her. He is carrying out tests. He suspects a UTI, but until he has confirmation he is treating her intravenously with a broad-spectrum antibiotic, and keeping her in isolation. She nods, and opens the chart. She is reading and listening at the same time, but most of her attention is on the small bump her mother makes in the bed, and her tiny hand, punctured and connected to a drip. Hardly the size of a mother at all, she thinks, then she rebukes herself for it. As if *mother* was something you could measure; no, *mother* is a concept, and it expands and shrinks according to the situation. After all, who is better qualified to know than she is: she has presided over the transition of thousands of women to *mother*. In the womb, *mother* is a child's whole world, vast and unknowable. Then motherhood begins, with a roar and a bloodletting, and from that point on it never lets up. In her hospital, they cut twenty-five or thirty umbilical cords a day, and it is often the father who enacts the symbolic severing of the baby from the mother, but his is an illusion of power, because a phantom cord remains, right up to the end.

Sheila has finished speaking, and is looking expectantly at her.

—Thank you, she manages.

Sheila leaves, and they are alone. She takes a seat. Her mother's breaths are so shallow they barely disturb the silence, but they are rhythmic, and she finds her own breathing falling in with it, and she is overwhelmed with the desire to sleep.

In her dream, she is delivering a baby. It has been a long labour, and a C-section has been suggested more than once, but she is confident that she can deliver the baby naturally, as the mother hoped. At last the baby crowns. She guides its head with her hands, and its body follows easily, in a last gush of amniotic fluid. That's when she realises that she is the one who has given birth, and that the baby she has guided out of her womb is her own mother. A shadow steps forward and as the father sets about cutting the cord she realises it means that both of them will die, but her scream is lost in all the other screams of the labour ward.

She wakes to loud ringing, and it takes her several moments to orient herself. The release from the dream lasts only until reality reasserts itself. She scrambles to turn off her phone in case it wakes her mother. It's Jeffrey again. This time she takes the call, because at least this time she has some answers.

—There you are, darling, he says, before she can speak. He sounds put out.

She tells him she's sorry for not getting back to him, then she fills him in, feeling only slightly guilty when she notices that she is making the situation sound more critical than it is. She won't be over this week. She needs to be here because, well, he knows how it is with old people and infections. He allows a wounded silence to precede his *Quite*, reminding her that he is actually a little older than her mother. Oh, to hell with niceties, she thinks. He knows *quite* well what she means, and is well aware of the differences there are between his health and her mother's.

—Sorry, she says again, insincerely. —And Jeffrey, I haven't had a chance to get back to Ken. He emailed to let me know they'll be offering me the job. Could you thank him for me, and explain that I may have to put things on hold.

She doesn't want to be any more specific than that. It is

enough for now. She pretends a demand on her attention and tells him she has to go.

The green-grey walls of the room have muted into shadows, with only the pattern of streetlight filtered through the blinds to alleviate the gloom. Small clicks and beeps from radiators and medical equipment are amplified in the silence. Far-off voices in the corridor grow faint and disappear, and even the traffic outside seems to grow still, until it feels as if the whole world is contained there in that room. This chair, this bed. This woman who gave birth to her, who fed and cleaned her then taught her to feed and clean herself, who taught her to read, and tolerated her when she was a brat. Who tended to her when she was sick. Who brought her back to life when everything had gone wrong. Because there was another bedside vigil, wasn't there, Mam? When I was the fevered, damaged one in the bed, and you were the one keeping watch.

Dublin, 1983

Adrian turned up at her flat the following day, while she was doing her bag work. He had persuaded the thugs he was involved with to wait, he told her proudly.

—They didn't have much choice, Jasmine retorted.

—So, here. He thrust a folded page at her.

She gave him a look.

—What's that?

—The venue. For the fight. Very hush-hush.

She held up her gloved hands.

—Maybe just tell me, Adrian, okay?

—Dollymount.

—The beach?

He nodded.

—When?

—Wednesday fortnight, 10 p.m.

She thought about it for a moment.

—In the dark?

—There'll be lights.

She nodded.

—What do you know about my opponent?

—Not much. Five foot ten, doesn't speak English. She's coming over with the gang from the UK.

—Does she want this fight?

—It's what she does. All over Europe.

—Great, Jasmine said through closed teeth. —Okay, now get out. I'm training.

She talked to George the whole time, trying to imagine the advice he would give. Get in there with your left hook. Then get out fast. Use your speed. Keep your focus. Watch for her weakness then exploit it. When it came to her first real fight, though, she would be on her own. She would not discover her opponent's weakness until she was in the ring, and it was terrifying, but somehow that fear had transformed into anger. These days she was angry about everything. She fuelled her morning runs with rage, and felt as if she still had miles left in her when she got back; she skipped in a fury; she attacked the punchbag like it was personal. Because it was. Everything that had happened – to George, to Cat, even to the Chinese girl, who made some kind of living out of fighting in secret, shitty locations – was personal, and come fight day, she had scores to settle.

On the day of the fight, Jasmine went to work as usual because she couldn't afford to piss Jock off, but she had so much nervous energy she didn't know what to do with herself. Bapty told her more than once that she was like a hen on a hot griddle, and she wanted badly to tell him what was happening, just so she would have someone to wish her luck. But she didn't want to drag him into anything illegal; it was bad enough that he spent his days in a bookies. So she cleaned things that didn't need cleaning, and fumbled change, and talked too much to the customers until, at last, it was time to lock up. She went home and had a feed of spaghetti hoops and sausages, even though she felt sick with nerves. It didn't help that she was probably pre-menstrual, but that meant that all her rage had gathered itself up like an ugly cyst that was ready to burst. She had her shorts and vest under her tracksuit, and her gloves and towel and gumshield were in a bag by the door, but it was still too early to leave. She slapped at the punchbag, then she skipped a little, then she flopped on to the bed. God, would it not hurry up.

At last. She treated herself to a taxi as far as the Wooden Bridge because she needed to save her energy. When she got out into the cold, drizzly night, she was seized by a sharp pain in her guts – nerves, she presumed – and she had an urge to turn around and run back to the flat. But she forced herself to put one foot then the other on to the wooden beams until she was on the island. The cottages were in darkness, and the Scout Den deserted. She veered into the dunes and followed the track until she got to the beach, but still she saw no one. She began to doubt herself, wondering if she could have got the night wrong, but knowing that she could not; she had planned every single minute of her training so that she would peak tonight.

She walked along the beach, her feet bogging in the sand and slowing her. The tide was in – she could hear the waves lapping close by – so it had to be near the dunes, if it was happening at all. Then she spotted them: men, making their way in twos and threes up the beach. They walked purposefully, as if they were on their way to a business meeting, with none of the excitement and high spirits of fans on their way to a fight. No one took any notice of her, so she put her head down and followed.

She was almost on top of them when she found the dozen or so cars, parked in a circle close to the dunes, with their engines ticking over. A dark cluster of men stood around, talking in low voices. That's when she spotted Adrian, standing on a box, no less, and they were giving him cash faster than he could take it from them.

—One at a time, gentlemen, she heard him say.

Gentlemen, my arse. She put down her bag, shelved her remaining nerves, and got down to business. First she took off the tracksuit, then she put in her gumshield and bandaged her hands. She would need help tying them, which meant she'd have to ask Adrian, if he could shift his focus from the pound signs in his eyes for one minute. While she waited, she kept warm by running on the spot and punching the air. They could find her when they wanted her.

She sensed, rather than saw, the approach of her opponent, a tall, silent presence. They nodded to each other in part acknowledgement, part sizing up. The Chinese girl was not gloved up yet, and when she spotted Jasmine's laces dangling she indicated that she would tie them. Jasmine held out her hands. Why not? This was women's boxing; they could do it their way. But before the Chinese girl could begin, two men separated out from the crowd and steered her away. Another man appeared from somewhere, a coach, he said, but he didn't give his name – of course, it was an illegal fight – and offered to tie the gloves. It was a comfort to know that there was at least one person there with an interest in the sport, not just the money, or the novelty, or whatever other pervy reasons the men had for being there.

Without any obvious signal, a lull fell over the crowd, and a space widened to let her through. She reached the centre clearing at the same time as the Chinese girl, who was coming from the other side. The car headlights were on, and she could see that they were in a sandy 'ring', marked out with tennis nets. The spectators stood a little way back, between and behind the cars. It was a strange atmosphere, but she pulled her mind away from her surroundings to the centre, and into her own centre.

The coach stepped between them, and said the things referees said at every boxing match, though she had never been close enough to hear them properly before: they should protect themselves, heed his instructions, and fight a good, clean fight. They touched gloves, and it was on. Instantly, her body adjusted to the sandy floor. She became her eyes and feet, her arms and gloves, moving in and back out fast, never losing sight of her opponent's moves, evaluating and re-evaluating instant by instant, all reflexes and instinct. Jab-cross-hook, move in, get out. Then a whistle sounded and the round was over. Just like that. She had done okay. Good, Jasmine, George would have said. Keep your mind clear, let your training do the work. Your body knows. Trust it.

She went to her corner and sat on the upended box she found there. No one came to tighten her gloves, or to give her water, or towel off the sweat. She was on her own. The car lights had been dimmed, but she knew the Chinese girl at least had minders. She turned to see where Adrian was, because even that useless imbecile would be better than no one, but she couldn't spot him in the crowd, so she had to resort to wiping her forehead with her forearm, and the only sound advice she got was the talking-to she gave herself.

She stood at the sound of the short, low whistle that announced the second round, but as she turned, she fell suddenly off-balance. She felt for the box to steady herself until the light-headedness passed. She must have stood up too quickly, that was all. Was she able to continue? the ref was asking. She nodded and got up again. She was fine.

But something was not right. She got in there, and got out, but the Chinese girl was strong, and when she made contact, Jasmine felt it. She compensated with her greater speed, to minimise the blows she was taking, but she could feel the fight getting away from her, and she seemed to be powerless to turn it around.

This time she was waiting for the whistle, and Adrian was waiting for her in her corner.

—What the fuck, Jasmine. Get it together in there. There's a shit load of money at stake. You just have to get through three rounds.

He sounded very far away, though his face was so close that she could feel his spittle landing on her. She didn't know what he was talking about.

—What three . . .?

—Stay standing, three rounds.

—Not a win? She was sounding strange to herself now, as if she, too, was far away.

—Just survive in there, all right? The Chinese is a pro, she's been in this game years.

Game. Pro. Years. His words were fading in and out, and she couldn't seem to understand their meaning.

—What's going on with you, you're out of it? Here. This will snap you out of it.

He threw water from a bottle at her face, making her splutter. But it shocked her alert so that she was able to get up for the third round when the whistle blew.

But this time she wasn't able to get away quickly enough, and she took the full force of the blows. When she fell into her opponent, she could barely release herself, and the ref ordered them to break it up. She threw wild punches, occasionally connecting, but most going wide. The noise of the crowd came and went. She really wasn't feeling well. The Chinese girl got her hard, below the ribs, and she gasped and stumbled back towards the net. Her feet somehow steadied her, but before she could move forward again into the fray she was hit from somewhere else. It came from inside herself, pain more intense than she had ever felt. She must have cried out, because as she fell she saw the alarm on her opponent's face.

It was excruciating. And there was blood, a black wetness soaking her shorts, and seeping down her legs. The lights were gone, the cars reversing, men moving quickly away, their low voices lost on the waves. Somewhere off in the distance an ambulance siren sounded. She was moving outside consciousness now, floating away from the pain, out across the dark water. And all the while the Virgin on stilts kept watch, over the Irish Sea and Dublin Bay and Dollymount Strand, over her where she bled to oblivion on the sand.

Rathlowney, 1983

Swanning around in Dublin, is it, then back here at the first sign of trouble? I don't know what happened, how could I the way that eejit Adrian babbles, and his father no wiser except to tell me he phoned him to come and collect you from the hospital. No doubt you'll tell me some story when you're back in the land of the living, Miss Rosemary. Or Jasmine, as you insist it is now, the good Christian name you were given not good enough for you, and your Uncle Adrian and Aunt Maureen, God rest her, standing for you. It was the decent thing to do, your father said, let bygones be bygones. Even with all that had happened he was always one to give in, to keep the peace – do you remember that at all, *Jasmine*? I'll admit to it, I was afraid for you. There was something intense about the whole ritual that'd throw you, you in the dress nearly to the ground and them holding you, and the trickle of water startling you into a wail, and the whole lot of them renouncing the devil. But sure isn't it really only a bit of drama so everyone can go on and get a bite somewhere and a drop of whiskey or whatever you're having to wet the baby's head, that's what I told myself while the priest was saying I baptise thee, Rosemary. That's Mary for the Virgin, with a bit of a twist because I love roses. But you know that.

But I'm getting ahead of myself. That's not where the story started. Didn't it start where it always starts: a girl meets a fella. And he was the tallest handsomest fella. I could hardly believe my luck, and he telling me I was the loveliest girl in the whole of Athlone, and he the luckiest fella going.

I was sixteen, coming out of the library holding my pile of books when he went by on his bike and didn't he nearly fall off, twisting his head around to get another look. I didn't let on to see him mind, kept my head down, only you couldn't miss the wobble of the bike and Billy Daly letting a roar at him out the window of his Morris Minor to take his eyes off the Murphy young one and watch where he was going.

When I got up the top of the town to our street he was already there – wasn't he after chasing Billy Daly to find out who I was and where I lived – and he blocked the path and asked if he could carry my books. Sure there was nothing to them, a few novels, I could carry them myself, I told him smartish, and kept walking. But wouldn't you prefer to let your arms swing while you walk? he asked. You see he was walking along beside me now, after turning his bike around, as if it was the most natural thing. Sure I'm nearly there, I told him. Then I put my hand to my mouth because it looked like I wanted him to know where I lived. Can I walk you home? says he, cheeky. You can if you want to meet the master, I said. That usually got rid of any lads I wasn't in the mind to have hanging around me, which up to now was the lot of them, raggedy bunch of yokes they were, but he only looked puzzled. The master is my brother, I told him. Well, that's as may be, but it doesn't bother me, he said.

You'd know he didn't know Adrian. Of course, it would have been a good long time since he was in primary school, well before Adrian was out of training college. It was the young lads coming up below me who were frightened out of their wits of him. Not that he was free with the rod – though he did use it as a last resort – no, it was the way he turned the threat of it into a game for himself. Well, this fella hadn't gone to school with Adrian and he wasn't ever his pupil, so he was as bold as brass and walked me right up to the door. I said right so, and he said right so, then he stood there scratching his head, not as cocky now, until finally he turned his bike the other way and made to go off, real slow.

I was putting the key in the door when it was opened for me and Adrian was out on the path looking down after your man on his bike. It's not my fault he followed me home, I said, stepping neatly past him as if to put an end to it. But Adrian kept watching, as if he could bore holes in the poor lad's back. Come in out of that, I told him, I don't even know the lad's name.

One of the McCarthys, he said, not looking a bit happy about it. And what of it? I said, I don't know them. McCarthys the bookies, he says, and you're too young to be carrying on with fellas. Well, I was stung. I'd never carried on with a fella in my life, only coming out of the library minding my own business, but I didn't let on to Adrian how annoyed I was, just got on with making his tea and doing my homework.

No matter how much someone thinks they control you, and God knows there are some who believe they can, they can't get into your head, and when I poured the tea, I imagined myself pouring it into Adrian's lap. Of course I wasn't going do it, but what I would do was give that McCarthy lad a piece of my mind if I ever saw him again for getting me into trouble.

He was waiting outside school with his bike the very next day, if you please. Miss Murphy, he said, pretending to take off his hat like someone in a film, only he wasn't wearing one. Well, I didn't want to be making a show of myself there so I started walking, knowing he'd follow. I didn't want to get home before I'd had a chance to say my piece, so I turned down the lower road, going the long way.

I didn't say a thing until we were well away from the clusters of uniforms.

You got me in trouble with my brother, I told him when we rounded the courthouse and turned down to the river. Your brother has a tight rein on you I hear, he said, which meant he'd been asking about me. I was pleased as punch inside but trying to be cross. You don't know the half of it, I said. Don't I now? he said. Don't I know your mother died when you were only a little one and your father died a few years back and your brother is the master up in St Brendan's, and all the aul' ones say he's like a father to you, and isn't he great. Then you get one who'll say, but he's a bit hard on her, a young girl like that should be out having fun, not inside waiting on that fella hand and foot.

Well, it was nice to hear that someone was thinking about what was good for me, but annoying all the same. What did they know anyway? Were they inside in our kitchen? It wasn't as if I was telling everyone because I wasn't, so I said it's a pity they haven't something better to talk about, and I said that I was perfectly fine. You are, he said, quick as a flash. I couldn't hide my thoughts then because I blushed like a tomato. I kept walking because I didn't know where to look. I won't go as far as the house, he said, I don't want to get you in trouble.

And that was all there was to it. He was there after school the next day, waiting at the courthouse, and he walked with me along the river, chatting away, not seeming to mind that he got no encouragement. But I suppose it was encouragement enough that I was going the long way.

It was autumn heading into winter, and the darker evenings were our chaperone, covering the awkwardness, mine anyway. I didn't know what to be doing or saying to a boy. Those were innocent times. A boy and girl might hold hands if they were doing a line, so when he took mine in the dark he couldn't see how delighted I was. It was coming up to Christmas when he kissed me, and I nearly died and went to heaven. It wasn't slobbery and awkward, the way the girls in school said, it was lovely.

He was lovely, not just kissing but talking too. Never before could anyone have accused me of being a chatterbox. With Adrian, with the nuns, the neighbours, even the girls from school, I kept my thoughts to myself, thinking, sure who'd be interested. But with him I talked about everything and anything that came into my head, chattering like a magpie, telling him all my plans and ideas – ach, they were only little plans and little ideas, everyday ideas, because the big plans were vague and daunting and besides, it seemed to me they were Adrian's to make – and he'd tell me stories from his father's bookies where he worked, some character of an oul' fella always up to something. We spent our time talking and laughing . . . that's the way I remember it anyway.

There was just the walk from school every day. Going to a dance or to the pictures was out of the question because Adrian would never have agreed. He tried to persuade me to ask, sure all he can do is say no, he said reasonably, but I knew there was no point, none at all. Aren't we grand as we are, I told him. But the truth was I was getting anxious that he'd get fed up of me not being able to do anything, that he might up and leave, take up with someone who wasn't a schoolgirl under her brother's thumb.

So I told him what I was worrying about. We were down the river as usual. He asked because I was chewing the ends of my hair; I had a terrible habit of gnawing it into rat's tails when I was fretting about something. That you'll break up with me because I can't go out in the evenings, I said, and I could feel myself blushing. I made to go on ahead of him, which didn't leave him too many choices. He drew me into step with him, and pushed my hair back, and put his two hands over my woollen hat – it was freezing – and the look he gave me I was nearly scared of him. Then he pulled me closer until our cold, dripping noses nearly touched, and told me he'd never break up with me, that he loved me.

And the long kiss.

After, I couldn't think about anything else day and night. There I'd be, cutting a loaf for Adrian's sandwiches, or wetting the pot for the tea, or making the beds, there I'd be in school, doing maths or listening to Sister Rosari reading *Paradise Lost*, and all I was thinking about was him. I couldn't keep the smile off my face, and passing the primary school with some of my friends, the children skipping *raspberry gooseberry blackcurran' jam, tell me the name of your young man, is it a, b, c, d* . . ., they were pushing me and teasing and laughing to go on, tell us, Margaret, tell us the name of your young man. That's all any of us dreamed about, a young man for ourselves. Silly, weren't we? But if the girls knew, so would the nuns and the neighbours, and so would Adrian eventually, if he didn't already. No matter, there wasn't a thing any of them could do about it.

Or so I thought, but I was only sixteen and what did I know? We went further, of course we did – even though the nuns preached at us to be lady-like and Mary-like and to mind our virtue, and the priests preached that it was a sin – because we had our young bodies, and we loved each other, and it made sense to love with our bodies. Sure they just leaped into life like nature intended them to. I was learning that the whole reason to be alive was the feeling of his hands on my skin under my clothes. We'd sit on the bench with his bike propped up against the back of it, and kiss and cuddle and tell each other everything. And when, one day, we turned up the field at the back of the convent and lay down on his coat on the ground in the copse to be out of the cold breeze, the whole world made sense, and it hurt only a bit, and he loved me, he told me again and again but I knew anyway because of the way he was so careful, as if he was afraid I might suddenly dissolve and vanish from beneath him. I think I would have vanished, I would have died, if he stopped moving the way he moved inside me.

It was after Christmas when I knew, I mean, really knew, because I think I knew straight away but I didn't admit it to myself. There were little tinglings in my breasts and in my womb, stretching, I suppose, so when my monthly didn't come I knew. I was supposed to be afraid and ashamed and a whole lot of bad things, but at first – only at first, mind, because the bad things came soon after – I was thrilled, for the way life happens, for him and me, love and life coming together.

He went quiet when I told him, but I trusted him. I never thought once that it wouldn't be the two of us together. What will we do? I asked him. I don't know, I don't know, he said. Little did I know that what he would decide to do would be based on the assumption that all humans share a common decency. But he hadn't lived with Adrian, and he didn't know the kind of a man Adrian was, hard as a shell. I used to excuse him for it; hadn't he raised me himself from when I was twelve and him only twenty-one and just out of training college. He got the job as master in St Brendan's and from that moment on he was the master of his house as well. And let there be no mistake, it was his house, and I was there on sufferance. I couldn't blame him. No one wants to be father to a twelve-year-old when they should be out sowing their wild oats. I was a good girl, as far as I could be, but I had my own ideas.

It doesn't matter what plans I might have been making because didn't he go and approach Adrian, face him like a man, he said. I jumped out of my standing when he knocked on the door, I was that nervous. Who is this coming at teatime? Adrian demanded. He didn't like having his meals interrupted. He went out with a mouthful of bread and jam and opened the door with his face already like thunder. Can I come in? I heard his voice and my heart sank. I might as well have gone on upstairs at that moment and put my few things into a bag because I knew I wasn't long for this house. At first Adrian said he was in the middle of his tea, and I let myself think I might be saved after all, but then he gave one of his long sighs and told him to come in and make it quick, but that if it was about getting him to change his mind about seeing his sister he could leave before he started and save them both the time and the trouble. It wasn't that, he said, and I could hear his voice faltering. It wasn't a small thing, what he was there to say, it was big and it was terrible, the most terrible thing could happen to a family, and the most terrible thing could happen to a girl.

I don't know what words he used, even though I was listening from the stairs, because what came after frightened them out of my memory. All I can remember is Adrian roaring for me to come down, and seeing my poor boy, broken and ashen-faced. And the look he gave me and him backing out the door, and I didn't blame him one bit. I didn't then, and I don't now. I had a whole life with Adrian to know what a bully he was.

The house was aching with its silences, words that had been spoken and were yet to be spoken, roiling in waves around us. Sure didn't I hear my own poor mother, God rest her, saying, will you go easy on the child, Adrian. But it was in my head and not his, that was the problem. And for all I know my father had something to say too, but if he did it wasn't to me. I never knew him, and maybe it was as well, maybe he was of a disposition to take a stick to my back, like Adrian did to me.

No one had taken a stick to me before – there was never a call for it – and it was more with interest than fear that I waited for it to fall the first time. But in the moment of that hot flash of pain, I had to decide whether to cry out or to hold it in, and I held it, until I realised it was making him more angry. You'd never have guessed he had the words, the master. Whore, slattern, bringing shame on his house, and I only there thanks to his good nature, anyone else would have thrown me into an orphanage and this was the thanks he got. Is it jack-the-lad who will put food in your belly and that thing's belly? Have you thought about it, have you? He was gone well past reason, and I had more than myself to worry about now, so I cried out like a banshee.

He stopped suddenly and sat down, his mad energy spent. You have choices, he said, his voice reasonable. Little did I know he was the more dangerous for it. You can still do your teacher training, get a job with me in St Brendan's. There's places they'll take care of it, couples in America dying for children from Catholic families to adopt. It'd have some sort of a life there, the best of everything. What would it have here, an illegitimate child? I'll have a word with Father Birmingham. He can arrange with the nuns above in Dublin. There's a place he knows, where he's had some dealings in the past, girls in trouble like yourself. He'll take care of it. Put it around that you're gone to help an elderly grand-aunt in Dublin. No one will be any the wiser.

Persuaded, he slid the stick back into its slot, behind the picture on the mantelpiece, and went on up to his room.

I was thinking of a him, a little boy blue, not an *it*. I was half knitting in my head little matinee coats and hats to match, but already my little boy was becoming someone else, maybe in a sailor suit in a black and white photograph that they would never send all the way from America to me, his mother.

I let Adrian have his way.

We travelled in the new Anglia, his first car, got specially for the occasion, and it was nothing short of a sin how proud he was showing it off going up through the town, big smiles and waves for any heads he managed to turn, when all I wanted was to vomit from the new smell of it, and the baby, and the motion I wasn't used to. I had to get him to pull over three times. You're lucky you waited till we were out of the town, he said, and you better not get the upholstery. This, while I was heaving and spitting, thinking my insides were being dragged out and maybe we wouldn't need to go to Dublin at all.

The main building was red brick with other bits tacked on to it, and trees out the front making it darker, even with the new leaves coming. We drove up the driveway and my heart sank. They say that, don't they? Only I could feel it fall as heavy as a stone down into my belly and there it stayed the whole time I was in that place.

There was a cup of tea and two Marietta biscuits for us in the parlour, and that was the last of the niceties for me. It was all for Adrian's benefit, of course, while he filled in forms which they made me sign. I didn't know what I was signing. I had a fair idea but I didn't have time to read it. My signature, sure you couldn't even tell it was me, my hand was shaking so much. It wasn't me, tell you the truth, but I had no choice so I did what they said and signed my stranger's signature and that was that.

I didn't know whether to be glad or sorry when the Anglia left, but I didn't have time to think about it. The nun said come with her and she led me down the corridor, black and red tiles, and red geraniums on plant holders the length of it. The strong smell of them. To this day they make me sick, and that's what happened; I got sick there on the chequered tiles. The face on her then. Leave it, she snapped. Hurry now. Another corridor, up a stair, more stairs, another corridor. I'd lost my bearings. I was wishing like Hansel and Gretel I'd had the foresight to leave a trail of breadcrumbs behind me to show me the way out when she stopped outside a door. In here, she said. Leave your clothes folded neatly on the bed, third from the end, put on the uniform.

The room was long and dark, with beds lining it on either side and only the one small window at the end. A panic ran through me because I had never shared a room before, with anyone. I was fond of my privacy. I walked slowly to the third bed from the end and found a neat ironed pile of clothes there. I sat on the bed beside them and thought, I'm not putting on those, I'm staying in my own clothes, how is that bothering anyone? I had on a modest dress, green with rosebuds: I can still see that dress, though truthfully it was starting to feel tight at the waist.

You hurry up in there, the nun called through the door. Holy God, was she waiting outside for me? The tone in her voice made me forget any objections to the uniform, and my hands were shaking as I undid buttons and stood out of my dress in my stockinged feet, and pulled the plain dark dress on, then a white pinafore over that, like a maid in olden times. Hurry up you, she said again, and I slipped my feet quickly back into my shoes and made a go of folding my dress and cardigan, then I gave up and half ran back to where she was waiting.

About time, she said. Come. I followed. At the end of the corridor we met a girl coming up the stairs. Her belly was huge and she was trying to catch her breath. I was afraid she was going to have her baby there and then. Mary Mulqueen, hurry along. On second thoughts, you can take this one and show her where to find the cleaning materials to clean up her filth. And you. She rounded on me. You needn't think you're special. I don't, I protested. Don't you interrupt me, madam. Your fine brother might have got you out of trouble but in here you're all as bad as each other. In here we don't interrupt our betters. Am I making myself clear? Yes, Mother. I can't hear you, she said. She was a tall woman, and as thin as a lath, looking at me down her long nose. Now get out of my sight, the pair of you.

Immaculata, she's a right rip, the other girl said when we were well away. What is it you've done to get on the wrong side of her? I don't know, I said. I said nothing at all to her. Well, the cleaning room is this way, you'll be able to find it soon enough yourself, because it's all we do in here, clean things that aren't dirty. What are you to clean? Well, I said, reddening, I was sick on the way, it wasn't much, it was the smell of the geraniums that got to me. The girl, Mary, turned, her mouth open half in shock, half amusement. You didn't puke in her corridor, did you? I suppose I must have, I said. Jesus, she'll have your guts for garters. It's her life. No one ever goes down that corridor except to come into this place or to leave it, or to polish those godforsaken tiles. She's there day and night, plucking dead-heads. You're lucky she didn't throw you back out. I wish she had, I said, I can't imagine sticking this place for another minute.

When was I due, she wanted to know. July, the doctor says. I'm over a week now, she told me. Then what happens? I asked. What happens is you have your baby across in the maternity unit, then you move out of the dormitory into the mother and baby wing. She dropped her eyes. Then they let you go home.

We both knew she was leaving something out.

The cleaning room had everything you could think of for polishing and scrubbing. There were big industrial tubs of bleach and barrels full of rags. Everywhere these rags were drying on pipes or lines or pegs. It was like something out of *Oliver Twist*, only this was the twentieth century, and it wasn't a story, unfortunately. I can still smell it to this day; that's how you know it wasn't made up, because there's times you think it must have been.

I got a basin with bleach. Where are the gloves? I asked Mary. She gave a half laugh and handed me a rag. For drying. You'll have to clean them after you're finished and hang them in here. So I picked up my basin and followed her back out along corridors and up steps and down until I was completely disorientated again, and we opened a door into that light-filled corridor. There you are, Mary said, I have to go, sorry.

I found my little bit of sick – it was nearly nothing because I'd got it all up on the journey – and I mopped it and made sure to do it right. I didn't want to be sent back for a second time. But the geraniums were getting to me again so I bolted out of there, and with a few false turns I got back to the cleaning room and did as Mary said. Then I didn't know what I was supposed to be doing.

A gong rang out somewhere. I was ravenous – if you're not throwing up you're eating rings around you when you're pregnant – so I went the direction of the sound, and soon I fell in with other girls who came in from outside, or out of other rooms. They were scurrying so I scurried along with them towards a smell of food. Well, it wasn't anything to be writing home about, big dishes with food for ten in each at the top of rows of long tables, and a nun overseeing them all. We filed in and the girls, standing behind their chairs, all went quiet. I did the same, not knowing what we were waiting for, and the food going cold. The nun lifted her right hand with a big gesture, like she was the Queen of Sheba, and brought it to her forehead. *In* the name of the Father, she started, making me jump. That made the girl beside me giggle and the nun looked straight at me as if she wanted to murder me. She started all over again. *If* everyone is ready. Everyone was staring, and me blushing beetroot. *In* the name of the Father.

I wasn't much in the mood for fathers, let me tell you, and us standing around one bump bigger than the other and not a father in sight. By the time we finally sat down I wasn't much in the mood for the food either, thick slices of fatty bacon and cabbage you could see wasn't washed properly, that's all I'll say about it. But I ate, for the baby.

We weren't there to make friends, though we did get friendly enough in a temporary sort of a way, united against the enemy, who was whichever nun happened to be in the room at the time. Though not one of us thought it was any nun alone who was responsible for our situation. It was mams and dads for some, and priests and school masters, and it was the fathers too, though we didn't talk much about them because if they were worth a damn wouldn't they be banging down the door to right the wrong of locking us up.

There were rumours that the odd one came, but he would have got short shrift; it was the times, people reasoned, but I say they're the times because of who's living in them. Because I'm not inclined to be forgiving, not even after all this time. No, because what they took from me was unforgivable, and I hope every last one who was to blame goes to whatever hell they're afraid of the most because that is what they deserve. I didn't know if your father was one of the ones that came. I told myself he was, we all did, because how else could we have borne the abandonment, how else could I understand that he had let this happen to me, when he said he loved me, and to his own baby? How else, in the night, could I have stopped myself from wanting to be dead, let mortal sin be damned? So, like everyone else in there I told myself he was one of them, out there, trying to break the doors down.

But we never heard anyone trying to break the doors down, that was the thing. At night we heard cars going by, or the awful screams of cats, and the shifting and tossing of the women who couldn't settle their pregnant bellies in the narrow, saggy beds, and the sighs and the sobs. Sometimes I couldn't tell if I was listening to myself or the other girls.

Then a sob would turn into a cry of pain and another one would be gone to the other side of the house to have her baby, to look after her baby, to give her baby away, and to go home to the remains of the life she left months before. And we got used to it.

We got used to it, can you credit that? You wouldn't see that girl again once she went down the drive, and if you did see her some day when you were up in Dublin in a shop, say, or on the street, you didn't let on to know each other.

The days were so long you could dream up twenty ways to do away with yourself only coming back every time to knowing that it was a mortal sin, probably a double-mortal, and you'd go straight to hell, not that you cared about that because it couldn't be any worse than being there, so even in your thoughts you were a prisoner. But if the days were interminable, the weeks passed quickly, until I got to be as slow as Mary had been that first day. Mary by now had had her little Miriam, a dote, with a mop of curly black hair on her, and Mary pure carrot. You'd be dying to ask about the daddy but it wasn't something you would bring up in there. The nuns didn't like it. I suppose it suited them better to imagine we were a pack of immaculate conceptions, they could get their heads around that easier.

My time came soon enough. The pain started and it wasn't too bad, I could cope. They brought me to the other side, where there was a bed with a plastic sheet and nothing else on it, and a bucket. And as soon as my waters broke . . . And I'll be honest, I hadn't a notion what was happening to me. I'd only the haziest idea of the whole thing from what you'd hear around the place. I didn't enjoy the gory conversations so I kept out of them, keeping busy with whatever I was supposed to be doing, weeding or scrubbing, while the girls exclaimed and put their hands over their mouths in disbelief. I figured I'd find out soon enough.

As soon as my waters broke, they stood me over the bucket, not to have to clean up.

Stand here, hold your whisht, is it trying to wake the dead you are? You'd swear you were the first girl alive to have a baby. And I holding it in, thinking I could cope, until the pain really broke through. My God, but it was like nothing you could have imagined. I can't rightly describe it, no woman can, or it'd be an end to the whole of the human race. The roars out of me would reach the devil himself, that's what the nun said, and she laughing. And I dying; I was sure I was dying, and it wouldn't have been unheard of, you heard stories about dying in childbirth. Then it'd pass for a while and the nun would get a sly look on her face between contractions, coming up close to me so I could see all the broken veins on her cheeks, asking with her thin, dry lips, was it worth it?

The human race goes on because there's the look between you and the baby that came out of you, and everything goes calm again, the pain fading to a shadow of itself, the pain before forgotten. That's the way it was when I had you, and the way it was when I had him. They handed him to me and he was gazing at me, full of trust, the terrible ordeal of being born all over and now he had his mam. He started mooching straight away, looking for a feed, I knew, without having to be told. We had it all figured out, himself and myself, before they even finished cutting his cord. Only I was wishing his daddy could be there to meet him.

I'm leaving for England to work, we won't ever see each other again, D.

Of course I put his letter in the bin the minute I had it read but my perverse brain wouldn't let the words go. Adrian would have had a hand in it, I knew that much, but it wasn't Adrian's handwriting, it was his. He had written me a note when we were walking out together, D and M in a heart, but I passed it back to him and said I didn't speak sign language. So he wrote it out for me, *I love you Margaret*, and signed his name, and I kept it until it broke at the four folds, and I kept it after. But it didn't come with me to Dublin, because what is love if it gives up at the first hurdle. Anyway, I knew the curve of his D as well as I knew my own M, and the letter was from him all right. England. It tore the heart out of me, seeing his words there on the Belvedere Bond, and the envelope that went with it, already open when the nuns put it into my hands, and the part of me that balled it up and put it in the bin hated him for being such a coward. But the part of me that was feeling an elbow or a knee pressing up under my ribs wanted to go after him and bring him back, and I think that was what was going through my mind when I walked out of the refectory where our post was distributed after lunch and straight down the corridor, right past Immaculata's geraniums – I didn't even notice the smell of them – then out the door and down the drive.

I had a notion I would make my way to where the boats left from, even though I had no idea where that might be, but I could ask, I told myself. And I did, once I was a few hundred yards from the front gates. Wasn't it funny, I remember thinking, all I had to do all along was walk out. I asked a man with a newspaper tucked under his arm – he looked nice enough – only he acted as if he didn't hear my question, just looked me up and down and hurried away. I hadn't thought about the uniform but his face told me I should have, so I pulled the apron over my head and balled it up and left it on a low wall as I passed. I was coming up to traffic lights: left, right, straight, where did it feel the sea was? I tried to smell it, the way we used to when I was small and we'd go to Salthill for a week, but there was only the dirty coal-smoke of Dublin.

Excuse me, miss? It was a Garda with a hand on my elbow, to help me cross the road, I thought, but he was steering me back around the way I came. But I'm trying to get to the ferry, I said. Only I already knew it was hopeless, the nuns had sent him, or the man with the paper, or a neighbour, someone who didn't know they were destroying a life, two lives, someone who couldn't have known, but if they did and brought me back anyway they deserve to go straight to hell with the rest of them.

After his feed they left me with him for a good long snooze, then they showed me where the nursery was, where the newborns went, and you could come and go and feed them and cuddle them. But then, after three days, they went where the babies went: a dormitory for babies. Is there anything sadder than that, all the little cots lined up in rows, all the babies crying and looking for their mam? You'd wonder how you'd know your own, there were so many of them, but of course you did; you went down to the newborns and went straight for him.

I went straight for him but Mother Immaculata was there first, with another in her arms. His mam isn't well, you can do him first. But Mother, I said. But Mother nothing, don't you but Mother me, and she shoved the baby at me. It was Imelda, another girl's baby, I thought, but I didn't know for certain because Imelda had gone into labour a week before me so I hadn't seen her with her baby yet. As it turned out I didn't get to see her again. She got some kind of an infection and she died in the place, God help her, and wasn't I glad then that I gave the little mite a feed and he starving. He was shipped off out of that place a few weeks later, away to America, poor little Irish orphan. Only he with a big farmery lump of a father hiding behind his haystacks down the country somewhere. Sure didn't Imelda tell us the whole story herself. But that was the way it went. What could you do? There certainly wasn't anything Imelda could do. And us, the rest of us, we had enough on our plates learning how to take care of a baby. It's not easy at the best of times, but in there . . .

I made the most of the time, and his gurgles and smiles never left me, or his sturdy little legs pushing into my thighs in his hurry to get out into the world, me wishing it was backwards we could go. His face was so familiar, my own and his father's in his. I did all I could for him, and did it gladly. Would he ever know? Would he remember, even in a dream? If we met would he know my smell? Every day for twenty-three years this is what I was thinking, even after you were born. When I was dressing you, or brushing out your hair, or wiping your face I was thinking, did they do this for him? Were they gentle with him? Do they know what he gave up to be with them? Do they know he's not an orphan at all, but a boy with both father and mother, a mother who is living and breathing and wondering? Do they care?

Ach, but the time went in a click of your fingers. The day came the way it had for the others, the warning to be ready the night before, the early call, the chill getting dressed, taking care to leave the little lamb asleep until the last minute, then feeding him and changing him and wrapping him up warm, and walking to the parlour – yes, the parlour, so you'd know you were both leaving, but where you had signed your name which meant you would not be leaving together – and handing your warm, sweet bundle to the tall, cold Immaculata. She took care to be the one going for the jolly to the airport.

I was left in the parlour with one of the other nuns. Watching them get into the car, I wanted to shout through the glass to be careful of his head. I heard the doors as they were banged shut, the sudden roar of the engine starting up, the roll of the tyres on the gravel. As the rear lights rounded the bend, there was nothing but the racket of the clock on the mantelpiece. I was shivering, not knowing was it the cold or the shock of it, wondering would someone not take pity on me. What had I done to deserve this? I tried to be good, did nothing wrong, just fell in love with a fella, that was all. Why did it have to be like this? I wanted to die. If I couldn't have my baby I just wanted to die, because the heart was scooped out of me when they took him out of my arms.

Have a cup of tea now. Your brother will be here any minute, and you need to get working on that smile, miss, the trouble you're after putting him to. And be grateful to him you're able to waltz back into your old life as if nothing had happened.

Back into my old life where? Which bit? The bit where I saw your father backing out the door? Or before that, when I knew? Or back some more, to me coming down the library steps and him going past on his bike? Where did she want me to go back to? There was no going back, there was nothing there for me. But I drank the tea for there was nothing else to be done, and I waited, and I put the smile on, and I got into Adrian's car, and we drove away.

Good girl, he said when I said will I put the kettle on, for that was where we were back to. And I did put it on, and I made tea. It was just a matter of passing the time until the right time came.

Adrian had it all worked out, how I would be passing my time, studying for the Leaving Cert, making sure to do enough to win the county scholarship, the *or else* left unsaid. Oh, you'd think I'd be excited about it, a chance to go away to college, to get away from Adrian for a while if nothing else, but I didn't care, staying there or going, it was all the same to me. So when he put a timetable on the kitchen table on his way out to St Brendan's and told me to get on with it, that he'd be testing me when he got home, I sat as obedient as a lamb and opened the books at the pages he had marked, and set about my lessons, the memorising and the working out. I did it all day, stopping only when it was time to make a start on the dinner. Then he came in and after he had eaten he was as good as his word, and I stood on the hearth and recited it all back to him and answered all his questions pat. Good girl, he said. More of that and we'll have you back on track in no time, and no one any the wiser.

I got on with it, because how do you decide which day is the one you'll do away with yourself? Adrian was watching my every move like a hawk, wanting to know where I was going and who I had bumped into if I said I was at the post office or the shop. The truth was he didn't want me leaving the house at all. Took to bringing the groceries home in a cardboard box himself, and to sliding the bolt across at half three every afternoon when he got home, as if to say that's that. Then he'd sit on at the table after his tea with his pupils' copies and his red Biro, and maybe the radio on for a bit of cheer. Is that bothering you, he'd ask, is it keeping you from concentrating? It's not, I'd say, because at that time of the evening I wasn't able to concentrate on anything at all, only going over every second I spent with him so I would never forget, reminding every one of my senses so that if I ever forgot the sounds he made I would remember instead his velvety skin, or the sweet smell of him. I sat and remembered, silently reciting my memories like a rosary, until it was a decent hour and I would yawn and say I was off to bed. I'd have to stop myself from skipping up the stairs, so much of a hurry was I in to get to my bed, where I could hold my phantom little boy blue in my arms and rock him to sleep.

He haunted my dreams but he was so welcome, little ghost. Even when the dreams turned dark and I tossing and crying in my sleep I welcomed the time with him. But morning always came and snatched him away, that day and the next and the next. They say time heals but that is not so.

It rained heavy one night and I lay awake listening, for sleep had long escaped me, and the sound of it echoed around my hollowed-out heart until it was more than I could bear.

I think I'll go down to the library, I said to Adrian in the morning, and he slurping the last of his tea in a rush; I timed it that way. I think I should get back to reading, something to occupy me when I'm not studying. He threw me a look, but he didn't have time for it. A good idea, I suppose, he said, it's a nice day after all that rain last night. But don't spend too long, you have exams coming up, don't you forget.

As if I could forget. There was only one way to forget every-thing. I hatched the library story on the spot, but the intention had been there every single day since leaving Dublin. I cleaned up the few things after the breakfast – why I did I couldn't say, but I wiped away the crumbs and washed the cups and the porridge bowls and the plates and rinsed out the rag well and hung it over the tap not to let it get stinky – then I threw on my coat and let myself out. The automatic patting of the pocket for the key before it closed making me laugh to myself because wasn't I beyond keys now. Then I walked quickly down the town. Not too sure of what I was doing, I went up to the library, but it wasn't open yet. As I stood trying to decide my course of action the last of the boys scurried up to the Brothers, and the girls to the convent. It was funny how separate from them I felt when I was one of them not so long ago. I was dreading that I might meet one of my own classmates, but they must have been a punctual lot because the stragglers were faces I only knew to see, and none of them noticed me. Still, I thought I had better move on, not to be drawing attention to myself.

I stepped smartly down those steps, a young woman about her business, crossed the road, then around by the courthouse I went and down the path I'd walked so happy another lifetime ago. I pushed aside all the memories not to let them get in my way. I was feeling purposeful now, keeping a nice brisk pace – getting a bit of exercise, if anyone happened upon me. The path was not gravelled now but a track worn in the grass, muddy in places where I used to side-step daintily, only now I splodged right through it. What did shoes matter, what did stockings? On I went, until I was making the track myself. The townspeople didn't come out this far, lazy lot, only the court-ing couples, and you know where that gets you. On I walked, thinking I'd know it when I saw it.

My company was the river, flowing the same way I was, only faster. It was a noisy companion this morning, swollen from the rain, sometimes spilling out on to the path so I had to move into the reeds, once frightening a duck from her nest, leaving behind her speckled eggs. The river now had taken over the path entirely, and the noise of it, with its tributaries swollen and gathering. I was starting to despair of finding what I was looking for, until . . . There, there at the weir.

Ankle- then calf-deep I was to get to it, with the water splashing up to the hem of my coat in its westward rush, and I in a near fever to be a part of it. Careful, careful, minding my step, for in the middle was where it would be the deepest, where I wanted to be, and all the while my coat was getting wetter, and that was a good thing, for it would pull me down until I became a part of the river, and Adrian would have no hold over me; no one would. I would flow with the water and merge into the sea.

Now, now, take it easy there, Margaret. I thought it was the river talking. I am taking it easy, I told it, and took a few more wobbly steps. Lord, but it was cold. I pushed on against the flow, but wasn't I pushing against flesh and blood, then there was a hand on my arm. Woah, woah, you'll take us both in. As if I cared. He would have to look out for himself, whoever he was, and damn him to hell for being here at all.

And then I was back on the bank among the wet grasses, and a man's face near mine. I thought I had gone in after all, that this was the afterlife, for it was him, Declan, only he was not quite himself. Then I thought it was my baby, grown up. You're all right now, Margaret, he was saying. But would he call me that and I his mam? What if it wasn't him? But if it wasn't, who was it? I was starting to get cold, and that was how I knew I hadn't done it, that I was here on the side of this godforsaken river with God knows who, and nothing had changed.

I was on my way up to Moloney's for spark plugs when I saw you standing on the steps of the library, he said. I was thinking it was good to see you out and about. Only then you made a beeline for the river, and it sounds daft but I had a feeling that I should follow you, Margaret. I'm sorry about what happened, what they put you through. I'm sorry about my brother.

Only I was shaking so much now I didn't rightly know what he was saying, and I hardly knew that he had taken off his coat and put it around me, then picked me up like a child and brought me back up the path and put me into the back seat of his car. He got in himself to the driver's seat and turned on the engine. The heat will soon get going, he said. I'll bring you up to the doctor's. I wanted to say no, bring me back, put me back where you got me, but I was shaking so much I couldn't say a thing.

The next thing, I was warming up under blankets and sipping at a glass of brandy, and I a teetotaller back then – medicine they told me – and there was something at my feet. A hot-water bottle, I said out loud, and there was a big relieved laugh from the two men. I knew neither of them, and I didn't trust them, why would I?

I want to go, I said, throwing off the blanket. I'd go home and bide my time and go again, more careful not to be followed this time. You can't, the stranger said, doctor's orders. This is Dr Lehane, our family doctor, the other one said, the one who was Declan's brother. I didn't know which doctor you went to yourself and you were in no position to tell me.

It was only now I noticed my coat missing, and I had a strange robe on instead of my dress. The nurse helped you out of your wet things, the doctor said, they're inside drying at the range. Don't worry, it was just yourself and herself, Declan's brother said. When you're feeling better I can bring you home. Bring me home, I repeated, wondering which of us was the stupid one. Are you forgetting where you found me?

He started pacing back and forth over the doctor's linoleum. I can't bring you back to our house because— He stopped short. I swallowed the last of the brandy and held the glass out for more because it was numbing my brain and I didn't want to hear what this brother of Declan was saying, or not saying. The doctor poured another glug.

He stopped his pacing to look at me and he was looking so hard I felt myself blush. Will you stay here? he asked me. Will you keep her here? he asked the doctor. Keep her warm. I think I know.

He didn't say what he thought he knew, then he was off, another man taking charge of my life. But what was I to do only wait, and with the brandy making me drowsy I slept, for half the day, I'd say it was. I half heard the doctor and his nurse coming in and out, keeping an eye, I suppose afraid what I might do. Then the nurse, Lorna, a lovely woman, brought me back my own clothes and said she'd leave me a bit of privacy to get into them. Hadn't she gone and bought new stockings for me – my own must have been destroyed – and my shoes hadn't a trace of muck on them, all clean and polished up as if I was on my way to Mass.

I was starting to panic because the clock told me that it was coming to the end of school time and Adrian would soon be home, and when he found me gone he'd be out looking. I couldn't think how I would explain myself, nor could I imagine what the consequences would be. But then Declan's brother was back, looking flushed. I'll take care of her, he said, and the doctor and nurse looked as if they knew he would. All I cared was that I wasn't going back to Adrian. Can you walk? he asked. Of course I can walk, I said. I was indignant, then I remembered that he'd had to carry me, and I was ashamed of remembering too the feel of my head resting against his chest.

I can walk, I said softer, but I let him take my arm and we walked carefully to his car. He had the engine running and the heat on, and over his free arm was the blanket from the doctor's office, folded neatly, which he tucked in around my legs. Are you right now? he asked, and I noticed that he had kind eyes. I am, I answered. And it was true, in a temporary sort of a way.

We drove for a while and the sun came out. It's to clear up, he said, but we didn't talk most of the time, him respecting that I must be exhausted, me not knowing what to say, or how to ask where we were going or what he had in mind. I fell asleep again at some stage, and when I woke he was pulling up in front of a house I had never seen before.

This house.

He told me about it when we had plenty of time for talking, how he bought it thinking he'd rent it out until such a time as he might start to think about settling down, only he hadn't got around to doing either. So this was where he was to install me. He had the fire already lit, and there was tea and sugar and a loaf of bread in the press, and butter and milk in the fridge. He'd make a list when I told him what I needed, he said, and a bed was all made up for me upstairs. He was embarrassed telling me. I'll be down here – he nodded at the couch – not to be leaving you on your own, not after.

In the awkwardness, all I could manage to ask was what town were we in, and he gave a big warm laugh and told me it was Rathlowney, which was a place I'd never been to. I felt safe enough to say have you a name? Michael, he said. I knew it all along from Declan, but I didn't want to be carrying anything over from Declan.

By the time Adrian heard and came over in his Anglia I was able to open the door bold as brass to him, because I knew Michael was coming back from the shop any minute. Hello, Adrian, I said. He pushed past me into the hall as if he owned it. What in the name of God is going on here, Margaret? So I said what Michael told me to say. I'm living here now. Oh, I hear you are all right, he said in his dangerous voice, with one of the McCarthys I hear.

You hear right, Michael said, coming in the still open front door with his box of groceries. His voice was quiet too but assured. But he doesn't know Adrian, I was saying to myself, the old anxiety flooding back. In sin, Adrian spat back at him, followed by a whole slew of words, language I won't repeat, but the gist of it being that I was not particular which McCarthy I bedded down with, and that no sister of his, and so on, and so on.

You won't use that language about my wife, Michael said in the middle of the poisonous spiel, and he grabbed Adrian by the arm and somehow twisted him around and pushed him towards the door, so fast Adrian didn't know it had happened. Then the door was closed behind him. I didn't know whether to laugh or cry.

That'll give him something to think about, Michael said, when the Anglia had driven off and the house was quiet, and we were stealing glances at each other to see what way to proceed. That was when the whole lot came tumbling out of him, how he knew I had no feelings for him, how could I when I didn't even know him, but what had happened weighed heavy on him. It wasn't right, he repeated several times, and I never should have been sent to that place. He knew nothing of it until Declan sent him a letter from England, more of a note really. Declan should never have let it happen, he said, but he had his weaknesses, and Adrian had persuaded him it was for the best. Nothing could make it right, he said, but at least he could try to make it better. You can't go back to that mad man, he finished, you would have no life at all with him.

He had a proposition, which was that we would get married and he would look after me, and people, Adrian, would have to let us be.

The registry office was a sad-looking place – no girl ever dreamed that her big day would be in a grey office above in Dublin with neither kith nor kin present – and after he brought me for a fancy meal, only I didn't have the appetite for it. Let's get you home then, let you get on with things. I don't want to be interfering, he went on, but if you want me to I can replace your school books. But I said that was a ship that had already sailed. Oh, I felt so old, but I was not yet eighteen, and I was young and silly too. He had a hard time sometimes, knowing how to balance the two with me.

So we came home here, husband and wife, and you can imagine the embarrassment that first night, him getting settled on to the couch, me heading up the stairs feeling as if my back was on fire with him watching. Of course, when I glanced over my shoulder he wasn't looking at me at all, just staring off into space, and I couldn't read his expression.

That night, and the next and the next. And in the mornings he'd drive over to Athlone to the bookies. He'd come back with boxes of whatever I had asked for, and maybe a few bars of chocolate thrown in, or a nice packet of biscuits. I was that glad to see him that I threw my arms around him one of the days, and he drew me gently away from him and held me at arm's length, then he let me go. Was there anything he could do that would make me happy? he asked.

Well, that shook me. Was I happy? Hardly, nor ever could I be. Sitting in a new house in a strange town from one end of the day to the other with nothing to occupy me, I took to going to the library, and I was getting through two books a day some days, and they left my head spinning, half of me in the moors of England or a hundred years back in the United States, while the rest of me was half alive here in Rathlowney. It was like living in endless twilight. I knew I would have to do something. Go back to the river, whispered a part of me, go back and do it right. But the other part, that was lively with foreign places and interesting people, persuaded me that there was many a marriage worse than ours. We were fond of each other, we made each other laugh, and that wasn't easy with me then, but he managed it. He was a good man, and I was ready to try.

I wasn't able to say the words so I kept hold of his arms and, backwards, walked him to the foot of the stairs, then up the first one, then the next. He cottoned on quick enough and picked me up carefully, like I was breakable, forgetting that I was already broken. When we got to the bedroom, he put me down beside the bed, but his courage seemed to be failing him so it was my turn again. I got under the blankets and waited for him to do the same.

It was a long while before anything happened under those blankets, many a week, but it was nice, after being numb for so long. It was nice to feel loved.

I loved him as a child loves a parent; that other part of me had closed itself off. He didn't seem to be disappointed with me, and that was important because no one would go on for ever disappointed. I know you're thinking, how could you? It wasn't fair to him. And it wasn't, in a way, but in another way he got what he wanted, and I got something that passed for a life, not the one I wanted – there was no going back to that one – but compared to going back into the river, it was something.

He was kind – well, you know that – the laughs, the jokes. He told the same jokes a thousand times but he enjoyed them so well you couldn't help joining in. He was forever dreaming up ways to have fun; that was his way. Even his job was more fun than work, listening to the old men spinning their yarns; they were probably more lonely than anything, going into that bookies day in, day out, and he was a welcoming face.

Not that I was through that door more than once. I'm bored here all day, I said sometimes, so one day he brought me. He was tense in the car, the laughing stilled for once, and when we pulled up to Moran's for petrol he lit a Woodbine and went over to the road and paced up and down, smoking the whole thing before Patsy Moran had the tank full. When we got there, there was nothing that I could see to be worrying about. The oul' lads were as friendly as could be, asking me about myself and where I came from, and Michael was proud, I could see that. So what was the matter then?

The matter turned up a few days later, looking the worse for wear, his suit crumpled as if he'd been sleeping in it, his hair needing a good barber, and dear God but he stank. There he was, larger than life, standing on the doorstep of this very house. Declan, back from England.

The sight of him. Nothing could have prepared me. My heart flipped and flopped and floundered, my tongue wouldn't shape any of the words I'd thought over the months, indeed it was nearly two full years since I saw him last, for he had the very look of his son, my son, our son. I shut the door on him and stood with my back to it, trembling.

I could hear him, I suppose not knowing what he would do. Then he said my name twice, Margaret, Margaret. Was he pleading or angry, I couldn't say, but I knew I was no match for facing whatever he was in the mood for. His steps moved away, and I knew he was trying to look in the window, so I stayed where I was. He'd go away if I stayed quiet and didn't answer, I told myself, hoping he couldn't hear my short breaths and my pounding heart.

Eventually it went quiet outside, but I didn't dare open up the door or go to the window. Instead I went up the stairs, on my hands and knees because I hadn't the strength to stand, and into the bedroom and I stayed there with the counterpane over my head, shivering, not able to warm up, until Michael got back. He called up the stairs when he didn't find me in the kitchen, then he was up in three bounds – worried, God love him, about what way he might find me. The relief on him when I came out from hiding. What is it, what is it? he asked.

When I told him he sat on the side of the bed, so quiet you could hear the ticking of the clock below in the kitchen. Are you all right? he asked finally, when I was beginning to think we'd never be able to move again. I don't know, I said truthfully, because it was one thing having a half sort of life and another to have the old one turning up into the middle of it. I'm a bit shaken. I can imagine, was all he said, and then he was gone, down the stairs and out and I could hear the car starting up again. I stayed where I was although I was getting hungry and I needed the toilet, but I hadn't the energy to get up, and I was too cold.

It was dark when I heard the car again. He checked in on me, and I mumbled something so he'd think I was asleep but so he'd know at the same time that I hadn't done anything stupid, then he went downstairs and rattled around the kitchen for a while. He was soon back up with a cup of cocoa and a cheese toasted sandwich, cut into triangles the way I like, and a hot-water bottle, and he helped me get settled with pillows behind me and slipped the hot-water bottle in at my feet. They're stone cold, he said. The cocoa was sweet and warm, and the feeling was coming into my feet, and it was only then I was able to take in the worried expression on his face, so I put a hand to his cheek and told him it'd be okay, it didn't matter, and would he not hurry up and get in and warm me up. God, but I felt sorry for him, for we both knew the truth of it.

We went on like that for another while, was it weeks, maybe months, until I got to being able not to think about Declan every day and started to imagine I might even be happy, content anyway. Of course that's when he turned up again. This time he came to the door a bare few minutes after Michael had gone on to work. I was washing the dishes and contemplating the walk I might take to the river for a few reeds, thinking I'd have a go at a St Brigid's cross, even though it was well after the 2nd of February; that's how much progress I'd made that I could think of the river in that way. But it was such a nice bright morning, and the blackbirds bursting themselves singing. Then came the tap, tap on the door. Jesus, but he put the heart cross-ways in me. Please, he was saying and I trying to shut the door on him, aren't I your brother-in-law? There was a funny look on his face when he said it. Will you not give me the chance to say my piece? He kept a pressure on the door just enough to stop me closing it.

Was I afraid? he asked me after, him turning up like that the first time, looking like something the tide had washed up. No, I had to admit, I could never be afraid of him. Just say it then, I said, letting go of the door. He stepped inside, and I closed it after him, wondering if Maureen or Breda across the road had seen him. I was making an effort to get to know them by now, and it'd be sure to set their tongues wagging, because there wasn't much else going on to liven things up.

The silence of the hall hung over the two of us until I said, a boy, we have a boy. He gave an awful cry then, like an animal, and with that he was on his knees, his arms around my legs, sobbing. I grabbed on to the newel to stop myself wobbling over then I eased myself down to the bottom step, and there we were for God knows how long, clinging on to each other and crying until we had cried ourselves out. Then he sat up again and wiped his face on his sleeve, and I took a hanky out of mine and blew my nose, and we didn't know what to say to each other again.

He took my hand and brought me up the stairs, paused at the door of our bedroom, mine and Michael's, then turned and drew me in to the next room – the spare room, I suppose, for it was surely never talked about as a room for a baby – and he kissing me and pulling the dress off me and I as bad; God, I had missed him. It was only when we were finished that I understood what I was after doing, and I married to his own brother. I broke down then, and he helping me back into my clothes. We'll think of something, he kept saying, taking that *we* for granted, we'll think of something.

He had to get back to the bookies by lunchtime for the busy stretch. I suppose Michael hadn't told me he was back working there because he knew how agitated it would make me. Imagine, they were working there side by side for weeks and saying nothing, or that's the way I pictured it. I spent the day half in shock at what I had done, making cups of tea that I forgot to drink, putting on my coat to go out to the town for a piece of bacon for the dinner then taking it off again because I was full sure that the whole town would know.

When Michael came home, he presented me with a big bunch of lilac that he was after picking in a hedge on the way. Get that out of the house, I screeched at him, it's bad luck. Jesus, Margaret. His big smile collapsed and he closed the door behind him with his foot. You'll have the neighbours thinking I'm murdering you. Look, I'll put it out the back, and he did. Will that do? he said when he came back, and I nodded it would, but the look on his face was full of hurt and confusion, and I burst into tears and ran up the stairs.

What is it, Margaret? He came and sat on the side of the bed where I was sobbing into the counterpane. He was always so kind, so good to me, no matter what new madness came over me, so I couldn't lie to him. Declan was here, I said, looking up at him. He frowned. When? This morning. I willed him to know the rest, not to make me say it. He didn't hurt you, did he? I shook my head. Then why are you in such a state? his expression asked, but without another word he lay down and draped an arm across my back and the two of us fell asleep like that.

When we woke it was already night. I'm starved, he said, will I go to the chipper? I must have nodded to that, and the next thing we were sitting up in bed licking salt and grease off our fingers and swigging on a bottle of lemonade. And when we were finished we went under the covers, still stinking of burgers and chips, and we made love. It was different to what I felt for his brother, but it was different to before, too. Something had opened up in me that I thought was long gone. What sort of a woman was I at all? I wondered, when I fell into sleep in his arms afterwards.

I saw Declan only once or twice a year, that way, but he came calling every Sunday and sometimes week nights as well, whatever kind of peace they were after coming to. For three or four years, I suppose, this went on, and I never knew for sure if Michael knew, but I think he did, and that it was the best any of us could do.

Until you were on the way.

Michael took in the news slowly and said nothing, only he took better care of me if that was possible, always making sure there was no draught on me, that I had an extra lean piece of meat, that there was a bit of chocolate or something nice for afters, driving me up to the doctor more times than I needed to be there. He's a good egg, Dr Lehane said, meaning Michael, and I nodded, but the doctor kept on looking at me anyway.

When you were born, Michael looked hard at you, wondering I suppose were you his, and you looked back just as steady. You were inseparable after that, thanks be to God, and poor Declan got shut out. He'd still come evenings and weekends and look at you for long stretches, lying there in your pram. He wanted to believe too that you were his, not to put too fine a point on it, and not to put too fine a point on it, it was possible that you were.

Michael made things worse when he announced, good Christian that he was, that he thought we should ask Adrian and Maureen to stand for you. Uncle Adrian and Auntie Maureen, your stand-in parents, what about that? he said into the pram to you, and Declan, there for his dinner, listening. He headed out, back home to Athlone on his bike, even though it was raining hard and he hadn't had as much as a cup of tea yet.

Adrian was well married by now, and she was grand, Maureen, happy enough to be the sort of wife Adrian wanted. I needn't tell you we didn't see a whole lot of them over the years, only by now we had you and they had little Adrian toddling around, and when Michael bumped into them one day in the street, he was convinced that Adrian was sorry about everything. God knows what gave him that impression, because I couldn't imagine Adrian ever putting himself in the wrong, but Michael begged me to ask them over for their tea, so I agreed and they came. Thank God for Maureen, because she was a chatterer and kept it all going. Little Adrian was doting on you, but you were only a few weeks old and I was afraid at first that he might hurt you, but she was careful to teach him how to be gentle. Still, I couldn't wait to get you back into my arms, and it was an almighty relief when they were gone. I let go muscles that had tightened up without my noticing. It went well, Michael said when we were at last on our own. They're your family, Margaret, and we can't choose our families. All we can do is make the best of them. He paused, and I could see that his thoughts had gone somewhere else, but you gave a gurgle and brought him back. Maureen dotes on her, and after all, little Adrian is Rosemary's only cousin.

Sure what could I say, though it broke Declan's heart, that fecker standing for you. I knew because he didn't come to the church. He turned up late to the hotel do, full of drink, and stood over your pram like a bad fairy. You needn't worry, it wasn't you he was making the spells over, it was Adrian. They stood at opposite ends of the function room, Adrian and Declan, and there wasn't a move one of them made that the other didn't know about. You'd nearly have expected one of them to draw a gun. But Declan was too much the worse for wear to do anything, and in the end he slipped a few pounds into the foot of your pram and stumbled away.

The next day, Michael came home and announced that Declan would be buying him out of the bookies. He said he had something else lined up for himself. What's the new job, Michael? I asked. Travelling with Armer Salmon, he said, going around the countryside talking to farmers. What do you know about farming? I asked. There was something about the new arrangement that I didn't like, though I couldn't have said why. Enough, he said. Then he remembered to smile. It's just a lot of sales patter, sure amn't I talking shite in that place from one end of the day to the other? Not in front of Rosemary, I said. If you're sure, I said. I'm sure, he said.

I was on my own a good bit after that. By the time you were five or six, Michael was gone half the week, staying up in the North, or over in England sometimes, and I was lonely. I had you, but I was lonely.

Then came that Saturday. I knew there was something about it when I woke to the rain pelting down, and I could feel something pressing down on me. God knows it was a feeling I got used to afterwards. It was so dark outside you'd swear it was still night but it was already late enough, and the wind, I was sure it would take the roof off. You were already up and pottering around downstairs, so up I got and got on with it. I was worrying that Michael wouldn't be able to get the ferry home from England, that it'd be cancelled with rough seas. I had the radio on the whole day, listening to Met Éireann. You were bored and contrary because you couldn't go out, and I was short-tempered with you, I admit that; when will Daddy be here? When will Daddy be here? – driving me mad. You were delighted when you heard the door opening, but I was more wary.

It was Declan, bringing the wildness in with him. He was after cycling over in that weather. How he didn't get blown off his bike into the ditch I'll never know. Shut the door, you eejit, I said, frightened and excited both to see him again, especially with the dark strange day it was. He must have felt it too, I thought at first, because he came in laughing. But I soon realised that he had been drinking. I closed up shop early, he told us. There wasn't a sinner in the town, all gone home to close in livestock and batten down the hatches. Is that not bad for business? I asked him, trying to look cross, but worrying about what might be happening. Feck the business, he said, and gave me a smack on the bottom. The child, I said, but I couldn't help catching the giddiness off him, we were cooped up so long in the bad weather. Ta-da, he said with a wink to me, pulling a bag of goodies out from under his wet coat and handing them to you. You'll ruin her tea, I said. Mammy won't mind if you have just a bit, he told you, and there's a new Secret Seven in there, they had them in at the Gem. Well, you snatched it away – you'd just got the hang of reading and there was no stopping you – off to your hidey hole beside the hot press.

She'll be all right for a while, Declan told me, laughing. He took me by the hand and up the stairs. Well, he made love to me like there was no tomorrow, the first time since you were born, and it felt like I had been waiting for him the whole time because, God help me, I loved that man like I never loved anyone.

It was over and I was coming down the stairs, pushing hair back behind my ear when I heard the car door slam, but it was too late for Declan; he was taking the last few steps down and shoving his shirt into his trousers as the hall door opened and Michael came in with a blast of wind and rain looking exhausted. He looked from me to Declan and back. Then you came running from your little nest. Look what Uncle Declan brought me, Daddy.

I'll drive you back, he said to Declan without a word to me. Declan must have known there was no point in arguing; he just followed his brother slowly. I closed the door on the two of them and the house went terrible quiet. I didn't know what to do with myself I was that agitated. You sensed not to bother me and went back to your reading. I thought about packing up a bag and leaving as soon as Michael got back. Then I thought about packing no bag but just going out the door as soon as you were asleep and back to the river, for all the problems I was causing. But I did neither. You went up to bed, glad I suppose to get away from me, and I sat on listening to the ticking of the clock and the howling of the wind. It had got itself up into a real storm now, but there was still no sign of Michael when the clock passed eight, and then nine, and I turned on the news then I turned it off again. I waited as the clock pushed on to ten, and by now I knew someone would be coming to the door, one way or another.

The knocking woke you and you came to the top of the stairs in your nightie. Go back to bed, I said. There was an accident, the Garda said, a tree down in the storm. I shouldn't be here on my own, was there anyone they could contact, any family members, neighbours?

All my family is gone, I told them calmly, my mother, my father, my little boy blue, and now Michael and Declan. So, no, there is no one, no one at all they could contact. Uncle Adrian and Auntie Maureen, you piped up. I hadn't seen you come down. Where does Uncle Adrian live, he asked you, as if you were the one in charge and I was the child. They're in Athlone, you told them, proud that you knew.

There was a drive in the back of the Garda car that I don't remember but you might, and back into my old room in Adrian's. If you're going to live in a nightmare you might as well do it right. But at least I had you. Rosemary can go into the back bedroom, Maureen said, meaning well; she had it all made up nice. I often wondered if Maureen knew anything at all about what Adrian had done. No. I said it loud enough and clear enough that she didn't ask again; this time I was keeping my baby with me.

They poured gallons of sweet tea into us over the days that followed. There was a church and a burial; they went into the cold ground, one beside the other, with their dead parents. I saw straight away that there was no room left in the grave for me. There was talk after. Declan had been the one driving, they said, and there was a branch down sure enough, but it wasn't on their side of the road, there wasn't even a need for them to go around it, just to make sure no one else was coming towards them, and no one was for the roads were nearly deserted that night. He drove straight into it, they said. Sure Declan didn't even drive, I was thinking.

There was a solicitor's office then, and a will. Michael had seen to it that things were in order before he moved jobs, and so it seemed had Declan, at some stage, though you'd never have thought he was the type; the two of them looking out for us. You'll want for nothing, the solicitor said.

But there was no describing the want they left me with, emptied out with the wanting, I was, but there was you. So even as all hollowed out as I was I had to keep going, thinking that maybe when you were grown I could take myself back to the river to float away at last.

Days passed somehow, and a month was up. I hardly knew who I was mourning, there were so many. So many that it started to come to me that I was cursed. You had your cousin to play with, and Maureen fussing over you, the girl she had not managed to have, brushing and brushing your hair until you'd yelp and wriggle away. I steered well clear of Adrian, I can tell you, but you were not a bit afraid of him. How I admired you, standing up to him for poor little Adrian, who'd be hiding with his mouth open, waiting for the fallout that didn't come. Sure it couldn't come now, and you only a little child without a father, and a shell for a mother lying in a darkened room upstairs; even Adrian couldn't lift a hand to you.

What a set-up. Temporary, that was the understanding, yet somehow the month stretched into three, and September came around and you wondering when you were going home to your friends, back to school. Sure we'll take her in with us, Uncle Adrian said, and I couldn't lift my head from the pillow. Why not? Maybe I was thinking, what difference does it make, what difference did anything make? And off you went, excited and annoyed, but soon you had new friends, and little Adrian, God help him, he was delighted to have you there. We went on like that past the anniversary, and there we still were coming up to the second.

Maureen's miscarriage then, her third, laid her low. We'll get out of your way, I told Adrian, because I was not able to be around him without her cheerful buffer between us. We would go home. A right state it'll be in, Adrian said, but he could see his power over me – over us – was gone. Besides, he had Maureen to worry about. You complained that you'd miss your new friends but I brushed your worry away, telling you you'd have your old friends. It turned out you were right, though, you never properly fitted back in, did you?

223

We were back less than a week, all the old things where we left them, the house full of memories we were hardly able to bear, when Adrian drove over to tell us about Maureen. They had found a lump, would we keep Adrian for a while? It was a welcome diversion, but poor Maureen went fast, God rest her, and when she was gone there wasn't much reason for him to stay on with us. He belonged at home with his father, that was what Adrian said, and there wasn't much arguing with that. And we were left with each other.

If I kept you at arm's reach it was for your own good. You were independent well before your time, making your breakfasts and lunches, taking money out of my purse to get the few messages on your way home from school, the things you could manage yourself: a few slices of corned beef, a tin of beans, packets of oxtail or minestrone soup. I couldn't stomach anything much, a few spoons of cornflakes for lunch, or a bite of the sandwiches you brought up to the room. I only forced them down to please you. And the cups of sweet tea. I always hated tea with sugar but I drank it and it warmed me. You'd open the curtains wide and tell me what it was like outside because I hadn't the energy to sit up to see for myself. Then you were off when you were satisfied that I had eaten something. Where did you learn to be such a good little nurse? Back downstairs then to do your homework, and on a good day you'd persuade me later with hot-water bottles and cocoa to come down and watch *Quicksilver* or *The Riordans*.

It was you who got me through it, you, and the foolish little hope that nothing and no one had ever diminished, that one day I'd see my little boy blue again.

We had some good times then. Do you remember going over to the Ritz in Tullamore, when we could get a lift? It was the raspberry ripple in the twist cups you always went for. And there were the annual trips with the parish to Knock, not what you'd call good for laughs but it was nice to get an outing all the same. You used to mither me non-stop to learn how to drive but how was I to get behind the wheel of a car after what happened? You'd get your licence the minute you turned seventeen, you said, and you trounced out in a temper. That was when it started to go sour between us, what with you getting into your teens and me getting through the days with the help of the drink.

It was discos up at the Rugby Club next, and you wouldn't be told to stay home. You wanted to be chasing boys, or whatever the attraction was, and let school work be damned – not drinking, I hope, though I never got the smell of it off you, thanks be to God – and once the rows started it seemed as if there was just no end to them. I didn't know what to do with you, to be honest. I was this close to sending you over to let Adrian deal with you, only I couldn't bring myself to do it. I'd sooner see you going off the rails altogether, and off the rails you were headed. Did you go to school at all in the end? I wonder, staying out late, hanging around street corners with the worst of the worst from Father Murphy Road, the ones you'd cross the street to avoid, with their smoking and spitting, and the language out of them. And one day there you were in the middle of them. I wanted to catch you by the ear and yank you all the way home. You must have seen it in my face because you decided you had less to lose by sauntering away from your new pals and away down the town.

I was waiting for you when you turned the key in the door. Up that stairs, young lady, and get into that bath, and wash that gunk out of your hair, sticking up like that, they won't let you through the school doors, and don't go wiping that paint off your face on to my clean towels. Make sure it's well and truly washed, and don't slather half the jar of cold cream all over yourself either, and give the bath a good wipe around when you're finished, don't be leaving a mucky tidemark there for me to scrub, I'm not your skivvy. Your dinner is on a plate in the fridge and I don't want you wasting it, and you can wash your plate and put it away, because I already did the washing-up and I'm not going to be starting again just because you finally decide to grace us with your presence.

Once I started at you I couldn't stop. The very next day you were gone, and is it any wonder you left?

Dublin, 2012

It was quite a legacy, Mam. There I was, half conscious on the bed – appendicitis, it turned out, and getting punched in the gut by a girl twice my size was the very thing to bring it to a head – and what lucid moments I had were filled with self-pity: George was gone, boxing was gone, my adventures were over and I was back in Rathlowney, at the mercy of my mother. I wanted to take a great big fistful of those tablets and die. But there you were, on your cocktail of Valium and gin, or whatever it was you were drinking those days, standing watch over me as if I were a prisoner and you a demented Scheherazade, telling your story that I thought would never end, in what felt like one long breath, never giving me the chance to do anything.

I suppose you didn't know whether I could hear you or not. You never alluded to your story again, and I never acknowledged that I'd heard it, but your words sifted and seeped through the haze in spite of me. Can you hear me now, Mam?

There is no sign. If it wasn't for your breathing you could be gone, you look that peaceful. I wouldn't begrudge you. You wanted to go for so long, yet you stayed, for me. It can't have been easy for you, sobering up enough to get me back fit and well, then putting up with me while I moped around declaring that my life was over, that there was nothing for me in Rathlowney. Only now I knew that there was nothing there for you either. It wasn't until years later that I understood that what was there for both of us was the other one.

But then, I was still groping around in my self-absorbed fog, and it was your story, the snatches that kept coming back to me, that gradually showed me that there was more to the world than myself. I pulled myself together enough to agree to do an early school leaver course, as long as it was in the next town over, and you pulled yourself together enough to see me on to the bus every morning, and to greet me every evening with a dinner. The rest of the time we worked around each other, like rescue animals, still wary of their new home. But we got there in the end, didn't we, Mam? The line of As on the Leaving Cert results sheet, the college acceptance. We had survived some delicate, critical, impossible stage, and now we could move on; in my case to college, and in yours to your sort of retreat from life.

I think it was a relief to both of us when I moved up to Dublin. I never told you what that was like. How could I, because I would have had to tell you everything that had happened before so you could understand the contrast between my old life in Dublin and my studious, funded, sheltered new life. I was grateful, but I kept myself busier than I should have, and I rarely made it back to Rathlowney. Then I had my years away with Médecins sans Frontières. I kept a check on you. I was surprised to hear that you'd made your peace with Uncle Adrian, I can tell you. *United in strife*, you wrote. I couldn't quite figure out whether you meant the antipathy between the two of you, or that you had found a bond in your wayward children. Because Adrian would have gone missing around then, wouldn't he? I was in Somalia at the time, so it all seems very unreal to me. I never believed he could just disappear. He was sure to turn up again at some stage, like he always had. It was just as well I was away, because that way I didn't have to withhold information from the Gardaí. Not that I knew much, just about the gambling. But Uncle Adrian had enough information about that. Poor Uncle Adrian.

I have him to thank for keeping me informed when you started to get bad again, and when you started doing things that were, as he said, out of the ordinary. He was the one who let me know that you couldn't go on living alone. He suggested that you live with him, but even with your newfound truce I didn't think you'd want that. That's when we tried living together again, in my place. It was a disaster, wasn't it? You were used to doing things your way, and you didn't like the city. I was worried sick about what might befall you while I was at work. Anita was a godsend for a while, then Yana. But it wasn't long before you needed more structured care. That's why we found this place, isn't it? It wasn't that I was trying to get rid of you, Mam.

—She knows you were not, Jasmine.

It's Ana. She must have slipped in.

—Ana. You must think we're starting to go a little bit mad in here.

—We're all a little bit mad, she says, laughing. —How is our patient?

Here, Jasmine is a daughter, not a doctor, and Ana is not expecting medical answers. Or any answers, really. She moves around, taking readings, doing her job.

—I'm trying to make sense of it all, Ana. How foolish that sounds, to wait until now.

—It is only at the end that we can look back with some perspective, Ana says, as she fills in the chart.

She looks at Ana curiously, wondering what it must be like to work with the dying every day – the opposite to her own, literally life-affirming job. What sort of existential crises must it induce? Or perhaps it brings this sort of wisdom.

—She doesn't have long, does she?

Jasmine is well aware that she sounds like every desperate relation of a sick family member who asks because they hope to be reassured, and Ana reassures.

—These little setbacks come and go, she says, settling the sheet neatly near her mother's neck, but not suffocatingly so. —She could be right as the rain in the morning.

Ana doesn't add what they both know, that a small development could finish off a patient with such advanced Alzheimer's.

—Thanks, Ana.

They both consider the tiny woman for a moment. To Ana, she must appear quite peaceful. But Ana doesn't know the demons her mother has wrestled with for most of her life.

—I wish I could do something.

The words feel useless even as she says them, and finish in a choking sob. Ana takes her hand and places it gently over her mother's wounded one and, with a small smile, withdraws.

Tennessee, 2012

A few minutes later, we're turning into an estate of tract houses. By now I know Kit is a medical student in UT, home for a visit.

—But my mom works a lot of shifts, so I've got the place to myself a lot. Which is good because I have finals coming up. You got lucky, today is her day off.

—I doubt your mom will see it that way.

Kit laughs.

—She likes taking care of people. If she could keep me at home, she would.

We pull up outside one of the houses, and we're still undoing our seat belts when the front door is flung open. Kit's mom is already at my side of the car, helping me out and quizzing me about my injuries, while Kit protests that I need to get inside first and lie down.

—Who's the nurse here? Kit's mom sticks out her hand. —I'm Sally-Anne. Not that Kit wouldn't make a great nurse. I've been telling her that her whole life but what does she do? Goes to the dark side.

—She means medicine, Kit says.

The shady room is cool and safe and for the first time since I left the marina, to my mortification I start to cry, great big unstoppable heaves. Sally-Anne puts an arm around me and lets me sob for a bit, then she magics some Kleenex out of somewhere. I dab my eyes and blow my nose and regain some kind of composure.

—Come on, honey, let's take a look.

She scans up and down, just like Kit did at the gas station, and just like Kit she works out plenty in seconds flat.

—Nothing life-threatening, but that's one ugly knee.

—Thanks. I manage a small smile.

—Here's what we'll do. I'll run you a nice hot bath. It'll sting, but it's the best way to get you cleaned up. Then I'll dress that cut, and we'll decide about your ankle and wrist. If you're lucky, you'll get away with a sprain, but we'll still need to bandage it up.

Kit has the water running by the time her mom gets me to the bathroom. Together, they sit me on a chair, and I'm totally dying because I know I'm going to bleed everywhere.

—Don't worry about bleeding all over the house, her mom says cheerfully, like she can read my mind. —We're used to it. Besides, that's what kitchen towels are for. And help yourself to anything else you need. Oh, and we'll find you something of Kit's to wear. Want some help getting undressed?

I shake my head, and they leave me alone. As soon as the door closes, I begin to cry again. They are being too kind. I start peeling off clothes, very carefully, because the blood has dried in places. With only one hand my progress is slow, and it hurts. I get my jeans off and get rid of the clumped and bloodied toilet paper. There's so much of it I'm worried it'll block the toilet, but it flushes away in one, and I already feel better. There's Tampax and stuff in the cabinet, and I help myself like Sally-Anne told me. I'm surprised that I feel sort of okay down there. I don't know what I expected. I guess the damage isn't physical. At least I have my period, which I think means I should be okay, but as soon as I'm done here I'll get to a drugstore and buy a test.

I work out how to get into the bath without putting weight on the right foot or the left wrist, and it feels so good to lower my butt into the water that I forget to watch out for the knee – *fuck*, it hurts. I gasp.

232

Kit bursts into the bathroom.

—What is it? Are you okay? Should I get my mom?

—I'm okay. It was my knee. Sorry for giving you a scare.

—Phew. That's a relief. She turns away, to give me privacy.

—Look, Ali. It's none of my business, but it looks to me like you want to get away from somewhere, or someone. I don't need details, but maybe I can help?

I'm pretty sure I can trust her, but I'm still scared.

—What makes you think I'm running away?

—Your paperwork. I couldn't help looking when I was picking it up. Who carries their birth certificate around, and their family photographs? And you acted scared.

So that's what's in there. I guess I already knew, but not for sure.

She hands me a towel from a pile on a shelf.

—Here you go. Better get that knee patched up. There's a robe on the door when you're done.

She starts to leave.

—Wait.

I manage to stand and wrap the towel around me, careful to hold it away from the still weeping cut.

—You're right. I am trying to get away. My mom died, and my dad's parents, who I never even met before, turned up and I had to go live with them. The bike . . .

—Not your brother's, I'm guessing?

—I don't have a brother. I don't have anyone.

—Except your grandparents? she prompts.

I shrug.

—Sure. Only I don't remember my dad. Plus, he was adopted, so they're not real grandparents.

—So you have no family?

—Nope.

—You just want to get away from your grandparents?

I nod.

—Okay. Well, let's get you fixed up first. Then we can figure something out.

Like having a bloodied runaway turn up is no big deal. I like these people.

Her mom has her big first-aid box out when I emerge after a good soak, and soon she has me bandaged and band-aided and ready to get dressed. Kit takes me to her room, where she tells me to choose anything. I pick sweat pants and a loose-looking T-shirt, figuring I'm probably a size bigger.

—Feel better? her mom asks.

—It feels great to be clean.

—And not bleeding, Kit adds.

I laugh.

—I bet you're hungry though, her mom says. —We were just about to have pancakes.

I must look doubtful, but Kit pulls an Aunt Jemima pancake mix out of her purse.

—It's why I went to the gas station. I was going to treat my hard-working mom to breakfast in bed, but as usual she was up before I left.

Soon we're helping ourselves from a steaming pile of pancakes, washed down with juice and coffee. Between us, we demolish the lot. Sally-Anne starts clearing up the dishes. She waves away my offer to help.

—I'm going to do some laundry. I'll put your things in, but they won't be dry for a while. You want to go take a nap?

—Yeah, go ahead, Ali, Kit says. —I have an essay I need to work on. What say you rest, I work, then we talk about what you want to do?

It hits me just how exhausted I am, and I don't even try to protest. Kit helps me to the bed in the spare room. She leaves me, and I have never felt so glad of a bed. The room is cool and dark, a safe haven where no one can find or hurt me, and I guess I was tense since for ever, because my body collapses on to the mattress and it feels like I might never be able to move again.

I don't know where I am when I wake. I can't remember what

I was dreaming, just that it wasn't good. I only remember my ankle when I try to get out of bed. That's when my brain gradually starts putting events together. It tries to slide over the part about Mom, and the storage park, and where was Mom when I needed her. I start shaking like it's real cold, and I'm crying again, and I guess I'm loud, because Kit and her mom come rushing in.

Sally-Anne pulls the comforter up around my shoulders and leaves her arm there. That's when I can't keep it all in any more, and I tell them everything, even the hard stuff. *Oh my*, Sally-Anne keeps saying, *Oh my God*. When I get to the part where she found me in the gas station, Kit asks me if I want to call the police. I'm confused.

—He should be in jail, she says.

For a minute I don't know who she means. I just explained how I'm running away from Danny and my grandparents. I don't want to deal with him again.

—I cut off his ponytail and stole the bike. They'll be after me. That's why I have to get going.

I make an attempt to get up.

—Oh honey. Sally-Anne gives me a hug, at the same time keeping me right there on the bed.

Kit spells it out.

—They're not after you, Ali. Right now they are going as fast as they can in the opposite direction of where they think you are. They are in so much shit right now and they know it. You do not have to be afraid of those assholes. If they come anywhere near here I'll have them strung up.

She sounds really mad.

—Well done on the ponytail, she adds, with a flash of mischievousness.

—It did feel good, I say. —But there's my grandparents too, they're gung-ho about the whole guardianship thing. I think it's their guilty conscience or something.

Kit shrugged, like this was no big deal.

235

—Give them a call. Tell them you're sixteen and you're getting married. This is Tennessee, after all.

We're all giggling now, but I guess she's right.

—So here's the deal, she continues. —You're staying here until you can walk properly and use your wrist. Mom's orders. I'm going to hang around for a week or so until I get these essays done, so you might have to watch a lot of TV. Think you can handle that?

Stay here for a while, in this cool, safe room, figure things out?

I try to hug both of them at once.

—Not so fast, Kit says. —We are also going to meddle in your business until you can't wait to get away. Right, Mom?

Sally-Anne smiles.

—Let's just say, it was quiet around here until you showed up.

—I could use quiet, I tell her.

They get down to business right away. Sally-Anne fetches a key for me, even though I tell them I'm not planning on leaving the house. They reinstate Kit's old desktop computer in what they're calling my room. They have to make several trips with arms full of cable and keyboard and monitor and speakers while I'm just laying there on the bed with my leg elevated – Kit's mom's doing – feeling useless. After one last trip for an extension cord, and some more hooking up, the computer whirrs into life. Kit sticks a Post-it on the top of the screen with internet and Netflix codes.

—There. Good to go.

I thank her yet again, but she cuts me off.

—New rule. No more thanks. Take something for granted once in a while, kid. I bet if I turned up at your mom's boat all beat up she would've done the same for me.

It was true. Mom collected strays, all the time. She couldn't help herself. It was way too crowded on our tiny boat, but it usually worked out. Strangers were angels in disguise, she used to tell me. I thought it was hippy new-age shit, but it turns out it's from the Bible. My mom, the heathen, quoting the Bible. Whatever. I'm just glad I washed up with folks who think a bit like her.

—Okay, I say.

—Good. Okay, I'd better get to work. You won't see me until I get my Introduction finished. You need anything before I disappear?

—Nothing. Go do your Introduction.

—Holler if you need anything.

—Your Introduction.

She gives me a grin and she leaves, and I hobble to the computer. I've been missing my phone, and it doesn't take me long to bring up Zombie Smash. Pretty soon I'm crushing zombies like it's the only thing that matters. I'm totally zoned out when Kit calls me for dinner.

—Yeah, I love that one, she says with a nod to the computer. —Banned it from my laptop though. Time suck.

—Yeah, works for me right now.

—I'm sure. You like pizza?

It's just the two of us. I guess I was too caught up in my zombie war to hear Sally-Anne leave. Kit shoves the frozen pie in the oven and I manage to make a salad, and soon we're eating dinner. She makes me laugh with funny stories about college, and I try to imagine what it would be like to have a sister. Or even a brother. I think it would be cool, less lonely. Especially now.

—So, plans? she's asking.

—I hope to get to the next level before I go to sleep. Zombies, I add when she doesn't understand.

—I like that you're ambitious.

—Thank you. I mock-bow.

—You'll be impressed to hear that my Introduction is now complete.

—I am.

—And that I am ready for my next project.

—Which is?

She turns serious. I have a feeling I know what's coming. I guess it had to, sooner or later.

—To help you figure out what you want to do. I mean, you can stay here as long as you want. My mom would totally love a surrogate daughter, but I'm guessing Johnson City wasn't the plan, as cool as it is . . .

We both laugh.

—No, I admit. —I just got off the highway to get gas. And pancakes.

—So you were headed towards Birmingham?

—I just needed to put some space between me and the bikers.

—You sure you don't want to call the cops?

I'd thought about it since she first asked, but I really didn't ever want to see any of those guys again. Only an idiot would have gone on the road with them in the first place. I shake my head.

—It's not your fault, Ali.

She's getting pretty good at reading my thoughts.

—I guess. But I don't want to see them, and I don't want to have to explain to the police why I was running. I'm scared they'll want to bring me back to Baltimore.

—So what's it like, at your grandparents'?

I tell her about the big fancy house, and how they don't actually like having me around, and about the school they want to send me to, and she just listens until I'm done.

—Let me get this straight. Your dad left your mom when you were little. What happened to him? Did you ever see him again?

—My mom told me they found his body in the Patapsco River. It had been there for days. No one had reported him missing. I think he had turned into sort of a drifter. He was a drinker. So he might've fallen in accidentally, or he could've killed himself. To be honest, he took off on my mom and me, so I don't care which.

Kit is nodding the whole time.

—So his parents figured they were responsible for you after your mom died.

—I guess. Only they're not his real parents.

—What about your mom's family?

—Her parents died before I was born. No brothers or sisters. I think my mom's mom had a sister, but I don't even know her name.

—Wow. So you really have no family.

—Thanks, I say. Then I'm sorry, because she's immediately apologising, and she's been so nice, so I start apologising, but she cuts me off.

—No, you're right. I wasn't being sensitive. It's just, I have a huge family. Not so much on my Dad's side, but my mom is Irish, so I have, like, forty cousins. We go there every few years. It's a riot.

—I guess I'm Irish too, I tell her. —It's where my dad was adopted from.

—See, that's our project right there.

I don't get what she means, so she elaborates.

—We trace your dad's family. That way, at least you know more about who you are.

I don't know what to think. My mom wanted me to have nothing to do with my dad after he left. But I'm still feeling bad for giving Kit a hard time, and besides, it'll probably turn out to be a dead-end. I push back my chair and stand up.

—Woah, woah, woah, where are you off to?

—To get that file. The one you picked up all over the gas station. I think that's our starting point.

—You're up for it?

—Why not? Maybe we'll find out we're related.

She laughs.

—Maybe. But you, lady, are going to sit back down and let me do the walking.

My ankle is pretty painful, so I sit, and Kit goes for the file. I can't believe it never occurred to me to do this before, but I guess until my mom died there was no need.

Kit comes back with the file, and right there, on her kitchen counter, we begin. She's real methodical, taking notes, sorting stuff, Googling.

—It used to be impossible to find this stuff out, she tells me as she types in her search. —It seems the Catholic Church in Ireland had it all sewn up. But I guess the nuns have been toppled or something, because you can find out all kinds of stuff right here online.

I lean in to read, but it's lists and lists of data, and I don't know what I'm looking for.

—You have his birth cert. That's unusual. It's pretty much all you need. If he had wanted to meet his birth mom, it would come down to whether she was still alive and if she wanted to meet him or not.

It's hard to think about a mom giving away her baby and not wanting to see him again. How ironic that he did kind of the same thing with me.

—Did he know he was adopted? Kit asks.

—The grandparents are the buttoned-up type who prefer to keep things secret. I think he only found out when he was an adult.

—That must have been tough on him.

—I guess.

It makes me think, though.

When Sally-Anne gets home we're still working, and she gets all excited when she hears what we're doing.

—I just knew you were Irish. It's your complexion.

My mom liked to say she was half Scottish, half Iroquois, and half sea-creature. *That makes you a mermaid*, she'd tell me when I was little. *Come let me comb your hair.* It was part of the never-ending battle to tame my blonde mane, which was

240

always in a tangle from the wind and the salt. Even now, unless I'm really good about brushing and conditioning, it still matts into dreads. It's why I keep it shoulder length. Mom's was the same. Everyone said I look a lot like her, so I never thought much about my dad's origins.

—So we've reached a dead-end here, Kit says, closing her laptop. —We have your dad's mother's name, and we've traced the Mother and Baby Home through the Adoption Authority in Ireland. Next, we need to find out if she's alive, and if she's willing to meet Ali. Sorry, Ali, she adds.

I shrug. It's not like I'm going to get sentimental about it. But it is weird finding out you maybe have a grandma, a real one. Weird, and kind of exciting. Kit and Sally-Anne think so too, because they're coming up with all kinds of ideas about trips to Ireland. They'll visit Sally-Anne's relatives, kiss the Blarney Stone, whatever that is, maybe find a nice Irishman for Kit in Lisdoonvarna. They're laughing like drains at that one, until Kit notices my expression. I've no idea what they're talking about, and besides, right now, a trip to the grocery store feels impossible, let alone Ireland.

—Hang on, Mom, not so fast. You're forgetting . . .

—Ankles heal, honey, Sally-Anne says, still giddy with plans.

—What if Ali doesn't want to go to Ireland? What if she doesn't have a passport? What about her other grandparents? Am I right? She turns to me.

I don't know what to say. Sally-Anne comes and puts her arm around me.

—Oh, honey, I'm sorry. I'm just talking crazy nonsense. It's just we had so much fun when we went a couple of years ago. And I'm not kidding about the husband. This old guy – heck, I thought he was too old for me – set his sights on Kit and wouldn't take no for an answer. He had the deeds of his farm back on some mountain *in his pocket*. Took them out right there in the bar. The whole place cheered. I never saw Kit so embarrassed.

—That's okay. Truth is, I don't know what to think.

—Hey, there's no reason to think at all, Kit says. —You could've gone your whole life not knowing, and nothing would be any different than it is now.

That's easy for Kit to say, but there's no avoiding the fact that my whole life has turned into *before* and *now,* and sooner or later I'm going to have to make plans of some kind. There's about a hundred reasons this trip is not going to happen: my wrist, my ankle, my lack of a passport, my other grandparents, who might this very minute be trying to track me down to take me back to Baltimore, and the big one: if this woman is even alive, who says she'd want to meet me. The last thing I need right now is some new-found relative who wants nothing to do with me. But Kit and Sally-Anne are waiting for me to say something.

—I guess there's no harm in finding out if she's alive, I tell them at last.

Kit's query to the Adoption Authority comes back at last to say that my dad's mom is alive, as far as they are aware, and her name is on their register, which means we can try to contact her. There's no email, though, just an address, so we send a letter by snail mail. It takes for ever to write. Where do you even start? But Kit tells me just to say whatever I feel like saying, so I get it done, and then we wait. Meantime, she decides I should get my passport, even if I decide not to go, because everyone should have a passport. She drives me to Birmingham and we get it sorted without any problems. The toughest job is telephoning my grandparents. Sally-Anne keeps telling me I'll feel much better when I do, so I bite the bullet and call. It's like Kit said, they can't force me to come back. I tell them I'm okay, but I don't want to live with them, and they sound kind of relieved. I tell them I'll write them, though I doubt I ever will.

—So, have you decided if you want to meet your grandma if she replies? Kit asks a few weeks later. She's home for the weekend, and I'm super-pleased to see her. I hardly see Sally-Anne because, like Kit said, she works a lot of hours. My injuries have healed, and I'm starting to get antsy from hanging around playing dumb-ass computer games. I've tried to come up with plans, going west like I originally thought, but now I know how it is to land up in some strange town, I'm not sure I want to. I couldn't have got luckier than Kit and Sally-Anne, but what are the odds of a repeat? I've been wondering what Mom would have me do, or, better, what she would do herself. *Let's take it out on the water.* I miss the boat. I miss my mom. But since I can't do anything about either, I've started to think this trip might not be such a bad idea. I even take out my new passport and try to imagine what an Ireland stamp would look like on one of its pristine pages, but then I get scared about the whole thing and put it away again. So, have I decided? I don't know until I open my mouth.

—If she's willing to meet me, I guess.

—Well, I have mid-term coming up. Mom will need to look at her schedule, start figuring out dates—

—Actually . . . I mean, you guys have been amazing, but I think I should do the trip alone.

Again, I didn't know I was about to say it until it was said. There's this long pause while Kit examines my face. I can feel myself colouring. She's probably thinking I'm a total ingrate, after everything they've done for me. Finally, she smiles.

—Good for you.

I hug her with relief.

—It'll be awesome. Broadens the mind. Then she draws back, and makes a stern face.

—But so does college. After the trip, you're coming back to Johnson for a bit. Your room will be waiting. Besides, we're going to want to hear all about it.

*

There's an email in Kit's inbox the next day. It's two lines, but it says everything I need to hear. *I was overwhelmed by your letter. Please visit us at the earliest opportunity.* It's signed, *Your Aunt,* followed by a long list of phone numbers and addresses.

Dublin, 2012

Although she has been expecting it, when the doorbell rings it makes her jump. She points the remote at the TV and plunges the room into uncharacteristic silence. She wants to absorb the moment, to gather her thoughts. But ever since the letter, forwarded by Uncle Adrian, she has been unable to do any such thing.

In practical matters, she has been more successful. She declined the job offer, which almost took care of the other matter: Jeffrey. She flew over, nevertheless, and explained, and he was as gracious as she knew he would be, and they parted civilly. The relief she felt as she got on to the Heathrow Express was overwhelming. She wondered if she would have felt the same way if she hadn't had her news, and the curious turn it brought about.

A few weeks before, she had left what she thought was her mother's deathbed, under instruction from Ana and Sheila to go home, have a shower, and get some rest. The next day, as she got ready to go back in, trying to prepare herself for what was possibly a last goodbye, a letter dropped on to the mat. She almost didn't open it, but the US stamps and the handwritten address to Mr Adrian Murphy, which had been crossed out and replaced with her address in her elderly uncle's shaky hand, persuaded her, and how glad she was. Its lines, covering both sides of a single page in a mix of question-statements that sounded simultaneously cocky and scared, reminded her of herself long ago, but it was their simple existence, rather than their content or style, that mattered.

She couldn't wait to get to the home, where she read it to her mother before even taking off her jacket; after all, it was really meant for her. Within an hour, the fever had dropped, and her mother was sitting up in bed. Oh, it was no Lazarus resurrection. She resumed staring at the walls, as she had done for years, but still it seemed – still seems – like a small miracle.

She moves into the hall like a sleepwalker. So much for collecting her thoughts. Automatically she looks through the peephole, and there is a girl, staring right back at her. She has never seen her before, but one look is enough. Even before she opens the door, the green-flecked-with-gold eyes are enough to tell her that there will be no need for exclamations and pretence. She knows those eyes, because they are the same as her own. She knows this Ali like herself.

Ali is starting to consider forgetting the whole thing, and making a run for it. The leafy Dublin street with its row of dark brick houses is getting more alien by the second while she waits for the door to open. Maybe she'll go west here in Ireland instead, find one of those old farmers to marry. Then it's too late. The door opens and a woman about her mom's age is standing there in the block of light.

—It's bucketing out here, Ali says, mostly to cover how nervous she's feeling.

Jasmine steps aside, and Ali goes past, throwing a mangled umbrella back out behind her. It lands on the pavement like a pair of broken wings.

—Thing is fucked anyway.

Jasmine shuts the door on the umbrella and the rain, and examines her guest. She's soaking wet.

—That thing really was fucked, she says. She hasn't sworn in years, but Ali's arrival has stripped her back to basics. She's humming as she goes to the hot press to take out a towel. She hands it to Ali, who uses it to rub vigorously at her dripping

246

hair, leaving it in tangles so familiar that Jasmine has to suppress the urge to run her hand through it.

—You're Ali, she says almost to herself.

—I guess we have some catching up to do, Ali says. She looks suddenly shy.

Jasmine nods.

There's no hurry. They'll drive to the home first thing so Ali and her mother can meet. She doesn't expect much – she must warn Ali not to expect much either – but she wants to believe that some part of her mother will understand; if Ali is not her lost baby, her little boy blue, she is the next best thing. She will explain all this to Ali. There is so much to know, and so much to tell. But there's no hurry. She's not going anywhere.

Acknowledgements

Thanks for making this book better to: Hilary McGrath, Ger Nichol, Mary Liz Trant, Mark Richards, and everyone at John Murray. Thanks to Tim, Mikey, Rafy, Georgia, and Alex for their continued support and patience.